SIDEKICK

THE TALE OF BILLY THE KID AND THE GIANTS OF COLORADO

EDWARD J. KNIGHT

MYTHIC WESTERN PRESS LLC

ACKNOWLEDGMENTS

This novel exists thanks to the help and support of many people. First, I'd like to thank my wife Sarah, for her unflagging support, and Griffin and Gwyneth for their patience with Daddy being off writing. I'd also like to thank Joe Schonbok and Mary Kay Dodson for early discussions and the Grand Lake Area Historical Society, the Astor House Museum staff, and the Cozens Ranch Museum staff for research assistance, and Marcia Knight, Elizabeth Knight, and Matthew Dodson for proofreading. I'd also like to thank Terry Mixon, Sam Sheddan, J. Daniel Sawyer, and Dean Wesley Smith for their encouragement and inspiration.

INTRODUCTION

The Jotunheim giants poured through the rift at Andersonville and annihilated both the Union and the Confederacy. Only the desperate efforts of a few heroes stopped them in the West, at the battle of Golden City, Colorado. Those heroes became legends.

So when Giant Killer Cassidy came to town, Billy McCarty swore he'd join Cassidy's team. No longer a kid, he'd do anything to be by Cassidy's side.

But "anything" could carry a high price, in both blood and honor.

In the Mythic West, where gunslingers battle monsters of nightmare, *Sidekick* follows the epic adventure that began a hero's rise.

Date	Event
April 12, 1861	United States Civil War begins.
April 9, 1865	Robert E. Lee surrenders the Army of Northern Virginia to Ulysses S. Grant.
April 14, 1865	President Lincoln is assassinated.
April 21, 1865	The Rift to Jotunheim is opened at Andersonville Prison, Georgia. Specific details are unknown as there are no human survivors.
April 27, 1865	General Wilson and his Union Army raiders become the first humans to encounter an army of Jotun giants in Georgia and have survivors. The human army is soundly defeated but is able to dispatch reports to Washington and Richmond.
August 6, 1865	A combined Union/Confederate Army under the command of Ulysses S. Grant, with Robert E. Lee as his second, fights a large Jotun army outside of Lynchburg, Virginia. The humans are defeated, but "Grant's Last Charge" kills the Jotun commander, temporarily halting the Jotun army advance.
July 13, 1866	Richmond, Virginia, falls to a Jotun army.
Sept. 2, 1866	Washington, D.C., falls to a Jotun army.
December 25, 1866	The Christmas Miracle. General Lee defeats a Jotun army attempting to cross the Hudson River into New York City. The Jotun make no further attempts to invade New England or upstate New York.
June - July 1867	Jotun cross the Ohio River in multiple locations. Fighting rages throughout lower Illinois, Indiana, and Ohio. The area becomes known as the Contested Lands.
August 10, 1867	The First Battle of St. Louis. Believing he has superior numbers, General Custer crosses the Mississippi from St. Louis and attacks a Jotun army. General Custer and his army are annihilated.
August 31, 1867	The Second Battle of St. Louis. A Jotun army crosses the Mississippi and sacks the under-garrisoned city of St. Louis.
September 1867 - May 1868	The Long Retreat. The Army of the West under General Sanborn makes multiple raids on St. Louis. The Jotun assemble a force to crush the Army of the West. The human army begins a long retreat along the Platte River. The Jotun pursue, as they believe that the Army of the West is the last capable human resistance.
May 24, 1868	The Battle of Golden City. The Army of the West lures the Jotun army into a trap between the Table Mesas outside of Golden City, Colorado. In a Pyrrhic victory, the Jotun army is destroyed.
1873	Plague sweeps New England and Europe.
June 1875	Giant Killer Cassidy returns to Golden City. Billy McCarty's adventures with him, as described in *Sidekick*, occur.
August 1875	Billy McCarty joins the Tennessee Raid, as described in *Sharpshooter*.
March 1876	Billy McCarty sets out for the Black Hills, as described in *Scout*.
April 1881	Beth Armstrong heads to Yellowstone, as described in *Gunslinger*.
February 1882	Beth Armstrong looks for ghosts in Saint Louis, as described in *Ghosthunter*.

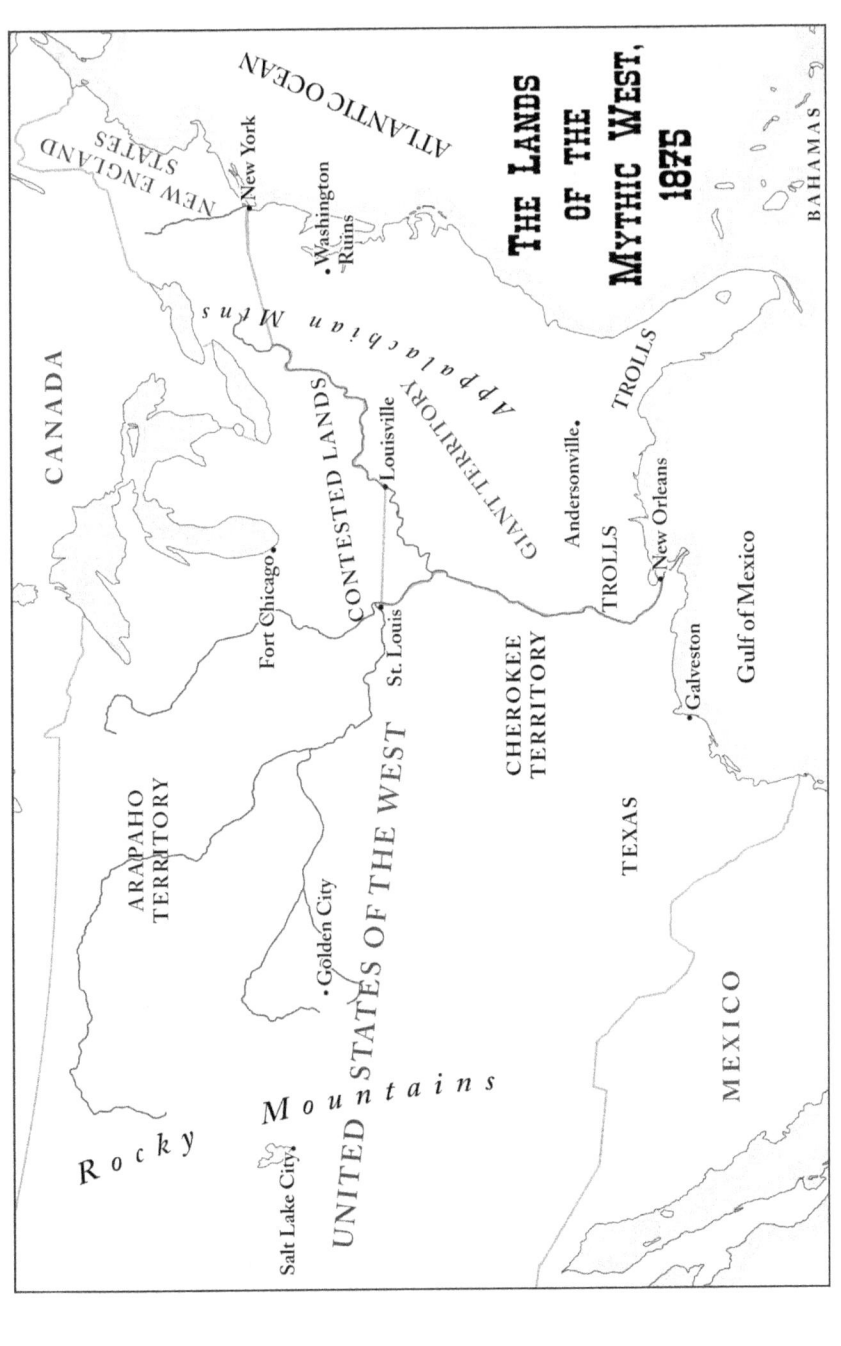

THE LANDS
OF THE
MYTHIC WEST,
1875

ATLANTIC OCEAN

NEW ENGLAND STATES

New York

Washington Ruins

BAHAMAS

CANADA

Appalachian Mtns

GIANT TERRITORY

CONTESTED LANDS

Louisville

TROLLS

Andersonville.

TROLLS

New Orleans

Fort Chicago.

St. Louis

CHEROKEE TERRITORY

Galveston

Gulf of Mexico

ARAPAHO TERRITORY

Golden City

UNITED STATES OF THE WEST

TEXAS

Salt Lake City.

Mountains

MEXICO

Rocky

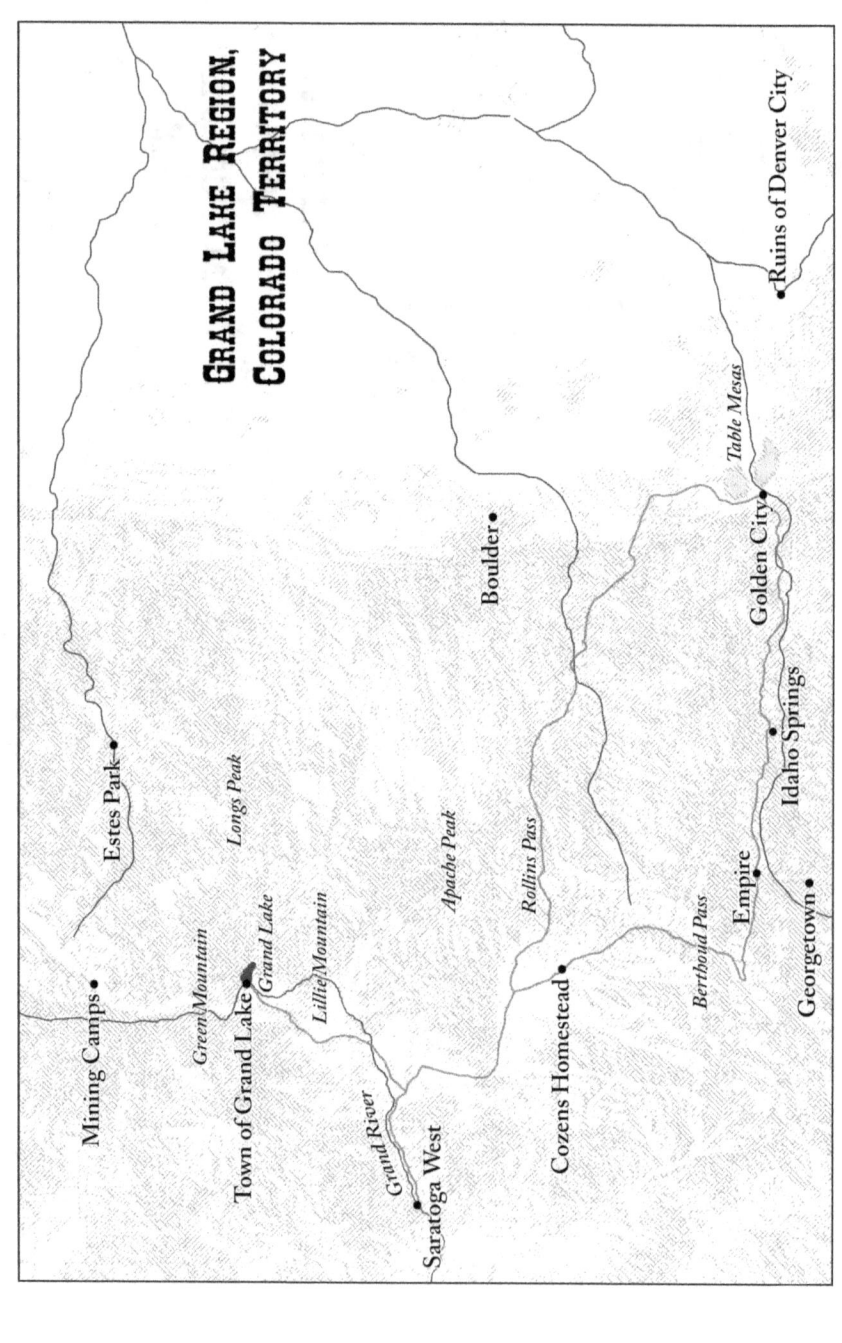

GRAND LAKE REGION,
COLORADO TERRITORY

Mining Camps •

Estes Park •

Green Mountain

Longs Peak

Grand Lake

Town of Grand Lake

Lillie Mountain

Apache Peak

Grand River

Saratoga West

Rollins Pass

Boulder •

Cozens Homestead •

Berthoud Pass

Table Mesas

Golden City

Empire •

Idaho Springs

Georgetown •

Ruins of Denver City •

PROLOGUE

I KNEW I wanted to be Cassidy the Giant Killer's sidekick the moment I saw him at the battle of Golden City.

As a lanky ten-year-old, I'd been assigned to one of the artillery crews nestled on top of North Table Mountain. There on the bare flat mesa, we did hot, dirty work. My eyes stung with smoke and cinders as I manned the two-wheeled ammo wagon, called the limber, with Tom O'Folliard, one of the kids evacuated from Denver City. We wrestled the bundled loads of gunpowder and cannonballs out of the limber and handed them to the runner, and did our best to act like we were twice our age.

The warm May afternoon had no breeze to blow the inky smoke away, which let it cling to us, sliding under our cotton shirts and wool breeches and into every crease of our skin. I'd wave the smoke away from my face, but the black acrid cloud always drifted back. Meanwhile the powder bags and rough wood of the limber scraped our hands and the sweat pooled under our ill-fitting caps.

We worked hard and fast, always trying to make sure the runner had the load as soon as he wanted it, knowing Sergeant Gallespie would cuss us out if we fell behind. Not that we could hear well enough to be bothered by his foul language. Despite the cotton wads jammed in our ears, the thunder of the guns in our company made talking all but impossible.

But at least the guns drowned out the shrieks and bellows from the broad valley below that stretched between the North and South Table Mountains. The troops manning the makeshift dirt and stone palisade that blocked the western edge of the valley, at the outskirts of Golden City, were getting the worst of it. The best that most of them could do with their rifles and spears was irritate the Jotuns, as we called the twenty-five foot tall giants that had come through the magical rift from Jotunheim in the waning days of the Civil War.

Still, that distracted the monsters from climbing the scrabbled sides of the mesas to where our artillery were. Without any trees or anything higher than sagebrush around, the giants would've destroyed us if they'd been able to make the climb. They didn't try the steep rocky slopes, in part because they had an easier enemy ahead of them, but also because we cannoneers weren't accurate enough against moving targets to be seen as a major threat.

But when we hit, we killed.

At the time, though, I was too busy to pay attention to what we did. Besides, I was too far from the cliff edge to see any of the battle proper. My legs ached from all the standing and the tension and the fear. My mouth gummed on saliva, desperate for water, but we'd finished the last ladleful out of the bucket an hour before. I yearned to sink down onto one of the flattened lumpy patches of scrub that grew between the hard stones and catch my breath, far away from the searing metal and splintery wood of the cannon.

But Tom and I were just two parts of the team, and the team had a rhythm. We'd get the load ready and the runner would take it to Sergeant Gallespie for inspection. Then the other men would put it in the cannon, aim it, and fire it. We'd all duck out of the way when the gun recoiled, and Tom and I'd help push it back into position. Then, while the number one and number two guys cleaned the embers out of the barrel, Tom and I'd prepare the next load.

Around us, fifty other cannon crews did the same.

The constant roar of the battle shook me. I fought back tears, not wanting to be seen crying like a little boy. Down below me, youths not much older than I were dying, trying to stop this invading Jotun army, the only giants to have crossed the Mississippi River in force. Bill Hickok had said that if we stopped them here, we could contain them in the East—keep the giants and trolls at bay across a river they were too heavy to swim. He'd sounded confident, and everyone at that rally in the Golden City town square had cheered.

There wasn't any cheering now. Those of us who weren't scared to our bones were too exhausted to say much of anything. Sergeant Gallespie barked orders, keeping our half-kiltered band on its battle rhythm. Everyone else just did their job.

I wiped the sweat from my brow and handed the runner the next load. He took it to Sergeant Gallespie. The men—some in their old Rebel uniforms, some wearing the blue of the Union—worked side by side to load and aim the big gun. It belched its iron and smoke and cinders, and then we did it again.

One by one, the eastern cannons in our unit fell silent. Sergeant Gallespie waved for us to stop, and then hastened to the rocky edge of the mountain. The other men quickly followed him there and stared down into the valley below. I looked at Tom, who shrugged. We closed the limber lid and jogged after the others.

Below, men in grey and blue spurred horses into the rear of the Jotun's lines. The cavalry men waved swords—steel sabers that the factories in San Francisco had feverishly been pumping out over the past year. The giants, who looked like oversized Vikings in their furs and helmets, slowly turned to face this new threat. As they did so, the cavalry split into three flying wedges—two slicing into the sides of the giants' forces and the third, slightly larger, plunging like a dagger straight into the heart.

Many men were swept off their horses by the axes, clubs, and even fists of the giants. Those that weren't ducked low and sliced their swords at the giants' legs. The monsters howled, and many of them dropped.

"They're hamstringing them!" Sergeant Gallepsie yelled. "Hamstringing them! Back to the cannon!"

I stared at Tom, not comprehending at first.

"The giants can't move," he said, "not with their legs cut up."

My eyebrows shot up. The adrenaline washed all the weariness away. We dashed for the limber with the same enthusiastic infection that the others had caught. The cannon began firing again—three, four rounds a minute. Each round was carefully aimed by Sergeant Gallepsie and the soldier serving as a spotter. From the way the spotter pumped his fist after each shot, our rounds had to be hitting home.

The roar of the battle faded as I focused on my job. Tom and I, more often than not, had the load ready before the runner had even turned around from delivering the last one. I bounced on the balls of my feet, eager, ready. The way Sergeant Gallepsie smiled when he looked our way said it all.

All too soon, we reached the end of our ammunition. Almost solemnly, we handed the last load to the runner and then closed the limber lid. Sergeant Gallepsie caught sight of us out of the corner of his eye and turned. I held up my hands, indicating we were done, and he nodded. Then he went back to aiming the final round.

Tom and I slowly stole up to the edge of the cliff. I blanched at my first sight of the carnage below.

Mangled bodies lay everywhere. Giants were twisted like macabre flesh trees, sometimes missing a limb or a head. Horses— crushed like overripe fruit. As for the humans, some limped, trying to escape the melee, some just twitched where they sat. All too many didn't move at all.

Closest to us, a cavalry squad circled a triangle of Jotun. The three brawny giants stood back to back, each waving an axe or war hammer at any horseman who dared to get too close. A distant rifleman plinked at them, but their kettle helmets protected their eyes and the bullets just ricocheted harmlessly off their iron breast-plates and drew only pinpricks of red on the few visible patches of sunburnt flesh. One of them, his dark brown beard swinging wildly as he swiveled his head, gave an evil taunting laugh.

The six horsemen kept their distance, always circling, always moving, their swords glinting in the sun.

That's when *he* approached. Cassidy rode his horse almost at a trot. His wide brimmed black hat, definitely *not* army issue, sat askew his head, his long black locks flowing behind him. He wore the same dusty black coat he'd worn in the photo on the dime store novel cover, but this time it was swept open. I could almost see the pearl handle of the pistol they said he always carried.

He pulled up just on the outside of the circling riders and sat tall on his horse. He studied the giants casually, as if there was no other fighting going on around them—no slaughter filling his ears as it did mine. He studied them, and then spurred his horse hard, riding straight at the nearest monster, the one with the laugh.

Two of the other riders swept close to the triangle, distracting the Jotun facing the other way. The giant facing Cassidy cackled hard again and dropped into a crouch, his axe almost bouncing in his hands as he waited.

Cassidy charged on, and on. Straight, hard, forward! At the last minute, he jerked his horse sideways and leapt from the saddle. The Jotun's axe buried itself in the horse's flank. The beast screamed and collapsed.

Cassidy somersaulted through the giant's legs. Somehow he bounded to his feet before the Jotun could free his axe. I couldn't see Cassidy's sword when he drew it, but a moment later, I knew the effects. All three Jotun howled and went down, clutching at their thighs or knees. The cavalry immediately charged in and finished them off.

Cassidy appeared at the edge of the butchery, his sword sheathed, brushing off his hands. He seemed to glow like a god.

Tom and I screamed cheers, jumping up and down. A moment later, the rest of our cannon squad did the same—waving their hats in appreciation.

Cassidy looked up. I swore he looked at me directly, but with the distance, I couldn't be sure. He tipped his hat back and nodded. A living legend, tipping his hat to me. Then he chased down a brown stallion that had lost its rider and returned to the battle.

Tom and I stared wild-eyed at each other, unable to keep our silly grins off our faces. When Sergeant Gallepsie sat down on a granite outcropping, we did the same, grabbing our own patch of dirt. The rest of the battle was too far away to watch closely, but it no longer seemed that the outcome was in doubt.

When it was over, only a hundred giants escaped, running east across the plains, leaving their fallen comrades behind. We'd won — the biggest victory since General Lee repulsed them outside New York City. Probably bigger, but at far higher cost.

Three quarters of the men and boys manning the barricade had died during the fight. So had all but twenty-two of the cavalry. They'd sacrificed themselves to keep the West free, a sacrifice we'd all remember.

Cassidy was one of the survivors. A few days after the last of the funerals, he gave a speech on the courthouse steps. He vowed revenge for the fallen. He promised to keep us safe by destroying all the remaining giants that had escaped. He even vowed to ensure that no troll or giant survived in Colorado Territory or anywhere west of the Mississippi. He'd hunt them down one by one. He swore it on the graves of the dead.

And I swore that, when I was older, I'd go with him.

ONE

THE DAY CASSIDY came back to Golden City, seven years later, I was hunting prairie dogs at the old battlefield. Most people wouldn't go there. Too many ghosts, they joked. But there's no such thing as ghosts, so mostly it was too many bad memories. I didn't share those. But then, I hadn't been on the barricade either.

I sat on a little rise of dirt and weeds halfway down the valley, perched on a hunk of granite as long as my forearm. It'd probably been a boulder thrown by one of the giants, but now it was a good seat for me to survey the prairie dog town that had grown up in the flat scrub. The rock was smooth on top, although a little small, so the edge would pinch my butt when I moved, even through my denims. It helped keep me alert. So did the light breeze that fluttered against my cheek, and the occasional call of a sparrow that broke the afternoon stillness.

Of course, the hot June afternoon sun also kept me from getting too comfortable. It beat on my back and arms, but my small sombrero kept my neck cool, especially when I tilted it back so I could get a better view of the prairie dogs.

Tom called them prairie rats. He said they caused plague and killed horses with their holes. Horses didn't come out to the battlefield anyway, so I figured he was just spouting nonsense he'd picked up at Vasquez's store.

Me, I saw them as stew meat. And good target practice.

It wasn't a great way to spend the afternoon. Sweat pooled under my shirt and I was stiff from sitting so long. If I needed it, I had a canteen in my beat-up leather bag, along with most of my other stuff, except for a change of clothes that was back at Tom's place. Still, as irritating as the day was, Mr. Boggs on North Washington Street would trade me the prairie dog meat for more bullets, which made it worthwhile.

About fifty yards away, a little to my right, one of the varmints poked his head out of his hole. Its head swiveled this way and that, before disappearing back down. I used its absence to raise my Winchester. I set the butt of the rifle against my shoulder, but kept my finger off the trigger.

The prairie dog's head appeared again. He looked around, then disappeared again.

I held still.

He came up a third time, and this time he popped all the way out of the hole. He was a fat little bugger, his brown fur sleek over his waddling belly.

I slowly lowered the barrel and took my sight.

His head swiveled back and forth, but he stayed up top.

I put my finger on the trigger.

He hopped once, and turned around. His tail wagged as he looked back and forth.

I fired.

He dropped. For a minute, I thought he'd jumped back into his hole, but as I ran over, I saw him. It'd been a clean hit. I scooped up the body, careful not to get my hands too bloody, wrapped it in the old ragged cloth I'd brought, and put it in my leather bag. Then I started the walk back to Golden City.

Tom found me just before I got to the edge of town, where dusty Tenth Street ran past the desolate shacks where the failed miners slept and then it petered out into ruts and thistles. He looked a little forlorn there, almost small, which wasn't him. While I'd never gotten very tall, he'd sprouted up over six feet, and added the muscle to go with it, working in the feed store. Small, he wasn't.

He brightened up when he saw me and started waving. "Billy!" he shouted. "He's back!"

I swallowed. There was only one person he could mean. Tom and I'd read the dime novels about Cassidy so many times they'd lose pages if we didn't keep them tied with a small piece of brown string.

"Where?" I asked, my mouth now dry.

"The Astor."

I nodded. It was the only place that made sense, since it was the best hotel in town and the only stone building to boot. I could easily imagine Cassidy sitting in the parlor with his team, around one of the dark oak tables with the red gingham tablecloths, drinking bottled beer from the Golden Brewery and playing cards. Poker, almost certainly, but not for serious stakes with his own men, according to the novels.

Still, my pulse began to race. I had to talk to Cassidy! For a moment, I worried he wouldn't let anyone in the room—the novels had talked about that as well—but then I took a deep breath. I wouldn't be just a gawker to be driven away. I did odd jobs time to time for the Astor's owner, Mr. Lake, and he also bought deer and rabbit meat from me when I had it.

"You gonna go see him?" Tom asked.

I nodded. "After I clean up."

"Yeah," he said as he looked me up and down, noting the dust coating my clothes and the blood smears on my hands. "You can use my place."

I let out a grateful sigh. Tom had a room in the Jefferson Boarding House. I slept ... wherever I could.

"Let's go," he said. "You want to be there before dinner."

I nodded. I needed to get there early if I wanted a word with Cassidy before the rest of the town showed up.

Washed and in one of Tom's white cotton shirts that had gotten too small for him, I nervously rounded the corner of the Boston Company store and started walking up Twelfth Street. I clutched the butt of my Winchester tight to keep it from sloppily swinging on the strap that held it on my shoulder. The late afternoon sun that was starting to settle over the mountains made me squint. I kept my eyes down and out of the glare as I strode up the dusty dirt road.

The Astor House sat just a block ahead of me. Its speckled grey and brown rough stone didn't show how fancy it was inside. Mr. Lake had everything—the best sheets from California and even a piano built by a company up in Seattle. The two-story building also hosted the only balcony I'd ever seen, though Tom said some buildings in Denver City used to have them, before the giants destroyed everything. About four feet wide and fifteen feet long, it offered a great place to sit and look at Castle Mountain, or even toward the old battlefield if you wanted to.

Sure enough, there was a small crowd on the Astor House balcony. I spotted Cassidy leaning against the nearby railing talking to a Mexican woman. My heart skipped and I picked up my pace.

Despite the heat, Cassidy wore a dark brown leather vest over his light blue long sleeved shirt. He didn't have a hat—instead he'd loosely tied his long flowing black hair back. He had a mustache now, and a small beard, which he'd trimmed, unlike the ragged bushes most men in town wore. He gestured animatedly as he talked, but I was too far away to hear.

I didn't recognize the Mexican woman. She was in a short sleeved yellow blouse with some frills around the cuffs and down the front. Her black hair was pulled back tight under some barrettes. She smiled a lot and nodded her head as Cassidy talked, but when she gestured or said something, he stopped and really listened to her.

Like I hoped he'd listen to me.

There were five or six other men on the balcony, but I didn't pay them much attention. My focus was on Cassidy, until I was so close it'd be obvious I was staring. Then I dropped my eyes and picked up my pace. I took a deep breath before pushing open the main door to the Astor. Then I bounded up the stairway two steps at a time before pausing one more time. I ran through the little speech I'd been preparing in my head for years before I stepped out onto the balcony.

I nearly bumped into a burly older man who hovered near the entryway. He was only an inch or two taller than me, but built like a bear to my beanstalk. Unlike a bear, though, he was nearly bald, with thatches of grey ringing his crown. He curled his lip at me, and the stink of beer on his breath was unmistakable. His eyes squinted nearly into a sneer.

"Where you hurrying to, kid?"

"I, um, I'm here to talk to Mr. Cassidy."

He looked me up and down, his eyes lingering on my rifle. "And what makes you think he wants to talk to you? Just who are you?"

"Oh, the boy's okay, Mr. McNab. He works for me from time to time."

I blinked. I hadn't seen Mr. Lake standing with the other men, in his light tailored jacket and holding a cigar. He nodded at me.

I looked Mr. McNab square in the eye. I spoke loud and clear. "My name's Billy McCarty, sir, and I'm the best shot in the territory. I can hit a gopher at a hundred yards and knock a sparrow out of the air. I figure I can be of use to Mr. Cassidy in his efforts against the giants."

The low murmur of conversation on the balcony died and everyone looked at me.

"Is that so?"

The voice came from behind Mr. McNab, who turned. I realized it was Cassidy who had spoken, and my mouth went dry.

The men between us parted, Mr. McNab pushing his back against the Astor stone wall, as the hero Cassidy strode over. He stopped three feet away from me, and planted himself, his balance casual, his face relaxed, his eyes full of challenge.

"That's so, sir," I said. "I'm the best."

His eyes went to my Winchester and seemed to slide down the barrel. He looked at my hands and then in the face.

"So ... Billy, is it?"

I nodded.

"If you're the best, how come I've never heard of you?"

I swallowed. "Because I've never had a chance to prove it to anyone outside of Golden City. And there hasn't been any fighting here in seven years."

"I know," he said, amusement on his lips. "I was there."

"So was I."

He cocked his head, waiting for me to continue.

"Cannoneer. I saw you take down three giants by yourself!"

"One of them," McNab muttered.

"Huh?"

"The hero worshippers," Cassidy explained. His eyes twinkled. "The ones that believe everything they read."

I swallowed, and my eyes darted between the two men. McNab seemed disgusted, but Cassidy just chuckled.

That's when I remembered McNab. He'd been in several of the books as part of Cassidy's team. I remembered him helping wipe out a pack of trolls that had crossed the Mississippi near Memphis. The book had said he was a cynical old cowboy who didn't trust anybody other than Cassidy.

"I can help," I insisted. I looked square at Cassidy. "I can."

With amusement still in his eyes, he nodded. "Okay. Prove it." He looked around, moved to the balcony rail and kept looking. "Can you shoot that?"

I stepped to his side and shaded my eyes. He was pointing at a small juniper bush about eighty yards away, across the street in an empty dirt lot.

"Yep."

He turned to Mr. Lake. "Do you have something he can use for a target?"

Mr. Lake nodded. "I'll have one of the boys put something out." He left the balcony.

I unshouldered my rifle and started checking it over, mostly out of nervousness. Cassidy eyed it appraisingly.

"That a Winchester 1866?" he asked.

I shook my head. "1874. Out of San Fransisco."

He nodded. "I knew they'd relocated there after the New England plague. I haven't seen one of the 1874's before, though."

My mouth went dry. I briefly looked him in the eyes, which were calm and warm, before dropping them to my rifle again.

"Um," I said, "would you like a closer look?"

"If you don't mind."

I handed him the Winchester. He held it up and examined it closely, sometimes getting his eyes inches away. Then he pointed it toward the juniper and sighted down the barrel. He tested the heft appreciatively and then handed it back to me.

"Mighty nice rifle," he said with a small tip of his head.

"Thanks." My heart raced—he'd given me a compliment!

One of the cooks put an old battered tin can next to the juniper bush. He waved and then hustled back to the Astor.

"Let's see you shoot, son," Cassidy said. He and the rest of the men moved back a respectful distance and turned to look at my tiny target.

I moved into my shooting stance. I raised the rifle and put the butt against my shoulder.

I took a deep breath and took my sight on the can as it glinted in the sun. I ignored the flicker of the breeze on my brow. When I was calm, I put my finger on the trigger.

I fired.

And missed.

TWO

"WELL, THAT'S TOO BAD," McNab said once the echo of my shot had died away.

The rifle suddenly felt heavy in my hands. I looked at Cassidy. His eyes were full of sympathy, and even a little pity.

All the other men had hangdog looks. Mr. Lake took a big swig out of his glass. A couple shuffled their feet where they stood and didn't meet my eyes. In the warm sun, it all felt like an oven of disapproval.

"Bragged too much," someone muttered.

That got my back up. I narrowed my eyes and looked around, but I couldn't tell who'd said it. My blood pounded, but not so much I lost control, like when I was younger.

Instead, I turned and looked for the tin can again. I raised my rifle, took quick aim, and fired.

The blast of the gun drowned out the sound of the bullet hitting the can, but it kicked up in the air. It flew about five feet and tumbled to the ground, bouncing off a clod of dried mud.

I sighted on it and fired again. The can skittered back and tumbled over, before rolling behind the juniper.

A bird cried in the distance, but the men behind me where quiet, until one cleared his throat.

I lowered my rifle and turned to Cassidy. I couldn't keep the grin off my face.

He nodded. "Mighty fine shooting."

He still seemed to be judging me, which knocked me down a peg.

"So maybe I'm not the best," I admitted, "but I'm good. I can help."

"Let's talk a spell." He gestured toward the back of the balcony, where he'd been standing when I first saw him.

I spotted his beer glass balanced on the wooden rail. The Mexican woman still stood nearby. She smiled prettily. The other men returned to their conversations, low murmurs all around.

Cassidy looked to Mr. Lake, who still attended us, nervously tapping his fingers on his glass. Cassidy nodded at our proprietor. "Some water for Mr. McCarty here, please?"

"I'd rather have beer," I said.

"If you want to buy a beer, go right ahead," Cassidy said.

I grimaced. "Water's fine."

Mr. Lake said he'd take care of it and Cassidy and I moved over to the side rail. McNab followed. I leaned my rifle against one of the wooden posts.

"This is Maria," Cassidy said when we reached the Mexican woman.

She was really pretty up close. Her black eyes matched her long black hair. Her smile captured the sun and her teeth were whiter than pure linen. She had a small mole above one eyebrow, but it somehow made her look more real and less like the prettiest little doll I'd ever seen.

For Maria was a half head shorter than me. Besides the bright yellow blouse, she wore a dark brown cotton skirt over what looked like buckskin leggings. I couldn't tell her age. She was older than me, but not as worn as Ma had been in her final days.

"How do you do, Mr. McCarty," she said. She extended her hand and made a slight curtsey.

I took her hand awkwardly and shook it. "Uh …"

"Uh, Mr. McCarty?" Her eyes filled with mischief. "You're doing 'uh?'"

My face flushed, and suddenly her hand was hot iron against my skin. I let it go. "I'm, uh, fine." I looked at Cassidy. "Just fine, I hope."

"Tell me a little about yourself, Mr. McCarty," Cassidy said. He leaned against the rail, his shirt crinkling. His eyes took me in, calm but firm. "Where are you from?"

I took a deep breath to steady my nerves.

"I was born in New York City, but Pa died when I was real young. Ma moved us to Indiana where my little brother was killed in a giant raid. We came out here just before the battle."

I steeled myself and looked Cassidy straight in the eye.

"I saw you then."

He met my gaze as if it was the most normal way of looking at another man. "So you said."

I felt embarrassed again and looked down. The rough bare pine wood of the balcony floor needed painting, I noted.

"Go on," Cassidy said gently.

I took a moment to calm myself before looking up. "I knew I wanted to be a giant hunter, then, you see? I knew it, but I wasn't old enough, and I had to help my Ma. But now, well, I'm older and Ma died of consumption last year."

"I'm sorry to hear that," he said. He sounded sincere. Really sincere, like he actually cared.

I tried not to choke up, but my throat was tight and the sun suddenly felt like it was scorching my neck.

"It was for the best," I mumbled. "She was hurting, real bad." I took a deep breath and steeled myself.

"So," I said looking Cassidy straight in the eye. "I've been practicing my shooting and everything else I could. I'm good with a knife and okay with a sword, though I don't own one. I can hunt, fish, trap, cook, and I even learned a little bit of Indian talk."

He nodded. "Which language?"

"Mainly Arapaho. A little Sioux."

17

"Know any Spanish?"

I looked at Maria, who still stood quietly smiling.

"Sorry," I said with a shake of my head.

She shrugged.

"Can you ride?" McNab asked from behind me.

I turned. He'd been standing quietly to one side behind me while Cassidy quizzed me, but he looked like he'd been biting his tongue the entire time. He cheeks were puffed out and his forehead was scarlet.

"I can," I said. "Not like him," I indicated Cassidy, "but enough to get around."

"Got a horse?"

My chest seized. "Uh ... no."

McNab snorted softly. "Uh huh."

"That's a problem, Mr. McCarty," Cassidy said. "We can't provide you a horse, and without one, you won't be able to keep up."

"Um ... uh, I can ... uh."

"Maybe next time, son." Cassidy's tone was clear, but I wasn't ready to walk away.

"And when will that be? When will you be back?"

"Maybe in a month, maybe never. We go where we're needed," McNab said. "Now run along."

My nostrils flared. I was about to tell McNab where he could stick his attitude, but Maria caught my eye. I thought better of cussing in front of a lady.

Instead, I picked up my rifle and clutched it close. "I'll find a horse," I said, with a glare at McNab. "I'll find a horse. You'll see."

McNab rolled his eyes.

My temper flared, but I fought it back down. Mustering every bit of self-control I could, I turned to Cassidy.

"Thank you, sir."

He nodded and flicked his fingers toward the door back into the Astor. And so, silently, I was dismissed.

I strode quickly down Twelfth Street, back the way I'd come. I kicked dirt clods when they got in my way, but I didn't slow down. I doubted anyone on the balcony was watching me, but I didn't want them to see me mad. I rounded the corner onto Washington Avenue, putting the fresh painted pine wood walls of the Boston Company store between me and the Astor.

Tom slouched against the wall there. He straightened up the moment he saw me.

"How'd it go?" he asked. His voice dripped with naive eagerness.

"He won't take me," I spat. "I don't have a horse. He says I have to have a horse."

Tom's eyes widened. "What ...?"

"I can't afford a horse!" I grabbed the butt of my rife. "Every dime I've earned went into this!"

Tom recoiled and took a half step back.

"Maybe I can steal one," I muttered in frustration.

Tom glanced around, but the only other folks on the street were a ways down, long out of earshot.

"You don't want to do that," he said.

"Why not?"

"What would Cassidy say if he found out you stole a horse? Remember what he did in *The Pennsylvania Raid?*"

I sighed. We'd loved that book, reading it over and over by the dim lamp in Ma's wash room. We used to take turns reading the chapters aloud while she ironed the laundry she'd taken in for a few dollars and smiled indulgently at us.

"He stole Traitor Jeb's horse back!" Tom said, as if I hadn't remembered. "Right when they were running from the giant lookouts!"

I hung my head. "Yeah." I took a deep breath. "Stealing wouldn't be a good idea."

"Do you think Mr. Lake would lend you one?"

"Nah. He's barely breaking even running the Astor. I know he likes me, but I couldn't ask him for a horse."

"So what are you going to do?"

I stood there, mulling my options. In the shade from the Boston Company store, the breeze seemed to blow away my temper. The tinkling of a piano from one of the saloons down Washington Avenue broke the stillness, but otherwise it seemed peaceful, which was surprising for the main street in the late afternoon. Maybe everyone was off getting their dinners.

But not everyone. A couple of miners slowly came up Washington Avenue toward us. They were covered in dust and mud, with small pouches at their waists and picks and mining pans strapped to their backs. The haunted look in their eyes meant they hadn't found anything panning Clear Creek. Their ragged hair and beards marked them for shack dwellers who hadn't found anything in a long time.

They gave me an idea.

"Maybe I'm looking in the wrong places," I said. "I don't have to buy a horse from Boggs or one of the other stables. Maybe there's a miner who'll sell me one for cheap."

Tom smiled, genuine and full of relief. "Let's go find out!"

We gave up at midnight. We'd walked every street in town, talking to anyone we saw with a horse. Most folks just scowled and shook their heads. A few called us names for daring to ask. "Stupid kids" was the nicest of those. One or two said they'd sell, but named exorbitant prices.

We went back to Tom's spartan room in the boarding house, exhausted and demoralized. I rested against the wall, thinking, while he sat at a tiny desk with a small oil lamp and composed a letter to his grandmother in Texas. He wrote her every week and sent money he'd earned at the store when he could, but shook off any suggestion to move there so he could take better care of her.

"She's doing okay," he always said, "and wages are better here."

I couldn't begrudge him that.

After he finished his letter, Tom tossed me a rough wool blanket. I stretched out on the floor, bundling my shirt as a pillow, and he blew out the lamp.

I tossed and turned. My mind just wouldn't shut off, thinking about how to get a horse. I finally slept, and slept late at that. When I did wake up, I realized what I had to do.

After some bread and apples, I put on my hat and grabbed my rifle. I slung it over my shoulder and we headed out. Tom and I walked down Washington Avenue, crossed the bridge over Clear Creek, and then trod down the muddy two blocks to Boggs's stables and store. Boggs ran a tight business. He was known for driving hard bargains, but he'd never cheated anyone. I figured he was my best bet.

We paused just outside the front. His store was a simple building made of pine planks and a wood shingle roof. There was one glass window up front that looked into a sparse front room. It had the counter he stood behind during business dealings, a few shelves with canned goods from Salt Lake, and hooks where tack, harnesses, and bridles hung. Most important, he wasn't there.

However, we could faintly smell smoke. After a minute, I gestured for Tom to follow me around the side.

We passed through a small gate in the split rail fence. The yard in back was formed by the stables, the store, and a small pine log lean-to that had a forge under it. Out of sight, the horses shuffled and snorted in their stalls but their scent now mixed with that of the smoke from the glowing fire at the forge, where the wood hadn't yet cooked down to coals. The light breeze blew the dark trails all around.

Boggs came out of the stables. He was a squat man—a barrel of muscles in a flannel shirt. His full beard and wild black hair made him look a little like a troll, but the last man to make that comparison out loud now permanently walked with a cane. Boggs hadn't been too mean—he'd only shattered one knee. The sneer under his fierce angry eyes deterred everyone else.

"Billy, Tom," he called when he saw us, "good morning."

I tipped my hat. "Good morning, Mr. Boggs. I'm here to get a horse."

He stopped short and frowned. "Get? You mean buy?"

I swallowed hard. "I was hoping more like borrow. With collateral." I unslung my Winchester from my shoulder and held it out. "You keep this until I come back."

Boggs blinked. He'd admired my Winchester 1874 before, but never seen fit to buy one himself. I could sense his surprise, but he recovered quickly and pursed his lips.

"No," he said. "No loan. You want a horse, you trade for it outright."

Tom paled. "But Billy," he said low and urgently, "you don't have another gun."

I looked Boggs straight in the eye. "Deal."

THREE

"BILLY!" Tom hissed. His eyes were wide with shock, his jaw tense.

I shook my head and my eyes narrowed. When he pleaded again, I glared at him.

Boggs stood with his fists on his hips watching. Then he held out his hand for my rifle.

I passed it to him. When I knew he had a firm grip, I reluctantly let go.

He inspected it closely, looking it up and down, his face an inch from the barrel. He then lifted it up and took his sights along the length.

"It's not worth as much as a horse," he said, "but I already have a buyer."

I grimaced. I'd hoped to be able to buy it back from Boggs later.

"Let me show you your horse," Boggs said. He gestured for me to follow him into the stables.

Inside, Boggs had opened a slat panel window near the hayloft, so we had plenty of mid-morning light. There was the usual loose straw here and there, with its musty smell filling the barn, but the place was tidy otherwise. Boggs had baled most of the hay and piled it against the wall leading up to the loft. Along the wooden slat wall near the door, he'd hung hooks with bridles all arranged by length. Two worn leather saddles sat on a low bench near a three legged stool, a tin bucket of water, and what looked like a can of polish.

Despite the open window, the air was still and uncomfortably hot, but not quite to the point where I was sweating. It did make the manure smell worse.

Boggs led me past five stalls with horses of various sizes and colors to the sixth end stall. There, a skinny black Morgan stood, eating loose hay out of a crude wooden trough. His ribs were visible and old welts criss-crossed his flank.

"Got him off one of the miners," Boggs said. "Abused the poor animal, stupid sod. But Blackie's sturdy and sure footed. He'll get you where you need to go in one piece."

"Is he fast?"

Boggs snorted. "What is it with you kids and speed? It doesn't matter how fast a horse is if he throws you along the way."

I grimaced. I briefly considered asking Boggs to let me have one of the other, nicer horses, but I knew his answer. They cost more, and I was lucky he was trading me at all.

"What about tack?" I asked.

Boggs stood up a little straighter and looked at me. "What about it?"

"I'm gonna need a saddle, bridle, saddle bags, some feed. The usual."

"That wasn't part of the trade."

My heart started pounding. "How do I ride a horse without that stuff?"

Boggs shrugged. "I'll throw in the bridle. After that—you got anything else to trade?"

I clenched my fists as my blood started to boil in frustration. But I wasn't stupid enough to take it out on Boggs, so I forced myself to take a deep breath.

"I've got a couple of boxes of bullets."

"Bring 'em in."

I nodded and then spun and strode out, without even a polite goodbye to Boggs. Tom hurried to keep up.

The wind had picked up on Washington Street as I stormed back the way we'd come.

"Billy!" Tom said as he matched my stride with his longer legs. "Why'd you do that? Why'd you trade your rifle?"

"I can get another," I said through gritted teeth.

"Where?"

I shook my head. "I don't know. But I do know that if I don't go with Cassidy now, I'll never get another chance! I *need* that horse."

"Slow up!" he said. "Let's talk."

We'd reached the wooden bridge over Clear Creek. It wasn't a wide bridge, maybe twenty feet total, but then Clear Creek wasn't very deep—about up to your waist if you wanted to wade into the freezing snow-fed waters. The bridge had been built for wagons and then rails added to protect the occasional drunk miner or cowboy from falling onto the sharp scattered rocks below.

I crossed halfway and leaned against the west rail, stopping in a place that had soothed me when I was younger. I stared out at the mountains, and Tom joined me at my side. He knew not to badger me immediately.

The cottonwoods Old Man Smith had planted back when were almost as tall as me, but still scraggly and scattered along the banks. They shook slightly in the cool breeze. Below, the creek burbled, sometimes being drowned out by the clang of Boggs returning to his forge.

Tom shifted his weight back and forth. He was too tall to lean his elbows on the splintery rail and be comfortable, and he never could just stand still.

Finally, after my pulse was normal, I sucked in my breath.

"I've *got* to go," I said. "Riding with Cassidy, fighting the giants —it's all I ever wanted. It's all I ever worked for."

"I know. I'd love to go too, but ..."

"Yeah, your grandma."

He nodded and picked a large splinter out of the rail. "I'm all she's got." He flicked the rough toothpick into the water below.

"Well, I wish you *could* come ..."

He grimaced. We'd had this conversation before.

"Forget it," I said. I took off my hat and wiped my brow. "You do what you need to do. It's okay."

He frowned and bit his lip for a minute. Then he looked at me, and it was like he was studying me. He took a deep breath before he spoke.

"You're my best friend, Billy."

"You're my *only* friend," I joked.

"Yeah, that too." He grinned when he said it.

We fell comfortably silent for a bit. Tom was thinking, like he used to when we were reading the Cassidy books together. He'd stop me, and not let me go on while he figured something out. Then he'd tell me what he thought would happen next and we'd turn the page and see if he was right.

"Do you remember that Hickok book? About the fight in St. Louis?"

"Yeah." We hadn't liked it as much, because Hickok was a shifty guy, not straight up honorable like Cassidy. And St. Louis had been one of the battles the giants won.

"Remember what he said when he was evacuating the women and children?"

I furrowed my brow. "Not exactly."

"He said, 'if we all stick together, someone will think of something smart.'"

"Yeah, well he was the one that thought of luring the giants into the trap at Golden City."

Tom pursed his lips, his eyes alight. He nodded.

"Look," he said, "I got something to do. I'll meet you back at Boggs's."

I frowned, but decided not to argue with him. "Okay."

We said our farewells and I headed to the battlefield.

My cache was right where I'd hidden it, under a cluster of rocks with old faded bloodstains on them. Giant blood, I'd decided, by the size of the stains. I figured most people were too superstitious to touch them.

No one had. The six cardboard boxes lay nestled where I'd left them. I pulled them out and hefted them in my hand, feeling the weight. It felt right. The problem was, 300 bullets wasn't gonna get me a lot of tack.

Still, it's what I had. Boggs wasn't gonna take my spare clothes and I couldn't give away any of my food any more than I could give away my canteen or travel bag. Cassidy would expect me to bring my own supplies if he expected me to bring my own horse.

With a heavy sigh, I tucked the bullets into my bag and headed back to Boggs's.

Boggs was inside his store this time, dickering with a ranch hand who wanted some rope, but was hoping to knock the price down. His tone was friendly but firm, while the cowboy blustered. Boggs nodded when I came in and I made a point of studying his inventory while they finished up. The ranch hand ended up paying Boggs's original price.

I plopped the boxes down on the counter. Boggs opened each one, even the ones that were still clearly sealed, and slowly counted the bullets. When he was satisfied that they were all there, he nodded.

"Two bags of feed for the bullets."

I grimaced. "That'll barely last me a day."

"So forage more."

"I have to keep up with Cassidy."

He tilted his head and looked at me. "You're going with Cassidy?"

I sucked in my breath. How honest did I want to be? Did I want to admit that I was only *hoping* to go with Cassidy?

"Yeah," I said, "I'm going with him."

Boggs looked surprised, but he shrugged. My obsession wasn't exactly a secret in town.

"Well, for a member of Cassidy's crew, I can make it four bags."

I blinked. For Boggs, this was like playing St. Nick.

"That's the best I can do."

I nodded. No point in arguing.

Boggs went in back to get the feed. I turned and rested against the counter, my mind racing. Doubts began to creep in—maybe I could wait until Cassidy's next visit. Maybe I could pass this time and catch up with him at the Ohio frontier later. He knew I could shoot—he'd take me then. And that'd give me time to rustle up everything I needed, including both a horse and a rifle.

But I'd have to wait. And I'd already waited seven years.

Even the thought of another day was unbearable.

I started pacing. I had to get the rest of the gear, but how? I just didn't see any way, short of stealing it.

Or stealing the money for them.

I shook my head to knock those thoughts out. If I was gonna steal, I should've just stole a horse. Stealing the gear now would be like adding the tinder after you'd started the fire. Just a waste.

I was still pacing when Boggs came back. He hefted the feed sacks onto the counter and was just about to speak when Tom hustled in.

"Here, Mr. Boggs," Tom said as he thrust a wad of bills at him. "This should pay for the rest of what Billy needs."

I turned in shock. "What?"

Tom recoiled at my tone. His shoulders folded and his eyes darted back and forth. He still held the money out.

"What are you doing?" I demanded.

His eyes widened. Despite being bigger than me, he seemed to be shaking. "Buy... buying you a saddle."

I couldn't believe it! "Why?"

"Because ... well, because you need one."

Boggs stood quietly, his eyebrows raised, but his face otherwise stone. When he saw my glare, the corners of his mouth turned up. "I'll come back," he said, and left.

I faced Tom again. "You can't afford this!"

He shrugged. "I've saved up some, and Grandma doesn't use all the money I send her anyway."

"But still ..."

"I told Mr. Lake I'd take over your chores at the Astor. That'll help. It'll be okay, Billy."

"But ... but ... but ..."

Tom smiled, as if my sputtering calmed him. "Relax, this is what I want."

"But why?"

He sighed, and for a moment looked out into space. The clank of Boggs pounding on the blacksmith forge filled the silence. The air inside the store was still.

"Remember reading all those books?" he said "The ones about Cassidy and all the others?"

"Well, yeah. We read them all the time."

He looked at me, a quirky smile with one upturned lip.

"You always wanted to ride with Cassidy or Hickok or one of the heroes," he said. "Heck, you wanted to *be* Cassidy."

"You did too!"

He slowly shook his head. "No, not in the same way."

I cocked my head and stared at him. Tom had always been more of a thinker than me, but he was good at explaining. He was the one that'd point out other choices Cassidy could've made in the books and how they would've been safer or smarter. I argued that since Cassidy had succeeded what difference did it make?

"You wanted to go on the adventures," Tom said. "I wanted to tell my grandkids about them, after."

"But ... but you have to go on the adventures first."

He shrugged. "So I'll tell them about you. My best friend in the whole world and what he did for all of us. Heck, I'll read to them from the book about you. 'Billy McCarty and the Battle of Memphis. Or Pittsburgh. Or wherever."

He turned and faced me square. The nervousness he'd shown earlier was completely gone.

"In fact," he said, "that's how you can pay me back. With an autographed copy of the first book about you."

I bit my lip to keep my chin from dropping again. "You're serious, aren't you?"

He met my eyes for an instant and looked away. "You're my best friend, Billy," he muttered, low and almost too soft for me to hear. "I'd do anything for you."

I sucked in my breath. I was Tom's best friend, and he was

mine. We'd been inseparable since the battle seven years ago. Except now, I was going to leave while he stayed.

The weight of that hit me, and my chest tightened. The air suddenly seemed stifling and hot. Boggs's hammer rang out a few more times and then went still.

"You have to go," Tom said. "You have to."

I let out a heavy breath. "I do."

He nodded, acknowledging my words, but then grinned. "Then kill a giant for me. You can do it. I know you can."

I snorted softly and couldn't help smiling. "You're the best friend a man could have."

"I am. Now let's go find Boggs and get your saddle."

There wasn't much more to say that wouldn't make things awkward, so we headed around back. The deal with Boggs went without a hitch. About an hour later, I was saddled up, with all the supplies I could afford meagerly filling my saddlebags.

Tom waved as I rode down Washington Street and across the bridge. I stopped and glanced back when I was on the other side, but he was out of sight.

I continued on to the Astor, which was quiet in the late afternoon. No one was on the balcony, so I hitched my horse to the post at the street and went inside. The parlor was also empty except for Mr. Lake, who was wiping down some tables with a wet cloth. He'd piled the gingham cloths on a nearby chair.

I paused in the doorway and cleared my throat. "Excuse me, Mr. Lake. Is Mr. Cassidy in? I'd like to talk to him. I have a horse now!"

Mr. Lake stopped his cleaning, stood straight, and regarded me. "Sorry, Billy, they left this morning."

I stared at him wide-eyed. "You're kidding."

"Afraid I'm not. There was a giant sighting up near Grand Lake. They went to investigate."

I sagged back against the doorjamb.

Mr. Lake gave me a sympathetic look. "Maybe next time, okay?"

FOUR

THE POUNDING of blood in my ears blocked out the quiet clanks of pots from the kitchen. I took a deep breath and fought down the urge to smash something. "Did they say which way they were going?"

Mr. Lake shook his head. "Sorry."

"Berthoud Pass or Rollins Pass?"

Mr. Lake looked a little exasperated. "I said I don't know. They weren't in a hurry, if that helps."

I nodded. It did help. They'd take Berthoud because it was easier, and there were more towns they could stop in along the way. Which meant I could take Rollins and beat them to Grand Lake.

"Say," Mr. Lake said, "Tom O'Folliard stopped by and asked if he could take over your chores. I was under the impression you'd already left town."

My chest tightened. "I was just on my way."

He cocked his head and looked at me. I couldn't read his expression.

"Tom'll do a good job for you," I said. "I don't know when I'll be back, if ever."

"Well, then good luck."

"Uh, thanks." I started to turn and then stopped and looked back over my shoulder. "And thanks for everything, Mr. Lake. You've been real good to me, especially since Ma died. I'm really grateful."

"You're a good young man, Billy. You take care, all right?"

I swallowed, more choked up than I'd expected. "I will."

He waved and then returned to his cleaning. I hesitated for a moment, looking at him, but he didn't look back, so I slipped out the door and got on my way. I had a lot of trail to cover quick.

As I rode up the trail to Rollins Pass, I fell into a melancholy. The light faded quickly as the sun dropped behind the mountains, which gave the few pines and aspen a ghostly feel. The crickets kicked up, not too loud, but just enough to make it seem a bit peaceful. Peaceful enough to think a bit. As I entered the mountains proper, the clopping of my horse's hooves echoed off the rocks covering the hills.

I thought about Mr. Lake. I thought a lot about Tom, too. My throat tightened as I thought about all the money he'd given Boggs for my stuff. He said he didn't mind, but it still ... it still didn't feel right. Not quite, at least.

Ever since Indiana, Ma and I had been alone, and she'd insisted that we make our own way. We weren't to be charity cases, no way no how. Not when either of us had two good arms and two good legs and a head on our shoulders.

But now Ma wasn't here, God rest her soul, and I was leaving my best friend in the whole world.

I shivered, even though the cool breeze was light.

I owed Tom, and I owed him big. If he wanted to read books about me, I needed to make sure there were stories worth writing down. I didn't know how, but I needed to do it.

I really didn't know how to do it, beyond getting Cassidy's help. I'd seen hundreds of men die, fighting the Jotun. Cassidy had lived. Was it because he was special? Or just lucky?

I had to believe he was special. I'd seen him take down three giants by himself! That wasn't even counting the stories in the books.

Cassidy was a hero. His whole band were heroes. As great as Mr. Lake and Tom were, they weren't heroes, and didn't want to be.

I didn't have any choice but to find Cassidy, and somehow talk him into letting me ride with him.

If I could.

I plodded on, lost in my thoughts, until it was too dark to keep going. I found a soft spot under a bushy pine and settled in for the night, with the hope that the next day I could make it to Grand Lake.

I started the final climb up Rollins Pass in the early afternoon. I hadn't stopped at the handful of cabins at the mouth of the pass —I didn't want to lose any time. My breaks were only long enough to keep my horse watered and fed. The climb slowed me down, though.

The pass itself was daunting. Not many people came this way, so the trail wasn't well worn or wide. There'd been talk of a road once, I'd heard, but it never came to be after the war. Instead, the dirt track just ran between scrub grasses and scrabbled bushes when it wasn't pure mud. Swaths of glistening snow still covered parts of the mountains on either side, leading to little rivulets of freezing cold water crossing the trail here and there and even running down its length at times.

Fortunately, only a few clouds filled the sky. As I left all shade behind at timberline, the warmth of the sun more than made up for the occasional gusts of wind off the peaks. The back of my neck even got hot at times, when my hat tipped too far forward.

Eventually, the steep switchbacks forced me to dismount. When I paused to catch my breath and drink some water, my horse grazed on little yellow flowers and spiny blades of grass. Then I led him by the bridle.

We worked our way around lichen-covered boulders in one spot where the trail had washed out from the melted snow, leaving a muddy mess. There were horse tracks in the mud, which helped me feel a little less lonely. I hadn't seen another soul in a long while.

Lonely, it kinda was, climbing the pass.

Now, I'd been alone plenty. Pretty much any hunting or fishing trip, or when I'd go to the battlefield to practice my shooting. But I'd never been this high up, where there weren't even trees. Not a hawk in the sky. Just me and the horse. Me and Blackie. I supposed it was time I started calling him by his name, since we were gonna be together a while.

Blackie and me reached the top of the pass just as the afternoon thunderstorms started to gather to the north. The little pockets of black clouds clumped together. To my surprise, I realized I was above them. That wouldn't be good, if more formed in the west, ready to float my direction.

I took a good look at the western trail. It wasn't much different than the one I'd just climbed, except it looped down instead of up. The same dirt and mud track twisted through the grass and turned with the curves of the mountain until it finally reached the pines.

There, at the treeline, something moved. I couldn't make out exactly what, but there was a flash of bright yellow.

I sucked in my breath. It was Maria's dress!

It was gone in an instant, and I couldn't be completely sure what I'd seen, but I knew. The yellow was the same as she'd worn on the Astor House balcony. Cassidy and his gang hadn't gone to Berthoud Pass. They were an hour, maybe two, ahead of me.

I started to run forward and slipped on some loose rock, almost falling. I took a deep breath. More careful then, I started to lead Blackie down the trail from the summit.

I reached timberline at dusk. The footing had been too treacherous to go as fast as I wanted, but I was past the worst of it. The breeze had died, leaving the air still and a bit chilly. My head ached a bit and I'd nearly emptied my canteen, even after refilling it in some of the snow run-off along the way. Still, I was too excited to stop. I remounted Blackie and urged him on.

An hour later, I spied flickering light ahead. Someone had started a fire off to the right of the trail. I swallowed hard and slowed Blackie to a walk. The last thing I wanted to do was surprise some lookout by coming in fast. That'd happened in *The Battle of Cincinnati* and Cassidy had nearly killed the man, thinking he was a troll. There weren't any trolls in Colorado Territory, but I'd be foolish to take the chance.

The trees weren't very thick here—mostly tall scattered evergreens with the occasional juniper and juniper bushes beneath them. The cloudless sky gave plenty of moonlight to avoid the branches thrust here and there in my path. I strained to hear voices, or anything, through the stillness of the night. The firelight still flickered far ahead.

So I nearly fell off my horse in surprise when a man stepped out from behind a scraggly spruce.

"Stop," he said.

I pulled up on Blackie's reins and froze. Still in shadows, I couldn't make out the man's features, but the rifle was unmistakeable. He held it up, though not pointed at me. I suppressed a tremble.

"Where are you going?" he asked. His voice was firm and powerful. The hair on my neck stood up. I didn't know this man.

"I ...," I said, "I'm looking for Cassidy."

"And who are you?"

"Billy. Billy McCarty."

"Who?"

I sucked in my breath, not sure what to say.

"Ah, hell," another voice said. To the right of the man with the rifle, another person appeared from the darkness. "It's that kid from Golden City. The hero worshipper who called himself the best shot in the West."

McNab's voice. I sagged in relief.

"Take his gun and his horse," McNab continued. "Let's see what Cassidy wants to do with him."

I swallowed hard as the man in shadows approached.

McNab led me on foot through the trees. He moved smoothly, without having to duck or swerve at the branches that jumped out and surprised me. He'd been surprised I was unarmed, but didn't ask any follow up questions once I'd made it clear I didn't have a pistol under my coat. He just muttered something about 'only fools go out' under his breath that I didn't quite hear.

'Shadows,' as I mentally referred to the other man, followed a few paces behind, also on foot, but leading Blackie. Shadows wore a long dark duster, a coal black hat with a wide brim, and carried a Henry rifle, which he wielded with ease. A trimmed black beard covered most of his chin but not quite all of his scowl. He didn't say much, but moved quickly and with confidence.

He made me nervous, even though he hadn't done anything threatening since McNab recognized me. At all, really.

We circled a small copse of Douglas firs and their campsite came into view. The fire crackled invitingly, sending small sparks dancing upwards to join the stars, along with the warm smell of burnt wood. A little bit back from the flames, three people rested on an old pine log. They stood, and I recognized Maria instantly by her dress. As McNab led me closer to the fire, the man to Maria's left stepped forward. It was Cassidy.

I sucked in my breath. Would I blow it a second time?

"What's this?" Cassidy asked.

"It's that kid, Billy, from Golden City. He found himself a horse and followed us."

Cassidy looked hard at me. Even in the dim firelight, his gaze seemed to take me all in.

"What are you doing here?" he asked.

"I …" I swallowed before continuing. "I have a horse. You said I needed a horse to ride with you."

He tipped his head an inch. "I did."

"But he's got no gun," McNab said. "No pistol, and not even that rifle of his."

"What happened to the Winchester?" Cassidy asked.

"I traded it for the horse."

The man next to Maria laughed, deep and hearty.

"Now that is rich," he said in a full deep voice. "He trades the one thing that impressed you for something that does not, simply to try and impress you again."

I looked at him, confused. As he stepped forward, into the fire light, my eyes grew wide. His white teeth shone against the darkness of his skin.

"Allow me to introduce myself," he said as he extended a hand, "I am Jeremiah Freeman. You may have read some of my books."

I swallowed hard. He wrote the novels about Cassidy!

I couldn't help myself. "But ... but you're a ..."

"Negro," Jeremiah said. "Yes, yes I am."

Cassidy nearly growled. "You got a problem with that, son?"

FIVE

THE HUM of crickets got loud all of the sudden, it seemed. I swallowed hard. "I ... uh ... no ..." I decided to shut up before I said something stupid.

Jeremiah still held out his hand. I took it and gave it a firm shake.

"Not what you expected, am I?" Jeremiah said.

I shook my head. "I, uh, I mean, we ..." I bit my lip hard.

Jeremiah's eyes danced with mirth. "There aren't many men like me out here in Colorado Territory."

Cassidy chuckled. "There aren't many men like Jeremiah anywhere."

I turned to Cassidy with a look of confusion.

"Brave and humble," he said, with a knowing look at Jeremiah.

Jeremiah rolled his eyes. "Just because I don't put myself in the stories ..."

"Which you should," Cassidy said. From his tone, this was a well-worn argument.

"It spoils the effect," Jeremiah protested.

"So what do we do with the kid?" McNab interjected.

"Show him where to tie up his horse and give him some food,"

Cassidy replied. Then he met my eyes, his expression firm. "He can ride with us to Grand Lake. Then he goes home."

My chest tightened. Cassidy's eyes brooked no argument. With a curt nod, I turned and stomped off to take care of Blackie.

'Shadows' name turned out to be Luke. He didn't talk much to me as I fed and watered Blackie at a small snow run-off stream he'd shown me a dozen yards from the camp. He just watched intently. He'd put his rifle away, but kept his jacket swept back from his Colt .45. Apparently the way I took care of my horse satisfied him, because he gave a small nod when I was done. We tied up Blackie with the other horses and he led me quietly back to camp, before fading into the dark to continue his watch. McNab pointed to a rock on the other side of the fire from the rest of the crew, and I sat.

They ignored me at first. McNab scraped the remains of what must've been their supper out of a battered tin pot and sucked on the spoon. Maria sipped what looked like coffee out of a small cup and leaned forward, listening, while Cassidy and Jeremiah bantered friendly-like, each holding a small canteen they occasionally took sips from.

"There's no way Lee would've gotten caught in that trap, if he'd been in command," Cassidy said.

Jeremiah shook his head. "You think it was just Custer's impetuousness."

"I *know* it was Custer," Cassidy said. He spat into the fire for emphasis. "The fool hothead never turned down the obvious target."

"But his scouts told him there were no Jotun or trolls north of the Ohio. Surely Lee's scouts would've said the same."

"Maybe. But Lee wouldn't have thrown his full force at the Jotuns. He would've held a reserve. He always held a reserve."

Jeremiah chuckled. "A reserve wouldn't have done any good with most of his army across the river."

I realized they were talking about the First Battle of St. Louis, which General Custer had lost. Badly.

"Depends," Cassidy said. "A reserve could've protected the cannons."

"Oh, please," Jeremiah said with a dismissive wave of his hand. "Custer didn't have enough cannon to make a difference."

I sat up straight at the mention of cannons and almost said something, but then stopped myself. I hadn't been invited into the conversation.

Cassidy saw and gave me a wink. "Depends," he said, "on how you use them."

Jeremiah swiveled his head and regarded me for a moment. Then he smiled and shook his head.

"The river valley was nothing like Golden City," he said. "No height advantage. Trees blocking your sight lines. The giants would've overrun the cannons in minutes. They *did* overrun the cannons in minutes. Golden City was as optimal as one could get, and even then you were lucky."

"You can make your luck. We did. General Lee does, or did."

I blinked. "Did? Is General Lee dead?"

McNab muttered something low I couldn't hear. Maria, who'd been sitting quietly looked hard at Cassidy, who took a deep breath.

"No," Cassidy said, "he's not. But his forces aren't in great shape."

I nodded knowingly. "The plague."

McNab snorted. "The plague was two years ago."

"Yeah, but—"

"So it wasn't the plague," McNab said. He spat into the fire.

"Won't hurt to tell him," Jeremiah said. He slowly ran a finger around the lip of his canteen, not quite looking at any of us.

Cassidy looked at the dark skinned scribe and studied him a moment, like he'd studied me out on the balcony at the Astor. Then he faced me, his jaw set firm.

"The Hudson froze in February," he said. "The Jotun took advantage of a blizzard and crossed the ice. Lee's army in Manhattan was destroyed."

My chin dropped and my gut turned to lead. "But ... but ..."

"Fortunately," Jeremiah said, "Lee and enough of his men were able to escape and start bonfires on the East River to melt the ice. The Jotun pulled back before they got trapped on the island."

"But ...," I said as my heart raced, " ...but with the New England Army gone, what's to stop the giants from—"

"Nothing," McNab said. "Not a gosh darn thing."

My gut tightened and my breathing sped up. "Not a thing ... but what about General Sanborn and—"

Cassidy cut me off with a wave. "Sanborn's going to attack across the Ohio. We hope that will distract them from hitting Lee again. But Sanborn needs more men, and more cannon."

"So give them to him!" I said.

"Tell that to Congress," McNab muttered.

I looked at him, confused.

He ignored me for a moment and scraped the last of the food out of his pot. Cassidy looked amused, waiting for McNab. Jeremiah smirked and took a long pull on his canteen. Maria remained sweetly silent.

McNab glanced around and grumbled when he realized he still held the floor.

"Those idiot Congressmen in San Francisco don't want to pay for more cannon and troops," he said. "They've forgotten we're in a war."

"It's been a long war," Jeremiah said.

McNab snorted. "That's no excuse." He spat on the ground. "They just don't care anymore."

"They care—" Jeremiah said.

"They have a lot to care about," Cassidy said, "and sometimes they get their priorities mixed up."

I couldn't hold back. "So somebody needs to straighten them out!"

Jeremiah chuckled. "What, young sir, do you think we're doing?"

I furrowed my brow, but then figured it out. "You're going to talk to them."

"We'll catch the train in Salt Lake," Cassidy said. "Which is why you're going home when we get to Grand Lake. After that, I suggest you get your rifle back and go join Sanborn at Fort Chicago. They could use a sharpshooter like you."

My shoulders sagged and I stared at the ground. The fire crackled a bit, but now it seemed like bullets going off rather than friendly kernels of corn. No one spoke, but I could feel their eyes on me.

I took a deep breath. "But ... but what about the giant sightings?"

"There ain't no giants in Colorado," McNab said. "Do you really think one could've crossed the Mississippi, slipped by our sentries, and made it all the way here without us noticing?"

I just studied the dirt at my feet.

"It's probably a bear, or something like that," Cassidy said, "but we'll check it out since it's on our way."

I nodded. It wasn't entirely on their way, but I could imagine the looks of the men in Golden City when Cassidy had said he'd take care of it. Sometimes the best comfort came from knowing a hero was on the job.

"Get some sleep," Cassidy said. "We've got a long day tomorrow and plenty of ground to cover."

Jeremiah and McNab muttered agreement and began preparing the camp for the night.

I didn't sleep. I couldn't sleep. My mind raced too much, my heart beat too hard. Jeremiah had curbed the fire down to coals, but with the moonlight I could still see the sleeping forms of everyone else. Luke had hunkered down at the edge of the clearing, now that McNab had the watch. Maria had her own bedroll a few feet back from the men, with Cassidy and Jeremiah close to the fire.

Mostly my thoughts were on Cassidy's dismissal. I kept coming up with arguments for why he should let me go with him to San Francisco, but none of them were that good. The fact was, I wouldn't be able to help with politicians. I was just a kid, even if I was a darn good shot.

But I didn't want to be just a sharpshooter, either. I had to find a way to persuade Cassidy to let me join him when he came back from San Francisco, on his way back to the front.

I didn't know how to do that, and my first handful of ideas were dumb. I realized maybe I could persuade one of Cassidy's companions, but I wasn't sure how to do that either. McNab didn't like me, and I'd barely spoken with any of the others.

But Cassidy listened to Jeremiah, I realized.

I thought a lot about Jeremiah being a Negro. I hadn't expected that at all. The ones we'd met in Indiana had all been escaped slaves, fleeing the Jotun onslaught. None of them could read, much less write. The stories I'd heard about Negroes described them pretty much like I'd seen. They'd led wretched lives, I'd been told, which is why the North had gone to war with the South, before the Jotun made that fight irrelevant.

But Jeremiah was not only smart, but well spoken and even knew military stuff. Cassidy sure respected him, and he'd written all those books, too.

If Cassidy liked him, then I'd better not have a problem with him being a Negro.

And as I thought about it, I decided I really didn't. Yeah, I'd been surprised, and he was nothing like anyone I'd ever known, but neither was Cassidy. If I couldn't handle being surprised now and then, there's no way a hero like Cassidy would want me on his team.

Besides, Jeremiah might be a real interesting guy to get to know.

And talking to Jeremiah was gonna be a lot easier than talking to McNab.

My mind whirled some more, but after a bit, the day's hard ride caught up to me and I fell asleep.

Dawn came early. The others were already up and moving. The men were off by the horses, getting them ready for the day. Maria knelt by the fire, stirring something in a pan. I rousted myself and ambled over. The smell of bacon arrived a moment before the popping sounds of it sizzling in the pan. Maria brushed a loose strand of hair out of her face and smiled at me when I crouched down. She forked two thick slices of the bacon onto a nearby tin plate and gestured toward it before returning to her cooking.

"Thank you," I said.

"There's biscuits and coffee, too," she said, barely looking up from her task.

"Uh ..." I glanced around and spotted them.

"Uh, again, Mr. McCarty?"

I blushed. "I, uh, see them." My face heated more when I realized I'd said it again. I took a dark brown biscuit, but decided I'd better use my own battered cup and scuttled back to my pack. I didn't look back to see if Maria was laughing at me or not.

I took a few deep breaths. I couldn't let her get to me. She was just a woman. A really pretty woman. But just a woman.

I focused on my food. The bacon was plenty salty and the biscuits were actually well cooked, unlike most of what I'd eaten since Ma had died. I went to wash it down and realized I'd never actually filled my cup.

I swallowed one more bite, set my plate down and went back to the low fire where the coffee pot nestled between two blackened rocks away from the flame.

Maria glanced my way, between pulling more strips of crispy bacon out of the pan and putting it on a nearby plate. Her eyes danced.

I nodded as I reached for the coffee. "Can I pour you some?"

"Thank you, no," she said with a shake of her head. "But it's polite of you to ask."

"Ma told me to mind my manners if I want to make a good impression." I filled my cup to the brim and slid the pot back into its resting spot.

Maria dropped two strips of raw pork into the pan. They sizzled and the grease spat from the sides into the fire where it fizzed.

"Your Ma was a wise woman," she said, barely breaking her focus on her chore to glance at me.

I nodded.

"Because," she continued, "Cassidy isn't the only one you need to impress." She paused and looked straight at me. "As long as you don't want to be sent home, that is."

I blinked, and my hand shook, spilling hot coffee all over my fingers.

SIX

I YELPED as I quickly set the coffee down. The burn stung bad across my knuckles and the web of my fingers. I shook my hand before wiping it off on my pants. The heat still seeped through and for some reason the sizzle of the fire was loud in my ears.

Maria just raised an eyebrow, her expression otherwise enigmatic.

"Kid can't handle his coffee," McNab said with an unsavory chuckle from somewhere behind me.

I leapt to my feet, full of piss and vinegar, and whirled.

McNab stood only a few feet away, his thumb hooked in his belt, a few inches from his revolver. His jacket hung open and his hat sat tipped back on his head. He smirked at me. Daring me.

I remembered Maria's words and took a deep breath.

"Sorry," I said, "you startled me."

Cassidy came up behind McNab, leading one of the horses. "Being startled can get you killed, at the front," he said, looking past the older man at me. "You need to be aware of everything around you, even when you're concentrating on something important."

"I'll remember that," I said, loud and firm.

"We need to get a move on," Cassidy said. "Finish up."

"I'll be ready in a minute," I said. I gave him a quick nod before crouching back down to polish off my breakfast.

Maria had finished the bacon and was rubbing a biscuit in the leftover grease to soak it up. I took several quick bites and chewed vigorously.

"Wash the plates and pans when you're done in the stream where you got the water," she said, not looking away from her tasks. "Be quick, but do a good job. Jeremiah will fuss if his plate isn't done right."

"Yes, ma'am," I said between swallows.

"I'm not a ma'am. Miss, or just Maria, will do."

"Yes ... Maria."

We didn't speak more as she collected the remaining biscuits up and put them in a small tin. I swallowed my coffee as quickly as I could without burning my lips. As I gathered the dishes, Maria handed me a bar of soap. I thanked her for it and headed for the stream.

The day looked to be fair. Now that the sun was up, the sky turned from grey to deep blue, with only a couple of high thin clouds hanging to the west. The light breeze was cool, but not as ice cold as the stream around my hands. The wind carried the scent of pine across the top of the water.

It didn't take me long to get the dishes clean. I'd had plenty of practice helping Mr. Lake at the Astor when he needed a hand. A full night of washing dishes got me dinner when he was done feeding his guests. Sometimes, it got me pie.

I hastened back to camp where everyone else was nearly ready themselves. I handed the dishes to Maria, who smiled and said thanks. I kinda wanted to say more, but realized I had to hustle. I was the last on my horse, but not by much.

As we rode, I couldn't help feeling like the poor cousin to the crew. Everyone in Cassidy's team wore long dusters and broad hats that would surely be warmer than my secondhand miner castoffs. Their saddlebags bulged and all the men had both cavalry sabers and rifles strapped to their saddles, as well as pistols at their waists.

I didn't even have a gun.

The trail wasn't wide enough to ride more than single file through the trees. Luke took the lead, with McNab and Cassidy right behind. Maria followed and then me, with Jeremiah as rear guard. Not that I thought we'd need it.

The day brightened as we rode. The wind was a little stronger than yesterday, but still not enough to chill. The trees spread far enough apart that we got hints of sun here and there as we made our descent. I tried to be alert, as Cassidy had said. We couldn't talk well, spaced out as we were, and just watching Maria's back was a bit distracting.

Still, my mind drifted.

Actually, it ran rabbit tracks this way and that, trying to find a way that I could convince Cassidy to let me stay. Nothing worked. There were no good reasons for me to go with him to San Francisco. None at all. As best I could figure, my only good option was to get him to tell me where he'd head after San Francisco and see if I could meet him there.

That at least was worth a shot.

Cassidy would be headed back to the front, probably to join Sanborn himself. It'd make sense for me to be there, and maybe I could convince him or Sanborn to assign me to his unit.

Maybe.

Except I had no idea how to do that. Did Sanborn make all the assignments himself, or have one of his officers do it? How was the Army organized these days anyway?

The Army at the Battle of Golden City had been a stew of crazy. Hickok had arrived with a squad just ahead of the retreating ragtag army that had sucked the Jotun into chasing them. He gave simple orders. Everyone was to build the barricade. After that, boys under twelve were to report to the Cannoneers. All the other men and boys were to man the barricade wherever they could. If a soldier in uniform gave an order, you followed it. If you didn't understand an order, you asked to have it explained. If you disobeyed an order, you'd be shot.

No one questioned it. We'd all heard what the Jotun had done to St. Louis.

There was just too much I didn't know.

But I could find out. And I knew just who to ask.

After a while, the trail opened up into a moraine, the trees fading away leaving just the long grass. I slowed and pulled to one side until Jeremiah caught up with me.

"Good morning, Mr. McCarty," he said with a nod of his head.

"Uh," I said, "call me Billy."

"As you wish, Billy." He looked around. "Fine day for a ride."

"Uh, yeah ... I was wondering ..."

He looked at me then, his eyes full of mischief. Embarrassed, I looked away.

"So what's on your mind, Billy?"

I took a deep breath.

"I was wondering, what happens after San Francisco? Where's Cassidy bound after that?"

"Thinking to meet up with us there?"

My chest tightened and I started to blush. But then I got irritated.

"So you read minds?" I asked.

"No," he said with a chuckle, "but any man determined enough to sell his rifle to follow us isn't going to give up just because Cassidy told him not to come to San Fransisco."

"Is it that obvious?"

"Yes," he said. "It's endearing, actually."

I hung my head, my face now red with heat. The sun on my shoulders didn't seem as hot as the skin on my cheeks.

"You're not the first hero worshipper to try to join us," he continued. "Probably won't be the last, either. At first, Cassidy let them ride with us, as long as they proved to be useful. But then ..."

He sighed.

"Then some things went really wrong," he said. "We lost a lot of good men because of a hero worshipper's mistake. Twice, in fact."

"Twice?"

"Yes. The first time, Cassidy just thought it was the kid. The second time ..." He gave me an indulgent smile. "Well, he told me to stop writing my books. He didn't want any more of y'all trying to join up."

"But you didn't."

He shook his head. "I convinced him that we needed the people in California and all those other places to keep being reminded what it was like and what we were fighting. It's too easy to forget about evil when it's thousands of miles away and other people are doing the dying."

"Oh."

We rode on, the light wind tugging at our clothes. The horses snorted and clopped along. Ahead, the final ridge before North Park rose up, scattered with pines and firs. Luke was already disappearing among them, a hundred yards ahead. We'd ride down them and then a few hours north, and we'd be at Grand Lake.

"So, um," I finally said, "where *are* you going after San Francisco?"

Jeremiah laughed, long and low.

"You don't give up, do you?" he asked.

"Nope," I said. "I don't know how."

"That's a good thing," he said, "a very good thing. Just make sure you understand the difference between backing off and giving up. Sometimes a retreat is the most sensible course of action. Even Custer knew that, even if he couldn't bring himself to do it."

"I learned that," I said. "Sometimes the hard way, when I earned myself a whooping."

"Lucky for you. Custer's men paid with their lives."

I nodded and fell silent. We rode on and grew close to the trees. The trail narrowed, and Jeremiah dropped back, letting me have the lead.

"Fort Chicago," he said just as I pulled ahead. "Sanborn's quartered there and we'll join up with him, if he hasn't already moved out."

"Thank you," I said, and truly meant it.

We stopped for food at a small stream just inside the woods, where we could water the horses and let them forage for a bit. I had some tack and jerky, and Jeremiah gave me some dried berries from his pouch. Most everyone just rested on rocks near the trail, with McNab even stretching out on the ground and closing his eyes for a spell.

Cassidy ignored me, mostly. I thought about trying to talk to him and almost started a handful of times, but Jeremiah's words came back to me. Did I really want to be just another hero worshipper?

Instead, I listened as he and Jeremiah continued their good natured conversation from the night before. They sat about three feet from me, a bit higher since I'd picked a clump of grass to squat on. Cassidy continued to argue that General Lee would've won the battle of St. Louis and even prevented the Jotun from crossing the Mississippi if he'd been there, instead of cooped up in the northeast. Jeremiah kept countering with arguments for how even Lee would've lost. They were friendly-like in their debate, but after a bit it itched at me.

"But if Lee was at St. Louis, we would've lost New York!" I interjected.

They both turned their heads and just looked at me.

"There was no way Lee could've known what was gonna happen in St. Louis," I continued. "He had his responsibilities, too! If he'd abandoned them and tried to get across Pennsylvania, what would've happened, huh? Either he'd have been killed on the way or the Giants would've noticed his absence and attacked New York!"

A smile danced in Jeremiah's eyes, but he curled his lower lip in, biting it.

"It's hard," Cassidy said, "to notice the absence of just one man."

"No way it would've been just one man," I argued. "Lee would've taken a squad, at least. And that would've been noticed."

I sat up straighter, emboldened by the way Cassidy seemed to be humoring me.

"We *know* they keep scouts in Ohio and Pennsylvania," I continued. "You think they wouldn't've noticed a squad. They noticed *you*."

I turned to Jeremiah. *"Giant Killer Cassidy and the Road to Harrisburg.* You wrote how they surprised you when you were sure there were none around."

"Yes," Jeremiah said with a huge grin, "yes, I did."

"We got through," Cassidy said.

"Yeah," I admitted, "and Lee might've, too. But it would've been a risk. A big risk. And why? As best he knew, the armies in the West had things under control. His job was defending New York and New England."

"Is that so?" Cassidy drawled.

"Yeah, that's so." I crossed my arms for emphasis. "Lee did the right thing by staying in New York."

A moment of silence hung in the air. I realized that Luke, Maria, and even McNab were all looking at me, quietly listening.

"Lee did the right thing," I said again, less confident now that my stomach was starting to flop around.

Cassidy slowly nodded.

"That he did," he said. "His orders were to defend the North, and he did it, and still does it, better than anyone."

"Then why are you arguing about what he would've done in St. Louis?"

"It keeps the mind sharp, Billy," Jeremiah said. "If you think through all the ways a battle could've gone, you're more prepared for the next one."

"I was at St. Louis," Cassidy said quietly. "I wasn't in charge, but I didn't question our plans, either. It's one of my biggest regrets."

I swallowed hard. Cassidy had regrets?

"Anyhow," Cassidy continued, "it's time for us to get back on the trail."

The others pulled themselves to their feet and I did a heartbeat later. I tried to ignore the soreness in my thighs. I'd only been riding a couple of days, but that was more than I'd done in a stretch ever before. I figured it'd have to get better after a while.

We mounted up, and headed up the trail the same way we'd ridden before. Luke in the front, the rest of us in the back. The breeze had died, making it a mite warm, but I wrapped a kerchief around my neck and that kept the sun off. We heard birds here and there, and what sounded like the call of a hawk. It was overall a pleasant ride.

After about an hour and a half, we topped the final ridge before North Park, the high flat valley where Grand Lake lay, many miles to the north of where the pass trail came out. We dropped down the hill, winding our way through the trees. Finally, we cleared the last of them.

The view was surprising. Ahead of us lay open grassland only spotted with pines, instead of a dense forest.

We picked our way down the last of the slope to the high moraine park. The trail joined the 'road' from Berthoud Pass, which was little more than a wide worn trail, and the combined track led north.

We spotted the south end of Grand Lake, the actual lake and not the town that had been named for it, around noon. We stopped on the shore to give our horses a rest and I walked down the mud to the water. The pine trees crowded the shore and so I didn't get a good view until we were on the edge of the lake itself.

I couldn't help gaping. The lake was *beautiful*. A mountain mirror, it reflected the sky and the far peaks. Small waves flowed across, breaking here and there, but mostly riding up and down. Trees on the far shore seemed tiny.

Jeremiah came and stood next to me.

"Magnificent, isn't it?" he said.

"I've never seen anything like it!"

He chuckled. "It's not as pretty as the bay outside San Francisco, but it's close."

"Never seen an ocean," I said.

"They're impressive. Usually not quite this pretty, but they have their own charm."

"And people take boats on these things?"

He laughed. "You really are a landlubber, aren't you?"

I shrugged, feeling a bit embarrassed but a bit not.

Jeremiah stopped and stared across the lake toward the western shore. He shaded his eyes and frowned.

"Cassidy!" he called. "You better take a look at this!"

"What is it?" Cassidy replied from where he was tending his horse.

"Bring your spyglass."

Cassidy strode to Jeremiah's side. He extended the tube and put the glass to his eye. Then he swore.

I peered in the direction he was looking.

Smoke, I realized. A lot of it.

Cassidy lowered the glass and looked at Jeremiah.

"Yes," Jeremiah said, "that's where the town's supposed to be."

SEVEN

THIN WISPS of grey coiled up from between the trees down the shore. I had to squint to make them out against the blue of the sky. The smoke was much clearer where it hung around the dark green treetops.

"Oh, God, Oh, God!" I said. "We gotta get over there!"

McNab gave me a sharp glance. Cassidy ignored me. Instead, he waved Luke over.

"Circle round the town, keeping out of sight, as best you can. Come into town on the far side," Cassidy said. "We'll be up the road in a bit."

Luke took off in a trot. Cassidy signaled for us to move out, but when we were all mounted, he led us at a walking pace.

My chin dropped.

"Let's go!" I said. "There could be people hurt!"

"It could also be a trap," McNab said.

"That much smoke means the worst has already happened," Jeremiah said. "If there's anyone alive over there, they'll still be alive when we get there. Or there won't be anything we can do for them anyway."

"And we won't be able to do a damned thing if we're dead," McNab spat.

Cassidy didn't say a thing. He just rode ahead.

I fumed, but racing ahead seemed stupid. If *Cassidy* thought this was the right pace, I had to trust him. I just fervently hoped we wouldn't regret it.

We did pick up the pace, though, as the trail rounded the lake. It still took a while to get to the west end. As we got closer, the smoke became more visible above the trees. It looked blacker, more dark and ominous. Various pines and spruces blocked the view, as they filled the small strip of land between the shore and the nearest hill, but the smoke was still easy to see.

My heart pounded in my chest, and it was all I could do to keep my horse steady.

Jeremiah drew even with me. We still rode behind the others, but McNab now was beside Cassidy, with Maria a short way behind. Jeremiah looked tense, his eyes focused ahead. He didn't look my way or speak.

My skin prickled under the hot sun, but I forced myself to take deep breaths. This was where I wanted to be, I reminded myself, riding with Cassidy.

Except I had no gun.

If we got into a fight, I'd be worthless.

Worse, I could be a liability.

My heart started to race.

Still, Cassidy kept us moving at no more than a fast trot.

I strained to see the town better, but we were just too far away to make out anything through the trees. I couldn't hear anything either.

But as we got closer, we could see some of the nearest buildings. They looked smashed, without any roofs and with walls knocked down, but not burning. The smoke came from some place more central. The wind shifted and we could smell it—acrid and biting—but just wood smoke.

That was good.

Finally, finally, we got close enough to make out details. Grand Lake wasn't a big town. It was mainly a bunch of cabins Judge

Wescott rented out, but also a supply stop for the miners and trappers working the area, with some long time residents trying to make a go of farming or fishing. It had maybe a triple handful of buildings, at the most, spaced out along the main road and abutting the lake shore.

But at least on this end, not a single one of those buildings still stood.

Cassidy held up his hand, stopping us, about a hundred yards back. We moved into a line, side by side, Maria to Cassidy's left, and McNab to his right, me and Jeremiah at the end.

"Anything?" Cassidy asked Maria.

She closed her eyes and took a deep breath. She seemed to be concentrating hard, and breathing hard. After a dozen heartbeats she opened her eyes.

"No," she said. "Nothing."

Cassidy frowned. He motioned to McNab, who began slowly riding forward.

Cassidy and Jeremiah pulled out their rifles and pointed them toward the town, ahead of where McNab was headed.

I held my breath. My eyes darted back and forth, looking for where trouble might be coming from.

McNab reached the the edge of town and he paused. Then he dismounted and walked over to the nearest wooden wreck, peering over a collapsed wall. He scanned the area again. Then again. He turned back to us.

"Nothing here!" he called.

I let out a deep breath. Slowly, we all rode forward.

The nearest building looked more like a ramshackle pile of kindling and lumber, the kind the carpenters back in Golden City would use for their scraps, except much bigger. Jagged boards poked this way and that. A few log posts still stood, with remnants of walls still nailed on them. The roof was completely collapsed.

The building across the road from the first was in similar shape. The front wall had caved in, bringing the roof down on top. It hadn't been as thoroughly destroyed, but the back corner support post had been snapped at ground level. It creaked in the small breeze.

The ones beyond looked much the same. Piles of broken up wood, mostly logs with a few ragged planks thrown in.

We all dismounted, and Maria stayed with the horses. For the rest of us, McNab led the way. We slowly edged our way into town. I kept looking around, but nothing much was moving. Some cloth that had been an awning flapped from one wreck that must've been a store at one point. At another, a squirrel raced over some logs, its nails clattering on the sawed ends. Soon, we heard the cackle of the fire.

Two buildings toward the center of town burned. One was mostly charred logs that smoldered. The one next was still a haphazard pyre of logs, with flames dancing throughout it. As we watched, it crackled, and a timber collapsed.

"Fire jumped from the first one," McNab observed.

Cassidy nodded toward the road ahead. Luke rode down it towards us, not in a particular hurry. We waited until he joined us.

"Anything?" Cassidy asked.

Luke shook his head. "No one north or west of town. No one at all."

"Huh," Cassidy said. He turned to the rest of us. "Spread out. See if you can find any survivors. Or any bodies, for that matter."

I shuddered. I hadn't thought of that. We'd only seen destroyed buildings. Where were the people?

"And Billy?" Cassidy said. "Walk around this fire and make sure it can't spread. We don't want to lose any more buildings than we have to."

I swallowed and nodded. It wasn't what I wanted to do, but at least it was useful.

The ground around the burning building was mostly dry trampled grass and dirt. There were a lot of trees scattered between the buildings, but fortunately none close to the one that was burning. I moved a couple of broken logs away, but there was little danger they would've caught fire anyway. I didn't think the grass itself would catch, there being so little of it, but I kept an eye on it.

The bigger danger was the smoke itself, which kept shifting this way and that. More than once it blew in my face, forcing me to duck and cough. I didn't get close enough to the flames to feel more than a touch of their heat, but it was enough.

But as I finished up, I wondered if I was doing any good.

I mean, if this was important, why was I the only one doing it? Jeremiah and Cassidy were poking through the nearby ruins, but they seemed to be taking their time. They weren't looking for survivors, I figured, at least not with any speed. And the others were all off in other areas.

But I supposed it was better than being told to just stand and watch.

I finished a second circuit of the fire and when I got back to the main road, Cassidy was standing there, hands on his hips, staring at the first building to burn. Now it was down to smoking embers.

"What do you think happened?" I asked.

"They had a cooking fire going when the roof caved in," he said. "Probably some sort of oven. See the brick?" He pointed to a lump two thirds toward the back.

"No," I said, "to the town."

"I don't know," he said. "There aren't any Jotun around here, and if there were, there'd be more human bodies. We only found two."

"What?" I said. "We did?"

He nodded and pointed over his shoulder. "Over there. A mother and boy, it looks like. Crushed when their house collapsed."

"Oh, no," I said, quietly

"They've been dead a day or two," Cassidy continued, "which makes me wonder about this fire."

"It hasn't rained," I said. It normally drizzled a little each afternoon this high in the mountains, but we hadn't gotten any as we came over the pass or the night before.

"Yeah," he said. "That might be it."

Jeremiah strolled over to us. Cassidy nodded to him.

"Maria doesn't sense anything," Jeremiah said. "We walked through the entire town. So no wights."

I stifled a shudder. Wights were *nasty*. At least in the books. Cassidy feared them more than Jotun or trolls.

At least that's what Jeremiah had written, I reminded myself.

"Not enough blood and corpses for trolls," Cassidy said.

"And a dragon would've burned the entire town," Jeremiah added.

Cassidy pushed the brim of his hat back and frowned.

"You want to set up in town or outside?" Jeremiah asked.

"By the lake," Cassidy said. "Tell McNab."

Jeremiah nodded and walked off.

I fidgeted, not knowing quite what to do. Cassidy must've noticed, 'cause he looked over at me.

"Why don't you go help McNab?" he said. Then he turned back to staring at the burning buildings.

I found McNab and Maria southeast of town, by the shore of the lake itself. They'd found a nice flat spot near a small stream that flowed out of the lake toward the river, giving us clean water. Some willow bushes grew on the far side of the stream and small pines dotted the area.

McNab had unrolled some bedrolls. A few feet away, Maria maneuvered rocks into a fire ring. The horses were all staked closer to the stream where some late spring grass grew deep green, about twenty yards away. Their saddles sat on the ground nearby. The beasts snuffled and shuffled as they ate, occasionally sauntering over to the stream to drink.

McNab looked up as I approached and frowned.

"Cassidy said I'm supposed to help you," I said.

He scrunched up his face as if he was about to say something mean, but then nodded.

"Well, kid, why don't you go gather some firewood for Maria?"

"I'm not a kid."

He snorted. "Well, you're not a man. Now get."

I sputtered, a dozen retorts rising to mind, but I choked them down. *Do not take his bait!* Instead, I stomped off, back towards the wreck of a town. I already knew there was plenty of burnable wood.

Still, I fumed. Who the heck does he think he is? Yeah, I was short. Not my fault. Yeah, I was young, but I was old enough!

I reached the nearest collapsed building. It looked like a log house, except most of the logs had been shattered like twigs. Not a single wall stood higher than my waist. The logs that must've been the roof lay in a fat disarrayed pile on the other side. In the middle was a mess.

Unfortunately, there weren't any good sized pieces outside of the walls. I leaned over the nearest one to see if there were some chunks of wood I could just grab. I spotted the remains of a bed a few feet away—the wool blanket on top covered with debris, the footboard shattered, the bottom legs snapped off.

The bed legs were the right size for fire logs. I clambered over the wall and gingerly stepped over to them.

Then I froze.

Sticking out from under the bed was the slim, small hand of a child. And it was moving.

EIGHT

I STARED at the dirty pink hand for a moment, stunned. The fingers curled slightly and then straightened.

"McNab!" I called. "McNab! I found someone!"

I rushed to the bed and knelt down. I had to duck my head to look under it and almost pulled back. A girl, maybe ten years old, lay there, her face pale and forehead caked in dried blood. Her eyes flickered open and then closed but she didn't seem to see me.

"McNab!" I called.

I started shoveling debris out of the way. I reached under the bed and tugged on her shoulder, but she didn't slide. Her legs were trapped. I pulled one more time, more gently, and she still didn't move.

Footsteps pounded behind me, and with a loud 'oof' McNab hurdled the wall and stood next to me.

"She's trapped!" I said, pointing at the bottom of the collapsed bed.

"She hurt?" he asked, kneeling down next to us.

"Yeah," I said. "Looks bad."

He grimaced. "We better not move her until we can see what's wrong. Let's get this stuff off her."

We started grabbing the debris on the top of the bed and chucking it deeper into the broken house. A few minutes later, Cassidy and Jeremiah ran up.

"What is it?" Cassidy asked.

"Girl trapped under the bed," McNab said. "Alive, but hurt bad."

Cassidy nodded and he and Jeremiah immediately pitched in.

We got all the broken boards and logs and large splinters off, me and McNab working one side, Cassidy and Jeremiah moving around to the other. Then Jeremiah knelt down near the foot of the bed and looked carefully underneath.

"I think," he said, "if we lift it, we can walk it this way until it's off."

"Better get the rest of that junk out of the way," McNab growled as he pointed to the stuff near the foot of the bed. I got it—we wouldn't be able to walk far without a clear path.

Cassidy knelt down by the girl's hand and looked underneath. He took it in his and squeezed it.

"We'll get you out," he said. "You'll be okay."

The girl didn't reply, at least not so that I could hear. But Cassidy stayed there with her while the rest of us got a space cleared for us to move the bed.

Then Cassidy stood. We each took one corner and lifted. I gasped under the weight, but it wasn't too bad. Slowly, we shuffled forward until we had the entire bed off of her.

Maria appeared as soon as we'd gotten the bed out of the way. She knelt by the girl's head, stroking it gently. Somewhere, she'd come up with a wet cloth that she used to mop the girl's brow.

I edged forward, next to Cassidy, to see better.

The girl herself still sprawled awkwardly on the floor. She had brown curly hair and wore a dirty white cotton nightdress and thick brown wool socks. One leg was twisted in an awkward position. Now that she was semi-conscious, she was flexing her toes.

That was good, as it meant her spine wasn't broken. I'd seen one of the men after the Battle of Golden City like that, and it had been a mercy when he'd died.

The girl muttered something low and quiet to Maria. The older woman snapped her head around.

"Water," she said. "Someone get a cup of water."

"I'll go," McNab said. "What else do you need?"

"My medicine bag," she said. "And start some water boiling."

Cassidy nudged me. "You get the water going." Then to Maria, "what else?"

"Check her legs."

Cassidy knelt on one side, and Jeremiah immediately did so on the other. McNab was already climbing over the wall out of the house. I quickly grabbed the broken bed legs and a few smaller scraps of wood and followed.

The dry wood caught fire quickly. I worked fast on building it up and getting a pot of water on it. McNab ran back and forth, taking stuff to Maria. We didn't speak—both too busy.

Meanwhile, I kept fervently praying the girl was all right. She'd had to have been trapped there, what, a day or two? That's what Cassidy or Jeremiah had said?

I really hoped she was all right.

And I was also mad that Cassidy hadn't moved faster, once we'd seen the smoke. But I bit that down when it came up. What mattered was the girl.

I'd almost gotten the water to boil when McNab hustled over and spread out a bedroll. A minute later, the others came, with Cassidy carrying the girl in his arms.

She had splints on both legs below the knee, and her right ankle was trussed with wood supports as well. Maria had also wrapped a bandage of some sort across her head. Cassidy laid her down on the blankets and then her head lolled to one side. Her eyes were open, and there actually seemed to be some life in them, even though her face was still a mask of pain.

"Go take over the watch from Luke," Cassidy firmly told

McNab. "Tell him to check all the buildings again with Jeremiah. We don't want to miss anyone else."

"Yes, sir," McNab said, and it looked like he was going to salute for a minute. Then he dashed off.

"Here," Maria said, thrusting a small leather pouch into my hands. "Pour half of this into the water and stir it."

I opened the flap. It looked like crushed berries and leaves, with a few chunky pieces here and there. I did as I was told.

While I stirred the concoction with a large wooden spoon I'd found in Maria's cooking supplies, she bustled about the girl, touching here and there. Long gone was the quiet Mexican woman I'd taken her to be during the ride. In her place was a whirlwind of energy that reminded me a lot of Ma.

Maria came over and tipped a tin cup into the soup I'd made. She swirled it, and then set it aside to cool.

"Can you sit up?" she asked the girl. "You need to drink more water if you can."

The girl wearily nodded but Cassidy was there instantly, kneeling behind her head. She lifted up a bit and he slid his arms under her back, supporting her just enough so she could open her mouth as Maria held a different tin cup to her lips. Slowly, the girl slurped the water and swallowed. After several sips, she leaned back into Cassidy's arms with a gasp.

"Good, very good," Maria soothed. "When you're ready, we'll try the medicine, okay?"

"What's your name?" Cassidy asked quietly.

"Beth Armstrong," the girl said quietly.

"Nice to meet you, Beth," he said. "I'm Cassidy. This is Maria and Billy. You're safe now. You're going to be all right." Her held her shoulder comfortingly as he spoke.

She gave a slight nod and her eyes darted to the water glass. Maria held it up for her to drink some more. When she was finished, she looked directly at the older woman.

"Where's Ma?" Beth asked.

"We don't know, darling," Cassidy said. "You're the only one we've found."

Beth's eyes went wide and she looked like she was about to burst into tears. Maria headed it off by thrusting the medicine cup towards Beth.

"Drink," she said. "Drink it all."

The gentle but firm tone was not to be ignored. Beth opened her mouth and let Maria put the cup at her lips. The girl drank, slowly but steadily until the cup was drained.

"We're gonna look for your Ma," Cassidy said. He continued to hold her as he spoke. "And we'll find her. Your job in the meantime is to get better, you understand?"

Beth nodded and sagged back. Cassidy gently lowered her to the ground, but not before Maria passed him another blanket that he rolled up to use as a pillow. Then he held her hand while her breathing deepened and she soon fell asleep.

"You didn't ask her what happened," I said quietly to Cassidy.

"I did that while we were getting the splints on. She doesn't know." Then he looked at Maria. "Is she going to make it?"

The Mexican woman nodded. "She'd be dead by now if she wasn't. The cut on the head isn't bad. Sleep, water, food, and she should live."

"Walk?"

Maria shook her head.

"Her legs are broken?" I asked.

"Just her ankle. Her legs are bruised, but they'll heal."

I let out a deep breath. The crippled soldiers in Golden City— well, saying they were miserable wasn't the half of it. I wouldn't wish that on anyone, especially a girl.

Cassidy looked similarly relieved.

"Anything you need?" he asked Maria.

She shook her head, so he turned to me.

"You stay with Beth," he said. "Do what Maria tells you."

"What are you going to do?" I asked.

His lip curled into a frown as if I'd challenged him, and perhaps I had, now that I thought about my tone.

"Dig some graves."

With that he walked off without looking back.

Maria set me to work preparing food and getting the camp set up. I spread out the bedrolls and cooked a couple of biscuits in the skillet under her close supervision. Luke came back to fetch a shovel, but otherwise none of the other men joined us. Beth still slept peacefully when they all returned at dusk. All except McNab, whom I guessed was still on watch.

I had bean soup ready by then, along with the last of the dried apples they'd packed from Golden City. Each man took a bowl and found a rock or old log to perch on. We huddled around the fire, kept low by McNab so it wouldn't show much, and ate in quiet.

At least the smoke from the burning buildings had lessened.

Jeremiah looked at the apples and raised his eyebrows. "We were going to resupply here," he said to Cassidy.

"We have enough tack and jerky," Cassidy replied.

"I could hunt," I said, excitedly. My mind raced ahead to what I might be able to bring to Cassidy.

After a moment of silence, Luke asked, "With what gun?"

That knocked the wind right out of me. I hung my head so they couldn't see the red of my cheeks.

"We don't want any gunshots," Cassidy said.

I looked up, momentarily confused.

"The sound would call attention to us," Jeremiah said. "We still don't know who or what destroyed the town."

"Uh, yeah," I said.

Cassidy set his empty bowl in the dirt. He took the last few swigs from his battered canteen and then stood. Luke ate another spoonful of soup and then did the same.

"Let's get to it," Cassidy said. "Jeremiah, go relieve McNab so he can eat." Then he turned to Maria. "Can you leave her long enough to join us?"

Maria looked at Beth, still sleeping soundly, and nodded.

"What do you want me to do?" I asked.

Cassidy looked at me, hard and long.

"Stay with Beth," he said, "and clean up camp."

I swallowed. It was menial work, but I was happy to do it. To do anything useful, actually.

Maria stood and joined Cassidy and Luke. They started walking back toward the town and, I knew, where the bodies were. They'd gone about ten yards when Cassidy stopped and looked back over his shoulder at me.

"And see if you can find a branch from one of these willow bushes that would make a good fishing pole. There's some hooks and line in my saddlebags."

I snorted softly. Of course. Cassidy would think of everything.

They continued on and I set about gathering up the dishes and boiling some new water to wash them in. McNab showed up, took his soup and apples, polished them off might quick, and headed off after the others.

Beth continued to sleep peacefully.

After thirty minutes of solid work, I had everything clean and either drying or stowed away. Maria returned and nodded, when she saw everything I'd done. It was almost dark, but I could still see the pleased look on her face.

"Did it go well?" I asked.

She nodded. She knelt next to Beth and felt her head. The girl continued to breathe regularly and deeply.

I found a willow branch, cut it, and began trimming it. I looked toward the town, expecting to see Cassidy and the others coming over too, but I didn't.

I waited a bit longer, but still didn't see them.

Maria still sat on the ground next to Beth, but now she was going through a pouch of herbs and leaves, sorting and counting and separating them.

"They're not done?" I asked. When Maria looked up, I gestured toward the town.

"It takes time to fill in a grave," she said.

"But you're back."

"My part was done," she said with a shrug.

"So what's your part? Or was your part?"

She gave me an enigmatic smile. "Making sure the dead pass on."

My chin dropped. At first I thought she was teasing, but then I realized she was dead serious.

"You can do that?" I asked, trying not to sound too much like a rube.

"Yes," she said. "Can't you?"

I stared at her. This was *not* something Jeremiah had written about in any of the books. Or anybody else had written about, either. It took a bit for my mind to stop whirling and for words to form.

"I didn't think anybody could."

"Oh. Some of us can."

"How?" I asked.

"How do you think? If they haven't already passed on, I talk to their ghost."

NINE

I STARED at Maria as we sat there by the cooking fire. With the sun down, it'd become quite chilly. Some insects buzzed in the willows, but otherwise all was still. Beth still slept quietly nearby. I realized I was still holding the rough willow switch in my hand and squeezing my knife way too tight.

"You mean ghosts are real?" I asked.

"Why wouldn't they be?"

I sputtered, trying to come up with a good reason.

"I don't know," I finally admitted. "I thought they were one of those made up things, to scare little kids, you know?"

"They're real."

"Uh ... oh." I dropped my eyes and cut off another sprout from my soon-to-be-fishing rod and tried not to think about the implications.

I heard Maria shuffling, and a moment later she laid a hand on my thigh.

"It's okay," she said. "Most people don't know about ghosts."

I frowned and set down my knife before I looked at her. Her eyes were clear and full of compassion.

"It's not that," I said. "It's, I mean, I've seen plenty of people die. But some of them are still here?"

"Some of them," she said, "but very, very few. Most souls move on right after death. A few linger for a few days. Very, very few stay in our world longer than that."

I blinked at her, digesting what she said.

"They can't hurt you," she said. "Most people can't even see them."

"But ... but what about *them*? Aren't they supposed to go to heaven?"

"We don't know exactly where they go."

That unsettled me. I thought about all the church sermons Ma had made me sit through. Heaven was what the preacher promised us for doing good, and for fighting the evil that was the Jotun and trolls. Holy warriors, he'd called the soldiers at the front, doing God's work.

And they might not go to heaven?

I'd always believed in heaven, and if I was good, that some day I'd go there. But ...

I stopped myself. Maria had said '*we don't know.*' That wasn't the same thing as saying people didn't go to heaven.

Beth stirred. The young girl turned her head towards us and opened her eyes. Maria immediately went and knelt by her side.

"How do you feel?" Maria asked.

"Thirsty."

I grabbed a canteen and hustled over. We helped Beth sit up enough to take a few sips when I held it to her lips.

"Where does it hurt?" Maria asked, her tone both soothing and surprisingly firm.

Beth grimaced. "My legs," she said. "My ankle. My head."

"Anywhere else?" Maria asked. "Inside, maybe?"

Beth slowly shook her head. Her eyes darted to the canteen and I brought it close enough for her to take more water.

"Good," Maria said. She squeezed the girl's hand.

When Beth had drunk, she looked at us both.

"Where's Ma?" she asked. "What happened?"

Maria hesitated for a moment, so I spoke.

"We don't know," I said. "When we got here, the town had been destroyed. You're the only one we've found."

"The only one?" her eyes went wide and her lips quivered, and then she burst into tears.

Maria pulled her into her chest and hugged her deeply. Beth sobbed and sobbed, but clung to the older woman as she did so.

I sat there awkwardly, not quite sure what to do. She was just a small girl. How was *I* to know how to take care of her?

Beth was still crying, though mostly just soft sobs, when Cassidy, Luke, and McNab returned a half hour later. I still sat dumbly when they approached, staring at Beth, my mind whirling as I wondered what I could do.

Cassidy immediately hurried to the girl's side. He joined Maria in soothing her, uttering kind words in a soft voice. They both held her until once again, she dropped off to sleep.

"Looks like it's time for us all to get some shuteye," Cassidy said. "I'll take first watch. Luke, Jeremiah—you get the other two."

They nodded and McNab let out a satisfied sigh. Maria curbed the fire and I decided to get my own bedroll out.

Despite a million whirling thoughts and all the excitement of the day, I quickly fell asleep.

———

When I awoke, just as the warm sun peeked over the eastern mountains, everyone else was already up. Maria tended to Beth, who looked a mite better as she drank from a cup. Cassidy cooked bacon on the grill but the others seemed to be out.

I ate quickly. Beth made small sobs between her sips, and Maria soothed her, though what exactly she said I couldn't hear.

I finished my coffee and biscuit and took the cup back to Cassidy. "What do you need me to do now?"

I expected him to tell me to wash the dishes, but instead he nodded toward town.

"Go see if McNab and Luke need any help," he said.

"Will do."

Beth's sobs increased. I turned and walked off, trying not to let the girl's crying get under my skin.

The fact was, Beth's problems bothered me, and they bothered me bad. When I'd lost Ma, it'd torn me apart for a few days, and I'd known it was coming. To lose her family, and her entire town, suddenly like?

That hurt. That had to hurt bad.

Really, it was more like Indiana when the giants had killed my brother Josie. That ... that had been a bad day. But Ma and I had been too busy running to grieve then. Not until later.

A fresh wave of grief washed over me. I missed Josie, but even more I missed Ma.

But I had to toughen up. A lot of people lost loved ones, once the Jotun came. That's what war did. And that's why we needed people like Cassidy to make sure we didn't lose any more, and especially not any women or children.

We had to keep Beth safe. She'd be sad for a while, but she'd live. That was what mattered.

I found Luke and McNab near the collapsed building with the awning. They'd stretched out two poles, that must've been support posts for that cloth, on the ground and were knocking off some wood that was still nailed to the top.

"Whattchya doing?" I asked.

Luke glanced at me. "Making a travois for Beth."

I nodded. I'd seen those pulled by refugees when we were crossing Kansas. Said they'd learned it from the Arapaho.

"Can I help?" I asked.

"See if you can find some canvas in there." McNab gestured toward the ruin. "Looks like it used to be the town store."

I approached the wreck. The front wall was completely knocked in, down to two logs on the bottom, and even they were broken in one place, like something had smashed them in hard. Beyond that, the wood from the wall and the ceiling stuck up in a pile that was higher than my head, with spars and splinters pointing every which way. The right side wall had fallen out, with logs rolling a half dozen feet away. The one thing that was weird was the gap on the right through the debris, running from the bottom front smashed logs through the side.

It looked like someone had run a train through there, shoving everything out of the way.

I stepped into the middle of that and looked around. Under some of the fallen roof beams and planks I could see broken barrels of wheat and dried corn, the grain spilling everywhere. I suspected the rats were having a feast, but I didn't see any.

Off to the right side were a bunch of smashed shelves and a ragtag of goods. I quickly spotted what looked like clothes, which meant there was probably uncut cloth nearby. I had to shove a broken ceiling beam out of the way, and then scramble over another one shattered from the wall, but that got me close to the shelves.

Yes, there were bolts of cloth there. I spotted four. After brushing off the dust and splinters, trying not to cough too much as I did, I was able to haul them out. Two were obviously too thin—simple colored cotton that looked like it was for ladies' dresses. The third was dark blue wool but the fourth was a gold mine—denim. I set the other three down, figuring I could come back for them later if needed, and crawled out of the wreck with the denim one for McNab.

He looked right pleased when he saw me. He and Luke had gotten the travois frame laid out in a triangle and lashed together with some rope. He hustled over and took the fabric from me. He and Luke started stretching it out under the travois, and it looked like they'd wrap it around several times.

"So ... uh ...," I said, "what do you need me to do?"

"We got this," McNab said. He tossed his head back toward camp. "Why don't you see if Cassidy or Maria needs anything?"

"They're helping Beth."

McNab furrowed his brow and rolled his lower lip into his mouth, obviously thinking.

"Why don't you get Cassidy's hooks," he said after a bit, "and see if you can get us some fish for lunch?"

I smiled. "Yes, sir!"

That I could do.

Cassidy was comforting Beth when I returned to camp. He held her upper body as she continued to cry softly. Maria was back at the fire, mixing something in a small tin pot.

I hesitated, not knowing quite how to approach. Then I saw the pole I'd made the night before. I strode to it and picked it up. When I turned back to Cassidy, he was looking at me. I glanced at the pole and then back at him.

"In my right saddlebag, in the small front pocket," he said.

I nodded and went over to where we'd laid out the saddlebags. Not far away, the horses contently grazed, only occasionally looking our way. That was reassuring, in a way.

I found the hooks and a length of silk fishing line, which made me smile. Back in Golden City, I'd mostly worked with horsehair line, which was too light to cast well. Cassidy didn't have a reel, which was too bad. But then, I realized, that would weigh a lot more, whereas the line and hooks were so small as to not be a problem as emergency supplies.

Without a reel, I'd have to use the old fashioned dink and dunk method to try and hook a fish. That required finding a steep shore-line since I couldn't cast too far out into the lake.

But first, I'd need bait. That meant soft ground where I could dig worms. I went back and quietly asked Maria if she knew where we might have a trowel or shovel, and she did, in with some of her camp stuff.

Beth had fallen back asleep. Cassidy still sat by her, lightly stroking her hair.

I decided to wander southwest along the river that left the lake, rather than fish in the still waters. I'd have a better chance of catching something dinking my rod in, if the fish were swimming by. I pushed around the willow bushes and a small stretch of river with few trees and mostly grass along it opened up. I followed the bank, keeping an eye peeled for a wash or other spot where there might be some mud I could dig through.

I walked about two hundred yards when I came to a flat muddy spot. It formed a wide wet bank, perfect for digging worms.

I started to walk out on that bank, but froze.

There in the mud, not too deep, was a booted footprint. A *huge* footprint. Forty, fifty inches long, at least.

I swallowed hard and nearly dropped my fishing pole.

Then I slowly set it down and ran back to get Cassidy.

TEN

I FOUND everyone in camp except Jeremiah, who was on sentry duty somewhere. Beth slept quietly by the low fire, with an old grey wool shirt of someone's rolled up under her head as a pillow. The travois Luke and McNab had built stretched out next to her. Maria still tended her pot on the stove, stirring constantly at a slow steady pace. Cassidy, Luke, and McNab stood a few feet away, talking quietly among themselves.

I ran up to the men.

"You gotta come see this!" I said.

Cassidy shot a stern look at me and then nodded towards Beth, so I lowered my voice.

"You gotta come see this!" I repeated. "A footprint! I found a footprint! A big one!"

Cassidy held up his hand, stopping me.

"Whoa there, Billy. Is there any danger?"

I shook my head.

"Then calm down and speak a little more slowly."

I nodded and took a deep breath.

"Over that way," I said, pointing, "I found what looks like a giant's footprint in the mud down the river. You gotta come see."

McNab snorted, but with a smile, and turned to Luke. "He finds Beth, and then proof of giants. Just how lucky is this kid?"

"I'm not a kid," I muttered.

"Nah, it's Billy the Kid," McNab said.

My blood rose, but Cassidy raised a hand.

"Embrace it," Cassidy said, his eyes mirthful, "once McNab gives you a nickname, it sticks."

"Unless Jeremiah changes it in one of his books," McNab said.

I blinked. I could be in one of Jeremiah's books?

"Let's go see this footprint, Billy," Cassidy said.

"This way," I said. I trotted back the way I'd come, with all three of them quick on my heels.

The footprint was still there—several inches of pressed down mud with clear edges. Cassidy stood a few feet back from it. He surveyed it carefully and then dropped to his knees for a different angle. After a bit, he walked slowly around it, making sure never to step in the mud itself.

Luke and McNab fanned out, looking for more prints. Everything was quiet, except for the buzz of insects and the sound of our own steps. The sweat beaded up on my forehead as I watched.

Cassidy completed his circuit and stepped up to the edge of the footprint. He knelt down and stuck his finger along one side, as if he was measuring the depth. He frowned and pulled back.

"Well, Billy," he said somewhat solemnly, "you've answered part of the mystery but created others."

"What do you mean?" I asked

"The town," he gestured back toward Grand Lake, "was smashed up by giants. This pretty much confirms it. But it raises the question, how did the giants get here?"

Yeah, I thought. Couldn't have been across the plains. We would've seen them.

"Maybe they came down from the North?" I suggested. "Through Indian territory?"

"Maybe," he said. "But how'd they get past Chicago then?"

Good question. They couldn't go through Canada because they couldn't cross the Great Lakes. Fort Chicago and the smaller forts west of it plugged up the only land passage to go around the Mississippi headwaters.

"What if they crossed through Cherokee Territory? From Memphis or something?"

He shook his head. After a pause, he looked around.

"McNab!" he called.

The burly man was walking a wide sweep above the shore back toward town when he heard his name. He quickly turned and trotted toward us.

"Memphis is troll territory," Cassidy said to me. "Even if the trolls let the Jotun cross through, there's no way the Cherokee would've allowed them to cross the river. And if they had, we'd've heard."

I fell quiet, thinking.

As I did so, McNab came up. He was breathing heavy, but didn't look at all winded. He only gave me a quick glimpse before his eyes followed Cassidy's finger, pointing at the footprint.

"Notice anything unusual?" Cassidy asked.

"It's bigger than usual," McNab said, "but within range."

"Yeah. What else?"

McNab paused, and then scratched his head. After a bit his eyes went wide.

"There's no heel. It's not a boot print."

"Jotun wear boots!" I said. "They do!"

"They do," Cassidy said, "at least most of the time."

"This is a moccasin print," McNab said.

"Maybe," Cassidy said. "All we know is it's not a boot."

"Cassidy!" Luke called. He stood further downstream, another two hundred yards or so, gesturing for us to come up.

I started to hustle, but Cassidy just strolled, so I slowed down. Several minutes later, we caught up with Luke. He stood on soft ground, some mud, but with a lot of trampled grass too.

"Lots of prints," he said, indicating the ground around us. "All look like this one. All headed west."

"Hmmm," Cassidy said. He knelt by the closest footprint and examined it. "Same as the first." Then he stood. "Let's get Jeremiah and talk back in camp."

We sat around the fire and talked. Well, I mostly listened after a glare from McNab when I'd interrupted for the second time. That turned out to be a really good thing. I had a hard time keeping my chin from dropping with what I learned.

I mean, I'd completely failed to notice that not only were there no people in town, but no horses or cows or other animals. Luke had found horse tracks headed north on the road out of town, but he couldn't tell how new they were. Same with the wagon tracks.

Which is when I almost slapped my forehead. Why weren't there any wagons? We wouldn't have to pull Beth in a travois if we had a wagon, and I'd completely missed them. Apparently there was one smashed up near something that Jeremiah called the stables, but there should've been more. Yet while the wagons were gone, no one had ransacked the buildings. If they had, they would've found Beth.

I'd missed all of this, but not Cassidy and his team.

Maria had managed to get Beth to talk a bit more, once she'd woken up in mid-morning. She hadn't seen anything and knew little. She'd been asleep when her mother woke her up and told her to hide under the bed. Then her parents had left the house.

Beth had lain there, scared and worried, for some time. She couldn't hear what was happening outside, but her parents didn't come back either. Then she heard crashing sounds and a few minutes later the house collapsed on her. She'd drifted in and out of consciousness until we found her.

Until *I* found her. I didn't say anything to remind the others, but Jeremiah did look my way and nod when Maria got to that part of Beth's story.

But that was my last chance to preen for a while. I'd found the first footprint, but Jeremiah had been looking for some, just on the other side of town, further north. The ground was harder over there, which made it impossible for him to find clear tracks, like I'd done.

Jeremiah pointed out that we also hadn't seen or heard any birds. That was just strange. When he mentioned it, I couldn't help but scan the skies, but all I saw were scattered clouds and blue sky. He'd seen fish, which reminded me of my aborted trip to hook us some dinner, and of course we'd all heard and seen the bugs, so the town wasn't lifeless. Just a lot quieter than it should've been, even with the people gone.

The conversation soon turned to what to do next. Cassidy listened to everyone on his team's opinions, and even asked Maria when she'd been too quiet. McNab was worried about the mining camps, supposed to be to the north, that had reported the giant sighting that had drawn us up here. Jeremiah thought we should ride to Saratoga West, the only other real town in the area, and either warn those folks or make sure they were okay. McNab pointed out that we might also need to let the folks in Empire know, or maybe even send somebody back over Rollins Pass to warn the folks in Golden City and get reinforcements.

He looked at me when he said that.

I pointedly ignored him. Cassidy only gave me a quick glance before turning to Luke and asking what he thought. The scout just shrugged and said whatever Cassidy decided was fine.

"The other towns come first," Cassidy announced when the debate died down a bit. "Luke, you ride to Empire, as fast as you can. Have them send a messenger to Golden City and get the militia called up. Jeremiah, you go north to the mining camps. Give them the same warning and tell them to get back to Golden City. If either of you encounter any Jotun, use your judgement on whether to go on or come back here."

The two men nodded.

"McNab, you and me will go to Saratoga West. We haven't met anyone from there, which has me worried."

"What about me?" I interjected.

Cassidy turned and looked at me, his eyebrows raised.

"You stay here with Maria and Beth," he said. "You do what Maria says, understand?"

"But I can ride real fast! I could get to Empire and back in no time!"

"And if you run into a Jotun, then what?" McNab drawled. "Gonna throw your fishing pole at him?"

My face burned. Why did he hate me so much?

"Billy," Cassidy said, his voice firm, "your job is keeping Beth safe. The Jotun could come back, or other things like coyotes could come in the night, if the rest of us aren't back by then. We need you here."

I was about to argue that Maria didn't need my help keeping Beth safe when I saw the stern look in Cassidy's eyes. Instead, I swallowed hard and nodded.

Cassidy turned to the others. "We have a lot of daylight still. I suggest we get started."

The men went to pack their things. I looked to Maria for what she wanted me to do.

"Go fish," she said with a small smile. "It'll be a good lunch."

I nodded. When the men rode out a little while later, I trudged down to the lake once again, looking for a good spot to hook some trout.

There's always been something peaceful about being out on my own. When I settled on the bank over a small pool that had some little brookies in it, it had actually turned into a nice day. The sun was bright but not too hot, with the usual mountain breeze to keep it cool. Some beetles flew near by and a couple of them buzzed, but I didn't know what type they were. Nearby some Indian Paintbrush grew, and I plucked a couple of their petal fronds, the green edible ones, and nibbled on them while I fished.

My makeshift pole wasn't really the best for what I was doing. It was way too floppy, but I didn't see a way to find something better without spending the whole rest of the day looking. It bent nearly double when I snagged my first fish, but I was able to bring it in and grab the line before it did so. But the other fish must've gotten smart then. I only landed one more before the sun was overhead and I knew I had to quit for lunch.

Back at camp, Beth looked better. She was sitting up and sipping something out of a tin cup. She looked at me and kinda smiled, or smiled as best she could through the pain that peeked out around the corners of her mouth and eyes.

I stopped at her side and knelt down. She had some color in her cheeks and a bit of life in her eyes, which was good to see. Her brown locks had been combed and her face washed, making her look more like a tired girl than an accident survivor. A giant survivor, I reminded myself.

"How you feeling?" I asked.

"I hurt," she said. "Not as much as before, thanks to Maria."

"Good for her," I said, giving the Mexican woman a smile. She nodded her head in acknowledgement and I turned back to Beth. "And good for you."

She tried to smile, but it had as much of a wince as anything.

"Cassidy'll take care of you," I said. "You'll be fine."

"That's what he said." She sighed. "I can't believe *Cassidy* is taking care of me." She looked at me. "He's even more amazing in person."

I blinked and leaned back, not quite sure what to say. Did *I* sound this sickly sweet?

"You must be thrilled to be part of his team," she said.

"Um ... uh ... yeah." I said.

She didn't notice my fumble, just heard my words. Fortunately, before things could get more than a bit awkward, Maria came over with a cup of what looked like tea.

"Here," she said to Beth.

Beth made a face. "More medicine?"

"Yes," Maria said calmly, "it will help you heal."

"Needs honey," the girl said.

"When we have honey, we will be sure to add it. Until then, please drink."

Maria held the cup close to Beth's face, but the girl took it in her own hand and sipped a little. She grimaced, but kept drinking.

Maria turned to me.

"Time for you to learn how to care for Beth. In case I'm not here."

ELEVEN

MARIA SAT BACK, her legs tucked under her. She smiled at me, a calm smile with those deep penetrating black eyes. She brushed a black strand of hair from her face and waited.

"Uh ... what?" I said. "Why won't you be here?"

She shrugged, but gave a reassuring smile to Beth.

"Let me show you how to mix the medicine," Maria said. She motioned for me to follow her to the other side of the fire. Beth sipped some more of her tea, but then set it aside and laid down again.

Maria had spread out a sheet of tanned leather, which looked like buffalo hide, and anchored the corner with rocks. A small mortar and pestle sat on the upper right, a bit apart from several small pouches, each about the size of a silver dollar. The pouches had decorative designs worked into the leather making each of them distinct. She also had two tin cups, one a little more dented on the side, both empty at the moment.

"This pouch is willow bark," she said, taking one with a stylized W on it. "Good for pain. You grind it into powder." She took a small piece of the bark out and demonstrated with the mortar.

I watched, but I'd seen Ma do stuff like this before, so it wasn't something I was worried about doing.

"No more than this," she said. Her pile of powder was smaller than my little fingernail. "At meals and halfway between meals. Understand?"

"Yeah," I said, "but ... why won't you be here?"

"I may," she said, "but it is foolish to have only one person that can do a job, no?"

I nodded, conceding the point. But then I caught myself.

"Wait," I said. "I'm new. If you need more than one person who can make medicines, you needed that before I came along, too."

She brushed some hair behind her ear and gave me an amused smile.

"McNab and Jeremiah can both do basic medicines," she said.

"So, why ...?" My mind whirled. She sat patiently watching me, while I thought.

"Because Cassidy might need you to go with him," I said. "For something you can do besides healing."

She didn't nod, but her eyes crinkled in amusement, which encouraged me.

"So what can you do?" I asked. "Jeremiah doesn't say in the books. He doesn't even *have* you in his books. Or if he does, I don't remember it."

"Jeremiah doesn't put everything in his books."

I snorted. That was true in so many ways.

"So what can you do?" I asked again.

Her eyes twinkled, and for a moment I thought she was going to refuse to say. As it was, she drew it out, moistening her lips and shifting her seat before she spoke.

"I," she said, "can detect rifts."

My chin dropped. "But there's only one rift. And it's closed, or at least that's what I hear."

"It is," she said, "but there have been other rifts. Cassidy's worried there could be one here."

That made sense! That made so much sense!

"If there's a rift here, that explains everything!" I babbled. "The giants couldn't walk all this way, not without being seen. McNab said so, and he's right! But they don't need to walk if there's a second rift. They could just, I dunno, *be* here! Walk through whatever it is on the other side of the rift!"

"Jotunheim," she said.

"Yeah! Jotunheim!"

Boy it made sense. It really made sense.

And then the implications sunk in. The Jotun had destroyed all of the Confederacy and most of the Union. The plague they'd brought with them had killed even more. It had taken everything us humans had to stop them, and we were still in a war with them and the trolls.

And if they were here ...

I sucked in my breath and started breathing hard.

Oh Dear God.

"This," Maria said firmly, "is ground chili pepper." She held up another bag directly in front of my face and shook it. "Mix it with bacon fat and smear it on her legs where they're swelling."

I nodded, but I was having trouble paying close attention. I kept picturing Jotun coming down from the mountains and overrunning Golden City.

"About the same amount as the willow bark in each spoonful of fat. Understand?"

I nodded, but I still struggled to listen. What would Jotun do to the Astor? Or to Boggs? Or to all the miners in their shacks? I did my best to learn about the medicines, and Maria must've believed it, because she didn't make me repeat anything back to her.

The three of us had a simple lunch of trout and biscuits, Maria cooking the latter in a pan while I fried up the fish. Beth ate a little, but mostly she drank some broth that Maria made. I excused myself when she asked for a bedpan, though Maria told me that was something else I needed to learn. I told her I already knew, having taken care of that awful chore for Ma, in her last days.

Instead, I wandered a bit into the town. The fire had finally died down. Just a few embers remained. Not enough smoke left to attract too much attention, but I realized that if the fire hadn't before, it certainly wasn't going to now. The Jotun had to know about it and just didn't care.

So I wandered through, looking at the wrecks and thinking.

Cassidy, and Maria, and Jeremiah, heck even Luke and McNab, all knew what they were doing, and were all good at it. They'd spotted so many things about this busted up town that I hadn't, and had even figured out there had to be a second rift, without even needing to discuss it. They did their jobs, and they did them well.

And what did that say about me?

I could shoot, yeah, but I didn't have a gun anymore. I could fish, but I'd needed Cassidy's hooks. I hadn't even thought to bring some of my own. I'd found Beth and the footprint, but McNab was right, that was just luck.

So what good was I?

I wasn't good for anything but looking after a crippled ten year old girl.

The only reason I was still here was because Cassidy didn't know where the giants were. I was sure that as soon as he did, he'd send me back to Golden City.

And maybe I should go.

But my gut rebelled at that. Every day, for seven years, I'd wanted to be here. Every day, I'd dreamed of being by Cassidy's side, fighting the giants. And now here I was—doing it!

I just wasn't doing it well. McNab didn't like me. Luke barely talked to me. Everyone else, well, they tolerated me. I was sure they wouldn't miss me when I was gone.

You could just go, I thought. Be a sharpshooter. Help the militia or maybe go join the army.

I shook my head hard, trying to cast the doubts out. I just had to work harder, do more to show them I was worth it.

I'd circled the burning building by then, and some puffy scattered clouds had rolled in. I figured the ladies were done with their business and headed back to camp.

Beth was asleep again, which I figured was a good thing. She'd shifted around a bit, as if she was trying to lay on her side, but couldn't quite make it. That had to be a good sign for her legs and ankle.

Maria sat near the coals of the fire, packing up her medicines and the cooking gear. She acknowledged me with a quick look before returning to her chores. I went over and checked on our horses. Blackie and Maria's mare seemed to have eaten most of the grass within reach, so I re-staked them a bit further down the shore.

It all seemed quiet. Peaceful like, if you didn't look too close.

After that, Maria suggested we take watches. She'd do the first shift and I agreed. When she woke me in the middle of the night, she said that nothing had happened.

Nothing happened for the first part of my watch either, but along toward dawn, I heard a horse riding hard down the road toward us. It came from the west, the way toward Saratoga West. I figured it had to be Cassidy or McNab, but I kinda wish I'd had a gun, just in case. Instead, I woke Maria and grabbed a long stick from the firewood pile, figuring I could use it as a club if needed.

I needn't have worried. After a few minutes, McNab surged into sight. He slowed, and then walked his horse to the edge of camp.

"Maria!" he called. "Get your stuff! We need to go!"

"What is it?" she asked.

"Ghosts," he said.

She grabbed her packed medicines and hustled over to the horses.

"What about the town?" I asked.

He looked at me. "Empty, like people left in a hurry. But there's also a lot of bodies."

I turned white. Oh, God.

"Help Maria get saddled," he said. "Then you stay here and take care of Beth."

I jumped to, and soon we had her saddle cinched and her mounted.

"Wait!" I said to Maria. "What about the medicines for Beth?"

"There's enough for tonight and tomorrow by the fire," she said.

"Okay." That meant she was planning on being back, which comforted me.

Maria brought her horse along side McNab's. He gave me one last look.

"Stay safe, kid!" he called. Then he spurred his horse and they were gone.

With all the shouting, Beth woke up. She was groggy, mostly, but wanted water. I fetched her some, and then lay next to her and held her hand while she drifted back to sleep. I myself was dog tired, but I couldn't rest. My mind just couldn't stop chasing squirrels and my heart thought there was a giant behind every bush. But it was quiet, with just enough breeze in the trees to be like a lullaby.

We talked some. I told her the news from Golden City and, after she asked, a little about my life there. She told me about coming to Grand Lake with her parents from Fort Collins. Her Pa had heard about silver, but hadn't found much. Instead, he'd provided for the family by taking his boat out into the lake and bringing back fish for the locals. Sometimes, his catch was salted and sent back to Fort Collins or Empire by wagon.

Which reminded me. We hadn't seen any boats, either.

After a bit, Beth started to feel tired again. I gave her some more water and medicine and then stepped away while she used the bedpan. Emptying it really wasn't much different at all than what I'd done for Ma. Then Beth tried to get comfortable on her side.

"Tired of sleeping on my back," she said with a worn look. She still looked like she'd been kicked by a horse.

I remembered the warning about bedsores Doc Richards gave me when I was taking care of Ma, and suggested we see if she could move some.

"You mean stand?" she asked.

I thought a bit.

"Why not?" I said. "If I had a crutch and I helped you, you might be able to take a few steps. Maybe sit somewhere a mite more comfortable."

She looked around our camp, which only had rocks and some broken logs McNab had pulled from one of the buildings to use as seats.

"Maybe for a little bit?" she said, eyeing the closest log like it was a possible throne. "After I rest?"

"I'll see if I can make you a crutch," I said. "While you rest."

She nodded wearily. I adjusted the blanket she was using as a pillow and pulled the blanket up around her shoulders. She closed her eyes but didn't drift off to sleep right away. Still, I headed into town to the building where we'd found her.

I didn't find a suitable piece of wood for a crutch as quick as I'd thought. I did find some blankets and some clothes, some of which were clearly Beth's and some her parents'. I also found a Bible and a broken oil lamp that must've been on a now-shattered bedside table near what must've been her parents' bed.

That's when I realized it. We'd searched the town for people, but not for supplies. We'd been eating the tack and bacon and dried fruit we'd brought from Golden City, but I'd seen the spilled corn in the store. If nothing else, I could probably grind it up in Maria's pestle and make the griddle cakes taste better. Heck, there was probably other food under that collapsed ceiling. And that didn't even count the rest of the town.

I needed a crutch, but what else could I find?

I decided I had to find out.

TWELVE

BETH RESTED QUIETLY under her blanket by the fire pit. She stirred when I returned and beamed in delight when I showed her the dress and unmentionables I'd found. They were hers all right, though she didn't want to change just then. Not in front of me. I left them within reach and went back to the town.

I remembered that the store porch had more support poles than we'd needed for the travois. As I walked there, I tried to guess what the other buildings had been. Most looked like houses, but one was probably a stable, because it had both a main building and a large barn, or at least what had been a barn once. In between sat a small corral, with most of the split rail fence pushed down.

No horses, of course, but I spotted some hay and some bags of feed. When Blackie finished grazing the grass near camp, we'd have some options.

At the store, I found a pole suitable for a crutch if I cut it down. That could be a problem, since McNab had taken his axe with him. Still, maybe I could find something.

I headed back to the corral area. Off to one side sat a small woodpile of pine logs, chopped in lengths for a fireplace. I poked around it, but didn't find an axe. Of course, the owner probably wouldn't leave the axe by the wood anyway, but keep it in his house or barn.

So I headed to the nearest collapsed wall of the barn. The wooden door had been blown out, but was largely intact. The posts of the doorway still stood, but the log walls on either side were torn and jagged and only about head high.

Still, the building wasn't as bad as the others. Now that I knew what to look for, it seemed that a giant had just walked into the middle and shoved the sides down. The walls hadn't been kicked to pieces like at the store or some of the houses.

Wooden pegs jutted outside of the inside wall on the right, and that's when I hit a jackpot. Not only was there an axe, knocked to the ground, but a saw, some hammers of various sizes, and tongs.

I definitely needed to search these buildings.

However, I also couldn't leave Beth alone for long.

I took the long pole, the axe, and the saw, and went to see how she was doing.

Beth waved when she saw me coming. She'd managed to pull on the new dress, this one a blue calico print. She still had the blanket pulled up to her waist but for the first time, she seemed to at least have a hint of a smile on her face.

"How are you feeling?" I asked once I got close.

"Still hurt," she said, "but it's nice to be in clean clothes!"

"I bet it does," I said with a chuckle. I checked the position of the sun. It was close enough to mid-afternoon.

"Would you like some more medicine?" I asked.

"Please?"

"Coming right up, my lady!"

She giggled, and it was like hearing a sunny brook. My own heart felt lighter.

"Yes, my lady?" I asked.

She still beamed at me.

"Why do you call me that?" She seemed earnest.

"Isn't that what you are? A lady in distress, like in the Camelot stories?"

"That's *damsel* in distress."

I nodded, conceding the point. She still smiled.

While Beth watched, I retrieved the supplies Maria had left from the small pack and spread them out, just as she'd shown me. The pestle and mortar to the right, the packets nearby. She'd separated out a little bit of willow bark into a wrapped waxed paper bundle, and I carefully unfolded it and began grinding it up. It turned out to be harder than I thought. Maria'd had a fine powder in a minute and after five, mine was finally to a level I thought would dissolve well.

It turned out it did, which pleased me. Beth didn't object either when I brought it to her.

"I should make you that crutch now," I said.

"Can you tell me about Cassidy while you do?" she asked.

"Uh ... sure." I took the pole I'd found and leaned it against one of the rocks we'd be using as a chair. Then I picked up the saw. "What do you want to know?"

"What's he really like?"

I shrugged. "You've met him. What do you think he's like?"

"He's really nice," she said. "And brave! He promised to get my Ma and Pa back."

"Hmm." I started sawing the pole, which gave me time to think. Cassidy had said he would, but could he really? We didn't even know if Beth's parents were alive.

I finished cutting the pole and took it over to lay next to Beth to check the length.

"So is he always that nice?" Beth asked.

"Uh ... well, I've never seen him be mean. Except to Jotun."

"Oh, I'm sure he's mean to them all the time! He hates them!"

I nodded in agreement.

"You've probably seen him in dozens of fights. Is he as amazing as the books say?"

"Yeah."

"Good!" Her eyes were fierce as she said that, as if it was a judgement. I kind of sensed that it was.

The pole was long enough, but then I realized it wouldn't fit under her arm well, without a crosspiece. I could make one if I could find a hammer and some nails.

"Be back," I said.

As I walked back to the destroyed barn, I started to feel a mite guilty. I hadn't exactly *lied* to Beth, but she clearly thought I knew Cassidy way better than I did. And I hadn't corrected her.

I took both the hammers and the tongs I'd found—no point in making another trip back if we turned out to need them—but didn't see any nails. I looked around a bit and even got down on my knees to push through the dirt and shattered logs. Then I laughed silently at myself.

There were *plenty* of nails around. I just had to pull them out of the wood they'd been nailed into.

Of course a lot of the log walls used a joist construction, but after poking around Beth's house, I found some nails through what must've been the front door frame. I was able to use the claw on the hammer and get two that weren't badly bent. Then it was back to camp.

I found Beth sitting up, looking out over the lake. She seemed sad, but not on the edge of crying again. I let her be and got to work sawing a cross bar and nailing it on. She continued to watch the waves on the water until I finished.

"What're you looking at?" I asked.

"Just the lake," she said. "Seems strange to not see any boats on it."

"We didn't find any boats."

"Most everyone kept them at the dock," she said, pointing north down the shore.

It was a ways off, but I could see a bunch of broken timbers there, mostly submerged. I hadn't walked that way before, but I guessed that Jeremiah or Luke had.

"Did you go out on the lake with your Pa a lot?"

"Uh huh. I helped get the fish into the buckets. Pa would dump the nets into the bottom of the boat and then we'd both grab the fish and try to get them into the buckets, without losing them over the side."

She pursed her lips, as if the memories were bringing the melancholy.

"You must've caught a lot of fish," I said as light as I could. I wanted her to stay a bit happy, as hard as I knew that must be.

"Lots. Big ones."

"I'm jealous," I said. "I only caught two tiny ones fishing this morning."

"The big ones don't come near shore."

"Yeah," I said. "I imagine that's true. But what can I do? I've got no boat, and all the ones by the docks are destroyed."

She looked thoughtful for a moment.

"Mr. Jenkins has a canoe," she said. "He keeps it by the side of his cabin."

"Really?" I said with a blink. "Which house is that?"

"The next one down," she said, pointing beyond the house next to hers.

"Huh," I said. "Well, maybe I'll have to take it out and catch us some *big* fish for dinner. If my lady would like that."

She rolled her eyes at me, but the corners of her mouth turned up still the same.

I held up the crutch. "Let's try this."

She nodded, and we worked together to lift her up. It was hard work, 'cause while she wasn't heavy, if we moved her ankle wrong, she'd cry out in pain. When we got her standing, mostly leaning on me and some on the crutch, she hissed and bit her lip. Her face was almost white with agony, but she didn't cry out.

With a few stumbled steps, we got her to a log seat five feet away and eased her back down.

"You gonna be okay?" I asked.

With gritted teeth, she nodded.

"I'll get you some water. Then I'll go look for that canoe."

She nodded again.

I refilled her cup, and realized I should refill the canteen as well. Once I'd taken care of that, I realized I also needed to put some more ointment on her legs. She let me, and as I did so, I looked them over. They looked awful—black and blue and swollen, but no bedsores and no infections.

That was really good.

Still, the move seemed to have taken a lot out of her. She slumped on the log and for a moment, I regretted the move. Before I could say anything, though, she asked for the blanket for her legs. That I was happy to do.

Leaving Beth relaxed, though not completely comfortable, I went down to the Jenkins house. The south wall had fallen over, and sure enough, under the rubble was a spruce bark canoe with two paddles tucked inside. It looked in good shape—no obvious holes— and so I dragged it down to the lake. It didn't sink, so after a bit I got in and rowed it back along the shore to camp.

Beth looked at me in disbelief as I walked up after beaching the boat.

"That was ugly," she said.

I bristled. "What do you mean?"

"Your paddling. You don't do that side push thing to steer a canoe. You change the end of your stroke, like this." she demonstrated with her hands.

"Uh, well, I've never been in a canoe before."

"You've never been in a canoe before?" She stared at me in almost shocked disbelief. "But Cassidy uses them all the time!"

At least in the books, I thought.

"You'll capsize for sure if you paddle like that!"

The blood rose in my cheeks and my pulse began to pound. *It's like she's making fun of me!*

"How can you never have been in a canoe?"

That stabbed me, the disdain in her eyes worst of all.

"Look, I haven't, okay?"

"Then why'd you offer to fish? That was stupid."

"Because I thought you'd like it!" I couldn't believe this girl! I'd been trying to do something nice, and now she was calling me stupid!

"It was still stupid."

That did it!

"Fine!" I snarled. "I'll go hunt us some dinner! That I know how to do!"

I stomped off north, making a point not to look back.

The sun was low above the western mountains. We had maybe an hour left before dusk, but all that meant was not looking to my left so as not to blind myself. It was cooling off, and I got maybe four hundred yards before I too cooled down enough to think.

That's when I realized how stupid this was, too. How was I gonna hunt without a gun? Besides, Cassidy didn't want any gunshots.

This was stupid. I was stupid.

So I stood there, catching my breath after the hard walk, staring straight ahead. Cassidy didn't make me feel stupid. Yeah, I wasn't as bright or experienced as them, yet. But that was *yet*. I'd learn.

I'd learn faster if they hadn't left.

That bugged me as much as Beth, I realized. It didn't seem like they were gonna be back by night, which meant they might not be back for a while.

I idly wished they'd come riding up the road right then. Any of them—Cassidy, McNab, Maria, Jeremiah. Even Luke. That'd set things right.

So I stood there, staring down the northern road, trying to think of what to say to Beth when I gave up and turned around and went back.

And as I stared, something caught my eye.

Movement, coming toward me.

I squinted. It looked like a man walking toward me. Jeremiah on foot, maybe?

But then it passed some pine trees lining the road and my heart froze.

The 'man's' head was even with the topmost branches.

We'd ridden by trees that height. The top branches had to be twenty-five or thirty feet up.

Oh, God, oh, God, oh, God.

The Jotun, and it *had* to be a Jotun, was headed straight toward me.

THIRTEEN

MY HEART POUNDED, and for a moment it looked like my legs were gonna go rubbery. My mouth went dry and I became real aware of how quiet the woods were, and how long the shadows were getting. For a moment, I hoped I was seeing something.

But then the giant stopped for a second and stared my way.

It started running.

My legs found their strength. I turned and fled.

I pelted into camp. Beth slouched on the log where I'd left her. At the sight of me, she started in alarm.

"Giant!" I cried. "Coming!"

Beth tried to rise in flustered terror. She dropped her crutch and sank back down in agony. I was at her side in an instant.

"What are we going to do?" she sobbed. "What are we going to do?" She threw her arms around my neck.

"The canoe!"

She clutched at me. I almost toppled over, but managed to claw for the crutch and shove it back under her arm.

"You can't paddle!"

"You can!"

She shrieked in pain as we hobbled forward and almost fell. I caught her and pulled the bulk of her weight onto me.

Beth gibbered and cried as we stumbled towards the shore. Tufts of grass were boulders to cross. All too often her toes scuffed through the dirt as I all but bore her weight. We stumbled, but I caught us. Then stumbled again, and again, I kept us from falling. She put some weight on her broken ankle and screamed. I jerked and we tumbled to the ground.

I rolled and landed on my back. Above, dark clouds blocked the stars. I looked back but couldn't see the giant.

Beth screamed and sobbed and grabbed at her ankle as she lay on her side.

"I'll carry you!" I said. I grabbed her arm and shook her to get her attention. "I'll carry you!"

She looked wild eyed.

"Sit up! Sit up!" I urged. With me pulling on her arms, she did so.

I flipped onto my hands and knees as close to her as I could.

"Crawl on my back! I'll carry you piggyback."

Still sobbing and crying, she reached for me. I pulled her arm forward until she could wrap her arms around my neck. I shifted my weight and helped her slide squarely on top of me.

I tried to stand. She almost slid off. I couldn't hold her in position and lift off my arms at the same time.

Fine. I'd crawl.

"Hang on tighter!" I said. I pulled her arms forward until she was able to get them completely around my neck. She almost choked me, but it was a solid enough grip.

I crawled. Stones stabbed my knees. Sand scratched my hands. I crawled.

Pain lanced my hand when I hit a thistle hidden in the grass. My shoulders throbbed under weighted agony. My ears deafened by Beth's cries of pain.

I crawled.

I hit the mud, mercifully not sinking in more than a half inch.

I crawled.

An eternity and a heartbeat later, we reached the canoe. Beth rolled off with a whimper, her face white, her eyes wide.

She'd stopped screaming. My heart pounded even harder.

I'd heard about battle shock. Read about it in one of Jeremiah's books even. This had to be it.

But I had no *time*.

I clambered to my feet and lifted Beth into the canoe. I did my best not to bang her broken ankle against the side. I got her lowered down into the bottom, her head on the bottom by one seat, her legs raised up on the other.

Panting hard, I turned and looked for the giant. In the dusky gloom, I couldn't see him. Blackie huffed and pulled at the rope that staked him to the ground. Our campfire, little more than embers, glowed like a lighthouse.

The medicines.

Gasping, I heaved myself forward. I stumbled as best I could toward the fire. I grabbed one of Beth's blankets and threw all of Maria's pouches and tools and supplies into the middle of it and pulled the corners up.

A bellow ripped the night.

My head whipped around. The giant was a few hundred yards away. He was running hard through the trees. He'd seen me.

I dashed for the canoe. Somehow, I didn't stumble and fall. I dumped the medicines in the front by Beth's feet and threw the blanket over her. Then I pushed the canoe off. I turned it so the seat with Beth's legs on it was away from me. I waded through the water until it was knee deep, and threw myself over the side, After a scramble where I made sure I didn't step on Beth, I got myself righted and sat up.

Behind me, the giant roared again.

I found the paddle and shoved water back as hard as I could. I may not've known how to steer, but I didn't need to. I just needed to get as far out into the lake as I could.

The giant roared again. This time it sounded like words, but none I recognized.

I kept paddling.

Ten feet to the right, the lake exploded. Water splashed feet into the air. The ripples died quickly.

Startled, I slowed only for a moment, before attacking my paddling even harder.

Something passed overhead and smashed into the water eight feet in front of us. Again, waves exploded in all directions.

He was throwing rocks!

I paddled.

The next splash was behind us. I didn't let up. The splash after that as well. I kept paddling.

I kept paddling until my arms ached and screamed and finally quit. I couldn't pull anymore. There'd been a few more splashes behind us, but not in a while.

I tried to turn my head and upper body to look, but nearly fell out of the canoe. I checked on Beth. She breathed shallow, her face still pale. I reached down and straightened the blanket over her so she'd be covered except for her face and feet.

Since I didn't know how to steer, I took the paddle and did that scuttle thing Beth had teased me about. It was awkward and didn't move us well, but eventually the canoe turned enough for me to see the shore.

The last of the sunlight had finally faded. I couldn't see much. Our fire was out, and so it was just black on dark grey on grey. But what I could see was the giant, partially silhouetted by the lighter sky behind him. He was also the only thing moving.

I couldn't tell what he was doing. He seemed to be walking back and forth. I sensed he was looking our way but couldn't be sure.

I waited.

After a bit, it became clear that he wasn't going anywhere. Whatever he was doing was going to take a while. Beth stirred below me, so I moved my attention from the giant to her.

She looked less pale, though it was hard to tell in the low light, and when I reached down and touched her cheek, it didn't feel as cold. I felt my way down her right arm and found her hand and pulled it up to her chest. That way I could lean forward and hold it.

As I did so, I rubbed her fingers, doing my best to get some warmth into them.

Jeremiah had written that there wasn't much you could do for battle shock other than keep the person warm and their feet a little higher than their head. They'd come out of it or they wouldn't.

I closed my eyes and prayed hard that Beth would. For both our sakes.

Sitting there in the canoe in the dark, wet below the waist and cold, I had to fight to keep my teeth from chattering. I also fought to keep the panic down.

We're safe, I reminded myself. Safe.

I forced myself to take deep breaths.

Safe.

I was still sore scared. I wished that Cassidy was there, or Jeremiah, or even McNab.

Somebody.

Beth needed help. *I* needed help. Where were we gonna get help?

I hadn't felt so alone since Ma died, and even then I'd had Tom.

I clutched Beth's hand tighter. She'd started breathing more regular, and seemed more at ease. I hoped she was asleep and not in battle shock anymore.

I hoped for a lot of things.

I wondered how long it would be before Cassidy or any of the others came back. Other than Luke, none of them expected to be long. How long would I have to wait?

But then I shook my head. For all I knew, they could be coming up to the camp now. Maybe stumbling on the giant.

That I hadn't heard for a while. I scanned the shoreline, but the giant was gone.

He could be hiding, I thought. Waiting for you.

I listened close, but all I could hear was the dripping of water off my clothes into the bottom of the boat. It splashed into little puddles there.

I never checked for leaks.

My heart froze.

One way or another, I had to get to shore. Soon. Somewhere the giant wasn't.

I let go of Beth's hand, put the paddle back in the water, and began stroking.

The canoe pointed north, toward a shadowed shore. I figured I oughta go that way a bit, just in case the giant was still near the destroyed town. The lake was too big to cross, especially in the dark. I paddled as best I could.

When I'd gone far enough that I had to look back over my shoulder to see the town ruins, or at least what I could make out in the dark, I did that side paddle thing until I turned. I splashed way too much, and I hoped the Jotun didn't hear, but I slowly got the canoe turned.

Beth moaned.

Startled, I reached for her, but then realized I was holding the paddle and so tried to move it to my other hand, while still reaching for her and …

I dropped the paddle over the side.

Beth groaned and shifted.

I lost it. I started laughing. Great bales of tension relieving laughter, rolling from my gut.

Hard laughter, long laughter. The 'hell with the world' laughter.

"Wha—what is it?" Beth said.

"It got too sad to be anything but funny."

"What?"

My gut hurt and soon so did my sides from the guffaws and tear-bringing bursts of relief.

"What?" she said again.

I forced myself to take some deep breaths, but they didn't quite still me. I took her hand.

"Can you sit up?" I asked.

"I think so."

We carefully shifted her around until she could lower her legs and lift her upper body. She still sat in the bottom of the boat with her back resting against the seat I was on. My legs splayed out on either side of her. The effort calmed me down enough that only a low chuckle escaped here and there.

"What's so funny?" she asked.

"Nothing," I said. "I just, well, good God, I started to list everything that's gone bad in my head, and it just started to become ridiculous."

"Huh?"

I stifled a last chuckle and took another deep breath.

"Well," I said once I felt I could control myself, "it's like this. We're in the middle of Grand Lake, without any supplies other than some medicine I grabbed. You're hurt, and I can't swim. It's dark. There's a giant on shore somewhere. We have no idea where Cassidy is, or if he's even still alive. The canoe might be leaking. And I just dropped the paddle overboard."

She snorted, which sent a wave of relief through me. She got the black humor, too.

"Well," she said, "I guess it's a good thing the paddle floats."

I couldn't stop from slapping myself on the forehead.

FOURTEEN

IT TOOK A WHILE, but we managed to fish the paddle out of the dark cold water and row back to shore. Beth wasn't able to do much herself, but she demonstrated how I should stroke the paddle through the water. We landed north of the dock ruins where we managed to get Beth out of the canoe and onto the ground without too much pain. The blanket had been splashed, but to my relief that and my soaked pants was about it. If we'd had a leak, it should've been much worse.

The shore was quiet. We could hear some bugs flitting around, and sometimes small waves lapping at the side of the beached canoe, but that was it. Our eyes had adjusted enough that we could make out a few low scrub brushes nearby as well as distant trees and the general debris of the town. But nothing was moving, and we couldn't see the giant.

"You better get out of those pants," Beth said quietly.

"What?"

"You'll catch the chills," she said. "The blanket's drier."

Well, I *was* cold. Nights in the high mountains were cold even if you weren't wet, and the clammy wool clung to my legs. The thing was, I needed to see if I could locate that giant first. We needed to be safe before I went around in my unmentionables.

"I'll be okay," I said. "What about you?"

"I hurt a lot."

"Yeah, the willow bark must've wore off. Let's fix that."

Thankfully, the medicines had remained dry. They were jumbled, and one of the pouches had opened up, spilling out some liquid I didn't recognize, but by feel and close looks I was able to find both the willow bark and the stuff for the ointment. I got 'em prepared and used the mortar as a cup to give Beth some water.

The problem was, we were about out. We had maybe enough until morning, when Maria had expected to be back.

I wasn't so sure about that anymore.

Still, Beth seemed to be doing better.

"You gonna be okay for a bit while I scout around?" I asked.

She nodded.

"Good. Stay warm." I tucked the blanket over her just to be sure.

I crept past the dock remains, and then over to the town buildings. I'd learned to move quiet, hunting prairie dogs. It was mostly a matter of going slow. That and checking your step before you put your foot down. Hard to do in the dark, but I made sure to move extra slow, especially near bushes or trees.

Nothing stirred as I worked my way from wrecked building to wrecked building. I made it all the way through town and didn't see a thing. I headed over to our camp.

Blackie was gone, which made me relieved and worried at the same time. The giant might've took him, or he might've escaped, but he hadn't been killed. The books said trolls ate horses, but that giants rarely did.

Our camp had been smashed up and a lot of things stepped on, but it looked like our stuff was there. I found my saddlebags still propped up against a tree where I'd left them, undisturbed. I owned one change of clothes and I decided that now was as good a time as any to get into 'em.

Finally dry and a bit warmer, I scrounged what I could find from camp in the dark—the old shirt Beth had used as a pillow, a pot that I kicked without seeing it, and her old bedpan. I figured she'd need that sooner than later. I looked around a bit more, hoping to spot some more medicines, but it was too dark to really tell, so I carefully, quietly, walked back to the canoe.

I didn't see any sign of the giant on the way back, either.

Beth was still awake, waiting for me, and she stirred when she sensed my approach.

"Got your pillow and bedpan," I said. "I didn't find a canteen, but I've got a pot we can drink from."

"Good," she said weakly. "Water?"

I quickly fetched her some and helped her sit up enough to drink. It was a bit of a struggle for her, and she strained even to just remain still.

"You warm enough?" I asked.

She shook her head.

I didn't have any more blankets. There was only one thing to do.

"How about I hold you?" I said. "Keep us both warm until morning."

The girl nodded and laid back down.

I stretched out next to her, trying to be close enough to share body heat, but not so close as to bump her bad legs. Her feet came to my knees when she was lying down, so it was no easy matter. But somehow we did it.

I promised myself I'd stay awake, listening for the giant, until she fell asleep and I could scout some more. But I'd had a long day, too, and I drifted to sleep before I realized I was even tired.

When dawn arrived, I blinked hard and opened my eyes. I stretched out the stiffness in my limbs and sat up. Beth continued to slumber.

We only had a slight breeze, enough to stir up the smell of the grass and tussle the water on the lake. The burning building had gone out, leaving just a hint of smoke in the air. Nearby, a bee flitted from Indian Paintbrush blossom to blossom. It would've been a really nice morning under other circumstances.

Actually, it was a nice morning anyway. We were alive.

I stretched and stood. My stomach grumbled, so I decided to go to camp and see what we had left in the way of food. I kept an eye out for the giant while I walked, but didn't see him.

I didn't find much back at our old campsite. I'd missed some smashed cook pots in the dark, and the travois McNab had built for Beth had been smushed several inches into the dirt. The rim of the footprint was still visible around it. The fire pit too was destroyed, but I lucked out and found my canteen, kicked off into a bush several yards from where I'd left it. I also found most of the tools I'd used to make Beth's crutch, except the axe for some reason. I'd left it buried in a log and the entire log was gone.

I wondered if I should move Beth and me to the camp, or set up a new one?

If Cassidy came back, he'd look for us at the camp. But so would the giant.

I decided we'd eat before we moved.

As for food itself, I didn't find any at camp that was edible. I had a little still in my saddlebags, but that was it.

Except, I realized, for what was in the town. I'd seen dried corn in the destroyed store. Maybe there was more there.

It took a while to move splintered boards, shattered logs, and the remains of shelves around, but in the end, I found a feast. They had plenty of dried pemmican and smoked venison jerky. Some mice had gotten into the corn as I'd suspected, and the berries were all smashed but there was actually some coarse bread that wasn't too stale.

Even better, a whole case of cider had avoided getting crushed.

I took everything back to Beth, who was awake and had used

the bedpan. She grimaced and bit her lip a lot, but I couldn't do much. I mixed up the last of the willow bark and gave it to her. She took it gratefully.

I frowned as I watched her drink it, mostly out of feeling helpless. There was plenty of willow around the lake, but I didn't know how to harvest the bark or turn it into the powder.

There was a lot I didn't know how to do, actually. A lot that Maria, and McNab, and Jeremiah already knew.

"So," said Beth as she started in on our breakfast, "when will Cassidy be back?"

"I dunno," I said with a shrug.

"Well how long does he usually take?"

I blinked. "Uh ..."

She waited patiently while my mind ran squirrel tracks trying to answer. Did I know from the books?

"Oh, I see," she said after a bit, "there's no usual time he's gone like this."

"Yeah," I said. "It could be any time, depending on what he found in Saratoga West."

"So what does he expect you to do while he's gone?"

That one I could answer. "He told me to take care of you."

"You've done that," she said with a smile. Then she grew serious. "Thank you for getting us away from the giant."

My face flushed and I looked away.

"I know," she said with a small laugh. "Just another day working for Cassidy, right?" She sighed. "He's *so* amazing."

I bit my lip. I didn't have any idea of what to say.

"What are some of the best things you've done with him?" she asked. "Anything as scary as last night?"

My gut started to churn. I fought to keep my breathing normal.

"You know," I said, "I'd love to tell stories, but we're not safe from that giant yet. I'd like to look through the town for more supplies, if I can find them, while it's light out and before he comes back."

Her face fell, but she nodded.

"We have food and some tools," I said. "I'd like to find a gun, if I can, and maybe some more blankets."

"Check the Jenkins house," she said. "He used to keep this old rifle from the War above the mantle."

I smiled, feeling relieved and hopeful for the first time in a while.

"You gonna be all right for a while?" I asked.

She nodded and shooed me off.

I spent an hour digging and clearing around the broken chimney at the Jenkins' place. The giants had knocked over the top half, probably with a punch I guessed. Broken bricks lay everywhere, along with a lot of dust and grit that got into my nose and made me sniffle.

Still, I found it! I pulled an old 1853 Enfield rifle-musket, like the ones the Rebs used, from under a long pine board that must've been the mantle. I brushed it off and climbed out of the wrecked house to give it a better look.

The good news was it was a rifle with good accuracy over long distances. The bad news was it was a muzzle loader.The really bad news was that it was empty and I hadn't seen any bullets.

Still, there had to be some.

With an annoyed sigh, I went back into the house and started moving junk and rubble out of the way again. I lost track of time, sweating and grunting as I moved stuff aside. My lips were cracked with thirst and the sun was high overhead by the time I found a small leather bag with four cartridges. The ramrod lay nearby, to my relief.

Four cartridges, that I'd have to load the hard way, one at a time.

At least I'd done it before. Long before I'd been able to buy the Winchester, Mr. Lake at the Astor had let me borrow an Enfield to go hunt. I'd had to pay for my own ammunition, which had led to me making sure I was really close before firing on a deer. I'd gotten good at moving quietly as a result.

Finally, I headed back to Beth.

I found her lying on her back, sobbing. I rushed to her side.

"What's wrong?" I asked.

"It hurts! It hurts so bad!"

I glanced down her body, but with the blanket over her, I couldn't see anything obvious.

"What hurts?" I asked.

"My ankle!"

I flipped the blanket back. The splints Maria'd fixed there had come loose and her foot had twisted. The ankle itself looked even more swollen than it had the day before. It needed some ointment, but we didn't have any.

But, I realized, I also didn't know how to set a splint over an ankle. How bad would it be if I did it wrong?

I took a deep breath. There was only one way to find out.

FIFTEEN

"I'LL FIX IT," I said. "I'll fix it."

Beth looked at me with wide plaintive eyes between sobs. Tears spattered her cheeks, and one rolled off and dropped to her shirt.

Gently I undid the splints on her ankle, making sure I held her foot to keep it from turning. I held her ankle and reached for the medicines, which luckily were in reach.

Should've gotten everything ready first, I chided myself.

Still, I managed to get the last of the ointment smeared on her ankle, and new bandages, also the last, wrapped around it. I put the splints back where I'd remembered them being, but I wasn't quite sure they were right.

But they'd have to do.

Then I gave Beth my canteen and made her drink. That broke her crying, which turned to deep gasps, which finished with a shudder.

"Look," I said, "we need Maria, and she's late. We can either wait here for her, or go look for her."

Beth's eyes went wide, with terror it seemed.

"We won't miss her," I said. "There's only one road to Saratoga West, and I can leave a message here just in case."

"I can't walk!"

I put a hand on her shoulder, comforting like I'd seen Cassidy do.

"I know," I said. "I'll figure something out."

She still looked on the edge of shaking.

"Look," I said, "would Cassidy let you down?"

She shook her head.

"Then why should one of his team?"

That seemed to relieve her, and she gave a small nod, and then snuffled, the aftermath of her tears.

"You just rest," I said. "We'll be ready to scoot in no time."

My problem was, I had no idea how to scoot. Beth couldn't walk and I had no idea where Blackie was, or if my horse was even alive.

So I decided to solve the problems I could. More scavenging through the general store turned up a ledger and an inkwell. My writing wasn't too good, but Ma had insisted I learn my letters, so I wrote out "Gone to Saratoga West" as neat as I could on a ripped out page. I nailed it to a stake that I plunged into the middle the remnants of our old fire pit. No way Cassidy or anyone in his team could miss it.

His team. Or our team?

I was contributing as much as anyone else, I reasoned, and I'd done a fine job of taking care of Beth, just as Cassidy had told me to. Probably better than he expected, even. No way Cassidy could've expected the giant to show up, and we'd beaten it. Escaped clean away.

Yeah, I figured I was as much a part of his team as anyone else.

At least for now.

But my gut churned at that. I didn't want to think it was only for now.

Not at all.

Still, I had a task to do right now. I had to figure a way to get Beth more medicine.

We couldn't both walk, and I couldn't leave her. We didn't have a wagon or anything with wheels. Though to be sure, I decided to do a closer look through most of the town. I didn't find anything that wasn't smashed.

As I wandered, looking at stuff here and there, I briefly thought about making a wagon or a cart, but while I could probably cut wheels out of a log, I couldn't figure out how to attach them to the cart without a lot of work. I could probably work up a bracket to hold an axle, but that could take all day and then some. I might be able to salvage enough parts, but that was a mighty big 'might.'

Besides, I knew the difference between riding in a well designed wagon, with springs and such, and what was basically a cart.

The more I thought about it, the more the travois had made sense. It wouldn't be much bumpier than a cart, if Beth could be strapped in well.

I scratched my head. I hadn't remembered any straps. I headed back to the travois in the mud.

To my surprise, it wasn't actually broken. It had been pressed down and was dirty, but all the wood and the denim was intact. So were the straps I'd never seen McNab attach. I carefully pulled it out of the ground, using the handle of the axe as a pry bar when needed, and the blade to knock off the biggest clumps of mud. It took some careful wrestling, but soon I had it free, and I stood it up on end. It looked okay.

It also looked like it would work, if I had anything to pull it with.

I wandered over to where I'd staked Blackie, before the giant came. All I could see was that the stake itself was gone. It'd been pulled out of the hole, but how or by Blackie or the giant, I had no idea.

However, his bridle and tack were still where I'd left them, in a jumble on the ground. That got me thinking—could *I* pull Beth?

I took them all and pulled the travois back to Beth. She was asleep, which I took to be a good sign. I started fiddling with the saddlebags, figuring how I could carry them like a backpack, and also how I could use the tack to bind the travois to my shoulders. I realized

I'd have to have the head of the travois closer to my waist in order to keep the angle down to something Beth could actually ride on.

I must've been figuring stuff out for an hour when Beth woke up. She stretched her arms and cocked her head. I had my makeshift harness on.

"What's that?" she asked.

"My harness," I said. "I'm going to be your horse."

"My horse?" she said with a laugh.

"Yeah," I said, "neigh and trot along, with you as my rider?" I smiled. "Well, maybe I'll just pull you along." I pointed to the travois.

"On this?" she asked.

"Uh huh. It'll work."

"Hmmm."

"You'll see," I said with as much confidence as I could muster. "How's your ankle?"

"It hurts."

"Better or worse?"

She paused and thought for a bit. "Better."

"Good. We'll get going as soon as you're ready."

It took a little while, but after we'd had some water and I'd cached the supplies I couldn't carry, we eased Beth onto the travois. I strapped her down, and we made sure they were tight but comfortable. Then I got my makeshift bridle gear on and attached to the top of the travois. It turned out to be easy to lift.

I pulled her a dozen feet just fine. We stopped and adjusted some things so I could pull better and she was more comfortable. Then, with a deep breath, we were off.

The day grew hotter, and I started sweating like a river. Still, I doggedly pulled Beth along. It was slow. Agonizingly, horribly slow. But I kept at it, one step after another, making sure to dig in and pull.

We made it out of the town of Grand Lake and down the road a good ways. The pine trees offered a bit of shade, so I set Beth down and we had some water. She didn't seem too good, but she also wanted to tough it out. When I was rested, we set out again.

The road grew bumpier, with old ruts here and there, as well as a washed out area. Still, I struggled on until Beth called out.

"Billy! Look!" She sounded excited.

I tried to glance back, but all I could tell was she was pointing at something. So I gently lowered the travois to the ground and turned for a good look.

And I almost let out a sob of happiness.

Jeremiah rode toward us. He was a ways back, at the edge of town, but it couldn't be anyone else. Not with those clothes. Not with that dark skin.

The exhaustion of the pulling hit me all at once and I sank to the dirt, sitting Indian style. Beth struggled against the straps, so I undid them so she could sit up. Despite her pain, she couldn't help grinning as we waited for Jeremiah to catch up.

But something in her face fell as he approached. She looked glum. She didn't say anything, so I figured I'd have to ask her about it later.

"My, are you a sight for sore eyes!" Jeremiah said when he'd caught up to us. He brushed his hat back as he grinned. "But what are you doing on the road?"

"We were attacked by a giant," I said. I quickly explained everything that had happened since he left.

He sat quietly on his horse while I talked, the horse shuffling a bit. When I got to the part about Beth's ankle, he said, "let me take a look."

Jeremiah dismounted and moved to Beth's side. She remained stiff, her eyes wide, as he gently unwrapped the outer bandages. She only winced once before he nodded and redid the wrappings.

"Not bad, Billy," he said. "We probably want Maria to examine it, but it should keep until then."

"That's the problem," I said. "We were expecting Maria back. We're out of medicine."

"Mmmm, that is a problem." He turned to Beth. "Anything you need before we get going again? Water, perhaps?"

"Water," she said.

I unhooked my canteen from my belt and handed it to her. As she drank, Jeremiah looked over the travois rig. He fingered the straps I'd used for my shoulder harness and snorted softly in appreciation.

"This is quite clever," he said. "I'm not sure I would've thought of it."

I blushed.

"We'll rig it for my horse though. You okay walking along side?"

"Sure."

Beth finished with the canteen and passed it back. Jeremiah patted her knee.

"You, young lady," Jeremiah said, "are one strong gal, letting this kid pull you across the rough ground like this. Quite strong."

She blinked in surprise.

He stood. "Let's get moving. I'll tell you what I found on the way."

Jeremiah didn't actually have much to tell. He'd found two large abandoned mining camps, both of which looked like they'd been occupied sometime recently. There were no traces of giants at either. He'd started moving further north and encountered a lone miner. He said the camps had been pretty full two weeks prior, but he'd been off on his own and had no idea where the men had gone.When Jeremiah told him about the town of Grand Lake and the giant footprints, the miner had started shaking in fear. He'd agreed to skedaddle north and tell anyone he met the news. Jeremiah had then turned around and headed back to join up with us.

"I found your note," he said. "I decided to leave it there in case Luke or the others came back as well."

"Good idea."

The road to Saratoga West followed the Grand River, for the most part. Dusty and dry, once it broke out of the woods near the lake, it was mostly a track through the high prairie grass. The cottonwoods and spruce all clustered along the river itself, so we got shade sometimes, when the road wandered close. We only got hot sun when the banks were too steep and the road stuck to more level ground.

It got comfortable after a while. Jeremiah rode slowly, pulling Beth's travois. I walked beside her, mostly to reassure her. Nobody talked, because we didn't need to say much. Instead, my mind buzzed with wondering where Maria and Cassidy and McNab were and what could've happened.

We made slow progress. We stopped three times—once for lunch, and twice for water breaks. By mid-afternoon we were still trudging down the road, though Jeremiah had reassured us we were close and would get there before nightfall.

Then Jeremiah halted. I walked forward, around his horse and tried to stare down the road at whatever he was looking at.

"What is it?" I asked.

"Something moved in those trees ahead, where the road curves back toward the river bank."

I shaded my eyes and looked hard. We'd been walking in an open stretch, with the river fifty yards to our right. The road curved back to the trees about five hundred yards ahead. There, a stand of large cottonwoods shaded the track.

I squinted, and saw something move, high up. Whatever it was, it was big. After a bit, it dawned on me.

"It's a giant," I said quietly.

"Yes," Jeremiah said, "yes it is."

"What's it doing?"

"Lying in wait for us, I suspect."

I swallowed hard. We were way too exposed to be able to run.

SIXTEEN

JEREMIAH SAT easy in the saddle, his arms bent, the reins loose in his hand. His horse huffed and snuffled and tossed its head a bit, but held its ground. Behind us on the travois, Beth began to quietly whimper. I reckoned she must've heard us mention the giant.

Jeremiah glanced at me and his eyes slowly travelled over me until they fell on my rifle.

"That loaded?" he asked quietly.

I nodded. "It's a muzzle loader, though. I've only got one shot."

"Then you'd better make sure it's a good one."

He turned and studied the distant trees. My eyes followed his. There, they must've been close to the bank for they grew thick— maybe a half dozen trunks within a few yards of each other. One sent two wide gnarled branches over the side of the road's ruts, and those bounced far more than the breeze could do. We could see something by the base, behind it and nearly as tall as the tree itself, but we couldn't make out what it was.

I had dozens of questions I wanted to ask Jeremiah, but my heart was hammering too hard for my tongue to work.

"Any good cover between here and the river?" Jeremiah asked quietly, not peeling his gaze from the distant trees.

I quickly glanced at the paralleling river, and then realized he wanted me to take a good look. I studied it a bit.

"Not much," I said. "A couple of small bushes. There are some saplings close to shore but most of the trees look like they're on the far bank."

"That figures," he said. He rubbed his chin as he continued to watch the hidden giant.

"Well," he said finally, "here's what we're going to do. I'm going to turn my horse and Beth's travois around and ride back toward Grand Lake. There's a chance he'll just let us go."

My heart pounded even harder.

"And if he doesn't?" I asked.

"This is where you come in," he said. "When I start turning Sampson here, you get yourself over to the nearest cover. If he starts coming after us, you're going to distract him. I want you to shoot him and then run for the river. It's not deep or wide enough to stop him if he decides to wade across, but I suspect he won't. The Jotun try to avoid that if they can."

He finally turned his gaze and looked at me. His smile was firm, but kind.

"If you can," he said, "shoot for the eyes. You'll only annoy him if you hit his body, but you can do real damage if you hit an eye."

His smile changed to pure amusement.

"Of course," he said, "we do want him to *see* you, so he'll chase you instead of us, so maybe you should aim for his mouth."

"I'll be lucky to hit him at all," I muttered.

Jeremiah chuckled. "I have confidence in you."

His words and tone reassured me, but only a bit. My blood still pounded and my knees quaked.

He seemed to read the doubt in my eyes.

"Are you okay with it?" he asked. "We could switch roles, but I'm better handling my horse and the travois."

I shaded my eyes and stared ahead at the trees. There seemed to be a bit more motion. I was sure the giant was watching us as we stood still. Probably getting suspicious, too. Jeremiah dismounting and me climbing on his horse would be even more so.

Besides, I realized, Jeremiah was in even more danger than me, with his plan. Even if the giant chased me, I could run, hide, and use the river to get away. Jeremiah couldn't do any of those things without abandoning Beth. There was no way he was going to do that.

"Nah," I said. "I just gotta decide if I'm going to shoot his right eye or his left."

"That's the spirit!" Jeremiah said. Even Beth, who'd been listening quietly after seeming to get control of her sobs, chuckled.

"So how do we do this?" I asked.

"I'm going to start turning around," he said. "You help adjust things so Beth's comfortable, but keep an eye on the trees. Hand me your pack as you do. You'll be able to run faster without it. Once we've got everything straight and pointed in the right direction, you scamper for cover."

"Got it."

We did pretty much as he described. I kept watching the cluster of trees, but they didn't change. It took me tugging a bit at the travois to get it around a rock in the road, but Beth looked grateful. She gestured at my canteen and I gave her a drink while Jeremiah checked that the harnesses weren't twisted. When he was ready, he looked hard at me.

"Good luck," he said.

"You, too." I replied.

Then he started down the road and I dashed for the nearest juniper bush.

I crouched, waiting, for a lot longer than I expected. My legs began to cramp up and more than once I had to shift my stance, or even sit for a second. The thin piney branches of the bush waved in front of my face and a few lower ones scraped across my knee, making me all too aware of their needles.

Still, the giant didn't emerge. I couldn't see him, and I had no idea whether he'd seen me run for cover, but it felt like a bit of a standoff.

That was good. Jeremiah had picked up the pace to as fast a trot as Beth could handle and was steadily moving away. He'd already gone probably a thousand yards before anything more than fluttering happened in the trees.

The giant stepped out.

I sucked in my breath.

He stood in the road, easily as tall as the trees he'd been hiding behind. At this distance, I couldn't make out much, but he didn't quite look right. Instead of the furs and armor most Jotun wore, he seemed to be in a ragged off-brown shirt and skirt, or maybe a tunic of some sort. He wasn't carrying an axe or war hammer or even a club. He stared in our direction and then slowly walked forward.

His moved slowly, deliberately. His head turned side to side. I ducked a little lower behind the bush, and then decided to peek around the side instead of the top.

I glanced back at Jeremiah and Beth. They were a good ways off, but no so far they'd be safe if the giant decided to run.

I took a deep breath. It was up to me.

I shifted to one knee, lifted the Enfield, and checked it over. Everything was as it was supposed to be. The question was, how close did I let the giant get? Too close and he'd be able to run me down. Too far, and I wouldn't be able to hit him.

What was the line? "Don't shoot 'til you see the whites of their eyes?" I decided to go with that.

Except that got harder the closer he got. He strode steady, looking firmly ahead. He'd balled his hands into fists and seemed fixated on Jeremiah.

But his strides were huge.

If I let him get too close, there was no way I'd be able to outrun him.

My hands began to shake. Then the rest of my body. I tried to steady my breathing, but it was hard, oh so hard.

I shouldered the Enfield and aimed down the barrel. I couldn't keep my sight on the giant's head, much less anything on it.

He kept coming.

A bit faster now, not quite at a run, but faster.

I had to shoot, I couldn't wait.

I took a last deep breath and dropped my aim to his torso.

I fired.

The bang of the gun was louder than I'd expected, and I hadn't set myself properly. The recoil threw me off balance and I fell.

I heard a roar as I scrambled to my feet. He was still a ways off, but now he was looking around and shouting in some language I didn't know.

I ran for the river.

The giant roared again as soon as I took off.

I scrambled. I jumped over rocks and dodged junipers. I dashed down a small slope and tried not to stumble. I dared not look back.

I didn't slow when I reached the riverbank, which had a rocky drop off to the water below.

Instead, I scrambled over and down, making sure to hold my gun and the dry powder high above the water. The cold chill shocked me as I sank to my knees in the water. I pushed through, pushing, pushing, pushing, until I spotted a couple of large boulders to my right.

I made for them.

As I scrambled onto the nearest one, I glanced back. No giant, but I was sure he was coming.

I slid off the far side into a shoulder deep spot and was nearly bowled over. As it was, I lost my footing and got swept a few feet down, before I was able to grab a sharp spine on the far rock with my free hand.

It was all I could do to not drop my rifle, but I managed.

With the strength of fear, I pulled myself to that rock, and then spotted a slower moving stretch on the far side. That was only thigh deep and I struggled through, constantly looking back, my chest on fire as I sucked in breath. The water got shallower and, gasping, I stumbled forward and collapsed on the far shore between two willow bushes.

The giant roared behind me.

With a groan, I rolled to my back.

On the far shore I'd just left, the giant stood, shaking his fist at me. I pulled myself up the shore. The tamping rod I'd strapped to my back was somehow still there and it dug into me as I slithered between the bushes.

The giant walked to a large rock half buried on the far shoreline. He started tugging on it, trying to dislodge it. His first few pulls barely got it to shift, but he kept at it.

I rolled to my knees and checked the Enfield. It looked fine.

I stood.

With shaky hands, I started loading the next round. It was awkward as heck, but I got the powder and the bullet down. I even managed to tamp it in place. One last check, and I knew it was ready.

The giant roared with triumph. The rock had pulled free.

I lifted my rifle and focused on the side of the giant's head. Thanks to some trick of the light, it actually looked like a prairie dog head when I squinted—brown and smooth and wrinkly.

I took a deep breath.

You can do this.

The giant lifted the rock to chest height and turned to face me. The one huge eye in the middle of its forehead seemed to look directly at me.

Which made it the perfect target.

It lifted the rock over its head with a roar.

I fired.

It screamed and collapsed to its knees.

The rock fell on top of its head, bounced, and then rolled forward into the river. The giant pitched forward and followed it, its face landing in the water.

It didn't move.

I lowered the Enfield in shock.

I'd done it. I'd killed a giant. Me. I'd killed a giant!

Then I remembered its eye.

No, I'd killed *a cyclops*.

SEVENTEEN

I SANK TO MY KNEES, suddenly exhausted beyond words. My wet pants clung to me, but I didn't care. I could survive the chill. So I sat, gulping in air, and stared at the corpse across the river.

A giant corpse.

That I'd killed!

I would've been excited if I hadn't been so dang tired.

Meanwhile, the river bubbled on, splashing here and there. It ran red downstream from the giant's head, but otherwise was as calm as if nothing had happened.

I snorted softly. I needed to go find Jeremiah and Beth and tell them everything was okay. Well, almost everything. My right leg was starting to throb. Somehow in the scramble across the river, I'd banged my knee on a rock, not hard enough to stop me but hard enough to ensure a good bruise. I probed it with my fingers and found it was already swelling up.

That was not good.

I stood and almost stumbled. I could put weight on my leg, but it hurt. I limped a few steps and grimaced. I'd never make it back across the river the way I came.

So I took one last long look at the cyclops. In the bright sun, sprawled face down a river embankment with his head in the water, he didn't look so scary. Not like he had last night. Presuming this was the same one of course.

And I killed it.

Yeah. Me.

I made sure I had all my gear, including the last two bullets and slung the Enfield over my shoulder. Then I walked upstream, looking for a place to ford.

My knee didn't get better as I trudged along, but I soon learned how to step without making it hurt too bad. I walked as close as I could to the river while keeping on level ground. Going up or down was what hurt the most.

Cottonwood and pine trees only dotted part of the riverbank, in clumps here and there. Willows and tall grass crept along the shore the rest of the way, and they were short enough for me to see the far shore and the road. I didn't spot Jeremiah and Beth. I figured I couldn't be too far behind them—the fight with the cyclops just hadn't lasted that long.

Eventually, I came to a jog in the river where it tightened and rumbled over some rocks, dropping maybe a foot or two. The bend created a quiet pool before the water got caught up in the narrower rapids. I could see the bottom, meaning it was only about two feet deep there, and realized I'd be able to wade at least halfway across with no trouble.

It was the other half I was worried about. There, the water moved *fast*.

There were enough rocks just under the surface that I was sure I could avoid sinking in deep. They were probably really slippery though.

I wanted a walking stick or a crutch.

I chuckled softly to myself. I knew exactly where a crutch was —back in camp, where I'd set it aside once we got Beth into the travois. The saw and hammer I'd used to make it were tucked into the pack I'd given Jeremiah. I had everything I needed—just not here.

Still, I could try to wade it, or look for something else.

Or maybe I could make it better.

The nearby trees were all pretty green, and I doubted I'd find any deadfall near them. I couldn't use wood for a bridge or a walking staff. But there were plenty of medium sized rocks in the shallow smooth pool. Maybe I could rearrange them.

It was cold going. I reached into the water and felt around the edges of one rock the size of my head, but tugging on it did no good. It was too heavy. Meanwhile, the cold water chilled my fingers to the point of pain. I checked out a few other rocks and realized none of them were going to work.

I'd have to wade it and take my chances or keep walking. Given what I'd seen of the river, this was probably my best bet short of the lake, where the water would be slower but deeper.

So with a deep breath, I waded in.

I crossed the shallow pool without a hitch. On the far side, I had maybe eight feet to go through the rapids. I lifted my rifle above my head and took a small step forward into the faster water, and slipped just a bit. I nearly dropped the Enfield as I did.

This wasn't going to work.

I needed to have my hands free so I could scramble if I needed to. That meant putting my rifle on my back and hoping I didn't fall, or trying to throw it to the far bank and hoping it didn't get damaged in the process.

I wasn't sure I could throw it that far.

So I strapped it onto my back, bent low, and started edging my way through the faster water. A couple of times, I steadied myself on rocks that stuck out, but then I hit a stretch where there wasn't anything to grab and the water looked deep. Real deep.

With a deep breath, I pushed on.

The rushing water against my legs almost immediately knocked me over. I struggled to move forward. I kept getting pushed downstream, pushed hard, and had to do everything I could just to stay on my feet. Inch by inch, I edged forward. I stumbled once, but caught myself. When I got to the deepest part, I had to stand still for what seemed like forever before I could move an inch.

I was just barely past that when I fell.

The water swept me down a ways. I banged into rocks and bounced off of pointed edges. I gasped and swallowed a mouthful of water.

Somehow I managed to keep my head up. Somehow, I managed to scramble to the side and half crawl out of the river on the far shore.

I collapsed, gasping on the shore.

When I recovered, I checked my rifle. It looked undamaged, but the cartridges had gotten wet. The paper wrapper stuck together and I could tell the powder inside was damp.

Hopefully I wouldn't have to shoot any giants soon.

I snorted and shook my head. I only had two cartridges anyway. Even if they were dry, I'd better hope I didn't have to shoot anything right away. I'd gotten lucky with the cyclops. He'd been standing still, and that one big eye was the perfect target. I suspected I'd never get a chance like that again.

But still … what a chance. I'd killed a giant!

I was a giant hunter now, even if Cassidy didn't take me into his band. That had to count for something.

But counting for something wasn't getting my pants dry or helping me find Jeremiah and Beth. After a tad more rest, I pulled myself to my feet and set out for the road.

Jeremiah found me, maybe an hour later. He trotted down the road toward me, just him on his horse. He rode calm, as if he hadn't a worry in the world. Neither the breeze nor the sun seemed to bother him a bit.

I stopped walking—my knee was a ball of hurt—and waited until he was close. He pulled up on the reins and stopped.

"Where's Beth?" I asked.

"Hidden in some bushes a ways back, resting."

I nodded. She was sick of the travois, I was sure.

"Where's the giant?" he asked.

"Dead," I said. I straightened up and looked him right in the face. "It wasn't a Jotun. It was a cyclops, and I shot it in the eye."

His mouth opened in surprise, but then quickly closed. He nodded with an amused smile.

"Of course," he said. "Can you take me to it?"

"Sure can. But ... can I ride? I messed up my knee." I pointed to it for emphasis.

"Of course."

He dismounted and came over to me. He checked out my knee first, and poked at it a bit. It hurt, but he said it didn't look like I'd broken anything. I'd figured that, but it was nice for him to agree. Then he boosted me onto his horse, mounted behind me, and told me to lead the way.

Jeremiah had us dismount about fifty feet from the giant's body. We approached cautiously through the grass and bushes, and then circled it a bit like Cassidy had done with the footprint. It was pretty clear the thing was dead. As huge as it was, if it'd been breathing at all, we would've seen it.

The cyclops had to be thirty feet tall. His tough brown skin was covered with thin black hair, even though his head was bald. He wore a tunic of what looked like wool, but was far thicker than anything a human loom could make. It was tightened around his waist by a rope belt that was thicker than my arm. His leather sandals laced around his ankles, though one had come untied, the loose end sprawled like a snake in the dirt.

He stank, mostly of sweat and crap. The flies had shown up, but that was about it. They buzzed about but, since there weren't any open wounds out of the water, they didn't amount to much.

"See any pouches?" Jeremiah asked as we walked around the corpse.

"No. Nothing except his clothes."

"We need to check under him."

I stared at him and then at the cyclops. Lying down, it came up higher than my waist.

"So how do we do that?" I asked.

"Roll him." Jeremiah strode back to his horse and unhooked a coil of rope. He tossed me one end.

"I'll tie this around his arm near the shoulder," he said. He pointed to where he meant. "You tie the other end to the saddle horn. You can lead the horse while I push."

I nodded. My knee was feeling a bit better, but I still didn't want to put much weight on it.

"Let's do it," I said.

It took us longer than we thought, though. Jeremiah had a tough time looping the rope under the cyclops's shoulder, given its size and how close it was to the ground. He actually had to get down on his belly and crawl a bit. Then when we started pulling, nothing happened. We tried a few different directions before we finally found one that worked. I stood next to the horse as it strained, soothing the animal and encouraging it. After what seemed like forever, the cyclops's arm flopped back and then, with Jeremiah pushing on its chest, the whole body rolled to its side. With another tug, it flopped on its back.

"No pouches," Jeremiah called out.

Dang. In the books, Cassidy's team often found useful clues or treasures in Jotun pouches. Of course this wasn't a Jotun.

I left the horse and did my best limp over to join Jeremiah. He had patted down the cyclops's tunic—a chore that required him to actually climb partway on the corpse, but he didn't find anything, to his obvious frustration.

Well, he found one thing. The tunic had a small spot of blood between the collarbone and the top of the ribs. Jeremiah sawed the cloth away with a large Bowie knife and shook his head with a grumble.

"Thick skin like the Jotun," he said. "Maybe thicker." He looked at me. "I presume this is your first shot. It didn't get through the skin and muscle."

I nodded. At least I'd hit the thing.

After he finished his examination and climbed back down, we both walked toward the river edge, where the top of the bank broke away and fell into the mud and water. The cyclops's head had flopped all the way over. The eye was a bloody crushed mess and almost unrecognizable. The jaw hung slack and open, a maw of rough and crooked teeth. You couldn't make out much more.

"Yes," Jeremiah said, "that's a cyclops. It can't be anything else."

Well, yeah.

"What's that?" he asked, pointing into the river.

A pewter medallion about the size of a dinner plate lay in the water. It had a hole at the top where a thick rope of a cord threaded through it and then around the cyclops's neck.

"I dunno," I said, "but I think we'd better find out."

He nodded and grinned. "You're thinking more and more like a giant hunter each day."

My face flushed and I looked away, even as Jeremiah started wading into the river to get the medallion.

EIGHTEEN

WE STOOD in the sunlight on the side of the shore and stared at the medallion. It glinted as we turned it back and forth. From the weight, it had to be pewter or something similar. As large as my forearm, it was actually hard to hold. Large words in a language I didn't understand covered one side and a lightning bolt symbol was on the other.

"It looks like Greek," Jeremiah said, "but it's probably ancient Greek. I can't read it."

"You can read Greek?" I asked, trying not to let my surprise show too much.

He nodded. "When I was a boy, my master insisted I do everything with his son, including sitting with his tutor. I was the whipping boy, you see. If the master's son broke the rules, they whipped me instead. That wasn't done much in Baltimore, but then, my master had some peculiar notions."

I didn't know what to say. I'd never thought about Jeremiah maybe being a slave.

"I ... uh, I hope they didn't beat you too bad."

"That's okay," he said with a friendly chuckle. "That was a long time ago. My master freed me when the war started—the War Between the States, that is."

Yeah, I thought, the one we all kind of forgot about when the Jotun came.

"A long time ago ..." His eyes grew distant for a bit, and then he shook himself. "But we have to deal with today's monsters. We'll take this with us." He patted it with one hand.

"But where are we going?"

"Well, your original idea was a good one. We'll go back and get Beth and see if we can find the others."

I liked the compliment, but then my mind jumped.

"Oh! We need Beth's medicine!"

"We do," he said, "but she'll be fine, at least for a little while. I always carry a little willow bark powder and I gave it to her."

I let out a deep breath.

"We should inspect those trees where the cyclops was hiding first, though," he said. "Just in case."

"Yeah." Once again, Jeremiah made too much sense.

The small copse of trees that had hidden the cyclops didn't have much else. We didn't find anything other than footprints. A few trampled kinnikinnick bushes implied the cyclops had moved around a bit, but not much since we hadn't seen him right away.

Nothing happened on the ride back to Beth's hiding place among a few junipers. She was both relieved to see us and irritated. She'd been sitting a long time, and even though Jeremiah had left her food and water, she'd found it uncomfortable.

She didn't want to get back in the travois. The straps chafed her and she hated the bumps. She also fidgeted and frowned the whole time Jeremiah was looking at her injuries. I took her disagreeableness as a sign she was feeling better. Indeed, it looked like the swelling was going down.

After a bit, we decided that we could put all our supplies and saddlebags on the travois and Beth and I could ride Jeremiah's horse. If she sat side saddle in front, she wasn't likely to fall off and it'd be a lot smoother that being pulled behind.

It took a while to figure out how to boost her up there. Jeremiah could lift the young girl, but it was awkward. That's when I figured we could set the travois on end to use as a crutch. It let her stand close enough to the horse so that all Jeremiah had to do was hoist her up far enough for me, already mounted, to pull her the rest of the way.

Finally, just as the shadows of the western sun were really starting to lengthen, we were on our way.

The sun dipped below the western peaks long before we made it to Saratoga West. We walked a bit, but as the gloom grew, we slowed. Jeremiah said he wasn't surprised, but I sensed he was on edge. Me, I was worried. We hadn't seen a sign of Cassidy or the others.

We camped near the river in a small cluster of pine trees. Jeremiah suggested we pass on a fire, so as not to draw attention to ourselves. We'd light one in the morning, he said, to boil some water for Beth's medicine and to cook any fish I could catch while he was taking care of her bandages.

Except in the morning, Beth asked me to take care of her. Jeremiah frowned, but joked that he'd be able to catch fish faster than me anyway. He made it clear he was teasing, so I just rolled my eyes.

But once he was gone and I was tending to Beth's ankle, I knew I had to ask her about it.

"Why didn't you want Jeremiah to help you?" I asked.

She wiggled a little, and jerked away from where I'd briefly brushed her shin. I gave her a meaningful look and waited.

"I'm ... I'm just not comfortable with him."

"Why?"

"Well ... he's ... well, he's a ..."

I grimaced, having a sense where this was going.

"You got a problem with the fact that he's a Negro?"

She visibly winced, and I wasn't even touching her. I figured it must've been my tone.

"It's just Pa and Mr. Jenkins were always saying ..."

I remembered the Enfield rifle had been Mr. Jenkins's. But Beth didn't seem to be going on.

"Mr. Jenkins fought for the Rebs, didn't he?" I asked.

She nodded.

"Well, I can understand why he might think some not nice things about Negroes, but Jeremiah's a good man."

"Why's he part of your team?"

Cassidy's team, I silently corrected.

"Well," I said, "he's smart and brave and a good fighter." I paused. I couldn't think of anything else immediately. Why was anyone a part of Cassidy's team?

"He does seem smart," she grudgingly admitted. "He talks good."

"Yeah," I said. "He also wrote all the books about Cassidy. He doesn't put himself in because he's humble that way."

Her chin dropped and she stared wide-eyed at me.

"It's true," I said. "He wrote 'em all. At least about Cassidy."

That got me thinking about some of the other books Tom and I'd read huddled under the blankets while Ma washed clothes.

"Did you ever read *The Battle of New Orleans*?" I asked.

"No ... is Cassidy in it?"

"No," I said with a shake of my head. "He wasn't there. Nobody from the army was there. When the trolls built those barges and floated across the river, the folks of New Orleans were on their own.

"They beat the trolls, though. And most of the men who did the fighting were Negroes. Even the leader was, a man named Cailloux. I think that's Cajun, so I maybe didn't say it right."

She looked suspicious. "They won?"

"They did. Pushed the trolls right back across the river. You don't hear about it much, 'cause it was happening at the same time as St. Louis."

"Oh." She still frowned.

"Look," I said, "one thing I learned in the Battle of Golden City is what matters is what a man does. Nothing else."

Her eyes went wide. "You were in the Battle of Golden City?"

"Yeah. And my commander was a real mean pistol, always swearing at us, but he knew what he was doing, and we respected him for it."

"Was he ...?" she nodded her head toward the direction Jeremiah had gone.

"No," I said with a shake of my head. "He was from Pennsylvania. Fought for the Union, back when that mattered."

She nodded and didn't say anything.

I finished with ointment on her ankle and rewrapping the bandage. It was now smeared with black dirt in places, but we didn't have anything better. I realized I should boil it, like Ma had used to do, to get it clean. I decided to do it after I'd prepared the medicine.

We didn't have much of that, though. Jeremiah hadn't had much time to harvest new bark, but I did what I could with it. Beth drank it gratefully. I started some new water boiling and undid her bandage once again to get it clean.

Jeremiah came back with a nice cutthroat trout just about when the bandages were clean. We boiled it with a few herbs he carried and the stale flatbread and had a nice soup for breakfast. Beth kinda stared at him when he wasn't looking, and he seemed not to notice, though I think he did. When she realized that I'd caught her, she had the grace to get red-faced about it.

Still, nothing was said. We packed up quietly, got Beth and me on the horse, and headed back on the road.

The wind picked up about mid-morning, making it almost chilly. Rumbled patchy clouds slid across the sky—not too thick to hint at rain, though. Jeremiah's horse clopped on, pulling its load and carrying us. Jeremiah walked alongside, his rifle across one shoulder but his eyes darting everywhere.

I tested my knee when we took a short break for water. It still hurt, but I could walk fine without pain. I said a small prayer of thanks before getting back on the horse with Beth.

After a bit, the road and the river both turned a bit, and in the distance we could see some buildings. No smoke, which I took to be a good sign, but we couldn't make much else out.

Jeremiah had us head over to some cottonwoods that were backed by some small pines. They made a small wall of thick branches that, with the limbs overhead, made it almost feel like a room.

"We leave the travois and our gear here," he said. "We may need to maneuver quickly if there's trouble ahead and it'll slow the horse down."

"What about Beth?" I asked.

"What about me?" she said.

I looked at Jeremiah. "Should she stay here, too? It'd be safer."

"No!" she objected. "I'm tired of sitting and waiting like a bag of flour."

"You'd be safer," Jeremiah said.

"I was supposed to be safer in Grand Lake," she said. "How'd that work out?"

"You had Billy with you," he said.

"Good thing," she said before turning to me. "You going to stay with me this time?"

I hesitated. I knew I should say yes, but I really wanted to go into Saratoga West with Jeremiah. How could I be part of the team if I was always getting left behind?

"It would make sense," Jeremiah said. "We only need one of us to scout around. If it's safe, you're not so far away. I could easily ride back and get you."

"Yeah," I said, "but …"

""Billy stays with me," Beth said. "If he goes, I go with him."

Jeremiah raised an eyebrow and studied her for a minute, but she set her jaw and glared at us both. Then he turned to me and tipped his hat back.

"Sounds like you stay," he stated.

My blood rose at his tone and I was about to say something, when I saw the grateful look in Beth's eyes.

"Okay," I said, forcing myself to be as calm as possible.

Jeremiah smiled.

"But I need more than this, then." I pointed at the Enfield. "I've only got two cartridges left, and they got wet when I crossed the river."

"They're probably fine by now," Jeremiah said.

"I'll only get one shot before any cyclops is on us," I said. "We both know I got lucky last time."

He chuckled. "You admit to that?"

I glared at him.

"Fine," he said with a pleasant grin. He pulled his Colt from his holster. "After what happened last time, I can understand. You take care of this, though, okay?"

"You make sure you come back."

"Fair enough."

He passed it over and I hefted it. It was heavy in my hand, but it felt good. I'd fired one a number of times, courtesy of Mr. Lake, but it still felt strange compared to holding a rifle.

"Don't worry," he said. "I'll hurry back at the first sign of trouble."

"You see that you do."

We nodded at each other, as it was clear we had an understanding. Then Jeremiah mounted his horse and set off down the road.

We had a nice patch of shade under the tree, and while Beth continued to look like she was getting better, she still looked worn out. After she had some more water, I suggested she take a moment and nap. She'd need her strength later and I was sure we had the time. She must've been tired, because she didn't argue with me. I tucked a blanket around her and she soon drifted off.

Me, I poked idly at the fire before I decided to get all our stuff packed up. When Jeremiah came back, we'd might have to move fast. Not that I expected any trouble. I was sure he could sneak up to the town without being seen by any cyclops.

In the meantime, I thought a bit about Jeremiah. I liked him. I liked him a lot. Of course, I felt I knew him through the books, even though he wasn't in them. Still, he wasn't what I expected. He was calmer, and spoke smarter than most men I knew. I could see him teaching at some fancy college if he wasn't a Negro.

And as for that ... Ma and I hadn't met many Negroes on our way to Colorado. I'd known a few in the fight there, and some still hung around mining and such, but many had gone on to Louisiana. We didn't get much news from there, but it did seem the trolls hadn't tried to cross the Mississippi since the Battle of New Orleans.

Yet Jeremiah rode with Cassidy.

There was a story there. I kinda wished it had made it into one of the books, because I was sure it was interesting.

In the meantime, I found a nice cool spot still under the trees but at the edge of the road where I could keep an eye out for Jeremiah's return. I put the Enfield across my knees, the Colt by my side, and waited.

The rest of the morning passed peaceful-like. I enjoyed listening to the bugs and relaxing. Once or twice I stood and stretched and tested my knee. It was getting better, all right. I figured it must've just been a bad bruise, which was good. The swelling was down and I could walk fine, though I didn't think I wanted to run.

Then along around noon, I spotted something out toward Saratoga West. It looked like a small dust kick-up at first, a thin cloud that hovered near the ground. It grew in size, though, and started coming toward me.

I stood and shaded my eyes to get a better look.

It wasn't a cloud, I realized. It was a flock of birds. Large birds, like vultures, that darted back and forth. They'd fly up and dive down, and after a bit I realized there was something ahead of them. I kinda wished I had Cassidy's spyglass for a moment, but all I could do was wait.

After a bit, they drew closer, and I saw what the birds were chasing. A man on a horse.

Jeremiah.

And he was in trouble.

NINETEEN

I DASHED BACK TO BETH. She still slept among our scattered gear, under the cottonwood limbs, between the trunk and the fire pit. She looked peaceful, but it couldn't last.

"Wake up!" I yelled. Wake up!"

She started and stirred. I grabbed saddlebags and threw them back toward the pines. They looked thick enough to at least slow down whatever was chasing Jeremiah.

Beth sat up and rubbed her eyes.

"Something's after Jeremiah!" I yelled again. "We gotta get under cover."

My words sank in and she whimpered.

"Let's go!" I ran over to her. I pulled her arms and lifted her up. She was heavy, but I realized we didn't have far to go—maybe fifteen feet.

"Hang on," I said. "I can carry you that far."

She nodded. She was breathing hard, but threw her arms around my neck and clung tight. I lifted her and was able to shuffle the short distance and set her down without bumping her ankle much.

My knee complained. It didn't give out. I did my best to ignore it.

After I'd shoved all the gear I could back next to Beth, I grabbed my Enfield and went back to where I could see the road.

Jeremiah still rode like a man possessed. He was maybe a thousand yards away, but the birds had caught up. They were diving at him. He waved his saber when they did. They would veer off rather than get bit by its blade, but one still managed to rake his back with its talons. He threw himself forward and didn't fall off his horse, but it must've hurt.

I shouldered my rifle and took aim at the top of the cloud. I didn't want to hit Jeremiah, and I was doubtful I could even hit one of the birds. But maybe I could scare them a bit.

I took a deep breath and fired.

The bang rang through my ears. A huge squawk went up from the funny birds. If I hit one, I didn't see it, but they all rose up higher in the air, leaving Jeremiah alone for a bit.

One of them squawked again and flew toward me. The whole flock quickly followed.

At least I got 'em off of Jeremiah.

I ran back under the cottonwood branches and stood a few feet in front of Beth. After shifting Jeremiah's Colt to my waistband, I reloaded the Enfield with my last cartridge. I barely finished when they arrived.

To my shock, the birds weren't birds. Their bodies and wings looked like birds, covered in brown and black feathers, except their wingspans were longer than any vulture I'd seen. Maybe as long as me. They had vulture talons, too. But their heads—their heads looked liked squashed human faces. Narrower with their cheeks pushed back, they had the eyes and nose of a woman but the mouth was full of sharp teeth and fangs. They had breasts, too—small bare lumps with human-like teats.

I'd read a book on Greek myths.

Harpies.

The nearest two squawked and dived down, but the tree limbs were too low to get past. They broke off and wheeled back, thwarted.

I raised my rifle, but the same branches that were keeping the harpies from diving on me also kept me from getting a clean shot.

Another made a pass, low, too low, and had to rise up to avoid the ground. As it did, I got a sense of its wingspan.

They were huge! Maybe eleven feet across, with talons as big as my hand.

One landed about ten yards from the tree. It glared at me and let out a ferocious squawk. It hopped forward, as if to walk under the branches.

I shot it.

We were so close, I couldn't miss.

Its chest exploded in crimson and it flew back with a loud cry, and flopped a bit before lying still.

The other harpies screamed. Like birds, not humans. A moment later, they filled the sky in front of me.

I threw the Enfield aside and drew Jeremiah's Colt revolver.

Two more harpies landed. I shot at them, but both took off again. One struggled, barely flapping on one side, so I must have winged it.

Literally, I thought. I couldn't resist a wry grin.

They continued to scream and whirl, far enough back from the tree to keep the limbs between me and them.

My ears rang. I was sweating hard. I had four bullets left, and there were more than four harpies. Maybe as many as a dozen, but I couldn't really count 'cause they moved so much. Still, I kept constant watch, especially to the sides. I couldn't have one sneaking by me.

The harpies to my left screeched loud, and the ones nearby turned and flew that direction. I couldn't quite see through the mess, but it was coming my way.

Then the black winged cloud broke apart and I saw Jeremiah, running hard toward me. A harpy dived at him. He threw himself to the ground, causing it to just miss. Then he clambered to his feet and kept going.

I fired at one of the beasts above his head. I missed, but it and another flew higher to get out of the way. That gave Jeremiah some room to run again.

A big one, its grey feathers fouled with black spots and a snarl of fury on its face, dove toward his back just as he got close. I took careful aim and fired.

Hit it in the chest. It flew back into another and they both tumbled to the ground.

The others shrieked and whirled away to dive back in. That gave Jeremiah a break. He stumbled, but kept running. I dashed out from under the branches and grabbed his arm. Quickly, we scampered back under cover.

One chased us, flying low, close to the ground. I pointed the Colt at it and pulled the trigger. I missed, but it pulled up and flew off.

Then they all circled back a ways and formed a cloud over something about fifty yards away.

"So much for my horse," Jeremiah said.

"You okay?" I asked.

He shook his head. "They got my back and shoulder." He turned so I could see the rents in his shirt and deep scratches. They oozed blood, which was already matting into the fabric.

"Oh, God!" I said.

"Can you hold them off?" He looked weary as he spoke, and for a moment I worried he'd fall.

"I dunno," I said. I hoisted the Colt. "I've only got one, maybe two bullets left." I'd lost count in the excitement.

"More in my bags." He gestured towards the back area where Beth sat.

She looked as white as a sheet, so much that I had to look twice. It wasn't battle shock though, as her eyes darted back and forth and she breathed hard.

"I'll get them," Jeremiah said. "Keep an eye on those birds."

I did, but only half an eye. They seemed content to feed on the dead horse for now.

Jeremiah said a few words to Beth I didn't catch, then found the saddlebag he was looking for and brought it back to me. He looked even more tired than he had just a minute ago.

"Here," he said, thrusting the pouch at me. "Reload while you can."

I took it and got straight to work. The pouch held a few dozen bullets, which would keep me going for a while.

As I reloaded, I kept glancing at both the harpies and Jeremiah. He didn't say a thing as he stumbled back to Beth. He handed her a canteen and another pouch and then thumped to the ground in front of her, sitting with his back to her. He said something to her over his shoulder. She winced, but reached for his canteen.

Two harpies screeched. They each had ahold of a large piece of horseflesh in their jaws and were pulling at it. Eventually, they tore it apart and each started wolfing down the pieces.

Like vultures.

And while they were feeding, they seemed content to leave us alone.

Still, we didn't want to get surprised. I walked backwards, never taking my eyes off them for more than a flash, until I was close enough to Jeremiah and Beth to talk. She was sponging his wounds with a ragged off-white cloth and cringing every time she touched him. He cringed too, but that was clearly from pain.

"You gonna be okay?" I asked.

"No," he said. "The stories say harpy claws cause disease. It already feels like they're burning with infection."

I fought down a moment of panic.

"What can we do?" I asked.

"Maria has some mold that would be good for this ..." His voice trailed off. He didn't have to say how that was no use.

"Um ...," Beth said. "Ma always used to say boiling water was good for infections."

The harpies were still busy with their feed.

"We can do that," I said.

Keeping an eye on the harpies, I rolled the rocks from our fire pit closer to Beth and Jeremiah, and then shifted the small pile of wood we'd gathered at breakfast. Jeremiah already had some wooden matches out. He dumped a canteen into one of the pots while she started pulling some bandanas out of a saddlebag. Jeremiah winced in pain, but he could move, so after a bit, I left him and moved back to my position at the edge of the overhead cover.

The harpies hissed and squawked at each other as they tore into the dead horse. They didn't use words, which caused me to scratch my head a bit. I'd thought they were supposed to be half bird, half woman, but these didn't act like that. Nothing they'd done seemed part human. They just seemed to be big vultures that looked part human.

Big nasty vultures. I've never seen any birds that mean. Or that persistent.

The one I'd killed lay not too far away. I couldn't see much more than a mound of feathers, but the others seemed to be leaving it alone. At least for now.

The ones eating the horse seemed to be in no hurry to end their feast either. I tried counting them—it looked like there were a dozen. With their huge wings, it was hard to tell. A couple hopped to the edge of their feast and stared in my direction, but they didn't come closer.

I hoped they'd learned their lesson.

But it meant we had a standoff. They couldn't get under the tree branches, at least I hoped, without me killing a couple of them. But if we left the trees, we'd be at their mercy.

I stood and watched them until I heard Jeremiah gasp behind me. I glanced back. With a grimace on her face, Beth was washing his wounds. His face was whiter than I'd ever seen on a Negro. He didn't look good, but then, did any of us?

I shifted my weight, testing my knee. It held just fine, with only some pain. I'd all but ignored it during all the fighting, which was good, real good. That meant it was just a deep bruise and I'd be okay. I could run if I had to.

The problem was, Beth couldn't, and judging by Jeremiah's shakiness, I wasn't sure he could either. No way they could outrun the harpies.

So how were we gonna get out of this?

TWENTY

I WATCHED the winged monsters for a while. They cawed and snapped at each other, and picked at the remains of the meat, though not so ferociously as they had before. They also seemed to laze about, sometimes looking our way, but otherwise ignoring us. A couple of them settled down into what looked like naps in the warm sun.

They weren't going anywhere.

They were too far away to shoot with the Colt. It might've been a hard shot with the rifle, too, but since I was out of ammunition for it, it didn't matter. I'd have to leave the shelter of the tree to attack them, and that'd be foolhardy.

But we couldn't stay here, either. Not with Jeremiah infected and us running out of willow bark and other medicines for Beth. At some point, even water and food would be a problem. The river was only fifty feet away behind the trees, but it might as well have been a mile for all the good it did us.

Except that got me thinking. The pines that formed the 'back wall' of our little shelter weren't too thick to push through, if you went slow, and had hands. The harpies couldn't manage it, but we could. Or at least Jeremiah and I could. Beth would still have problems.

"Hey, Jeremiah," I called, not taking my eyes from the monsters still devouring the horse corpse, "did you find Cassidy in Saratoga West?"

"No." His voice was rough and ragged. "Those beasts were on me as soon as I reached the edge of town."

It figured.

"You think he's still there?"

"Might be," he said. "It looked like most of the buildings were still standing. They might've holed up in one of them."

"Think you can hold them off," I gestured back towards the harpies, "if you have this?" I hefted the Colt.

Jeremiah looked shaky. His eyes darted to Beth. She'd frozen in tending his wounds and was staring at me, wide eyed.

"We need to get the medicines Maria has," I explained. "I think the harpies will be busy for a bit, so I figure I can sneak out the back way and get up to town. If the others are there, I can lead them back."

"There has yet to be a creature that can be two places at the same time," Jeremiah said with a forced grin. The pain choked away all the humor from his voice. He shifted his weight and winced.

"Will you be okay?" I asked.

"Do we have a choice?" Jeremiah asked. This time he managed a more genuine smile.

"Nope," I said, even though an answer wasn't needed.

I quickly handed him the Colt and the pouch of bullets. I glanced at his back—the gouges from the harpy claws weren't deep, but they were ugly, deep black and red with obvious smudges of filth.

Beth still held the bloody rag and the water, but she too was shaking, from fear as much from pain I suspected. She looked scared, real scared.

I put my hand on her shoulder.

"I'll be back, I promise," I said. I gave her a comforting squeeze. "We're all going to be all right."

She looked me in the eye, but then slowly nodded.

I had to get moving. The branches were thick, and I didn't think I could get my rifle through them, so I gave it to Jeremiah. Then I slowly pushed my way through the wall of pine limbs, stepping over and around them as best I could. I had to go slow and protect my face from needles slapping into it, but after a bit, I was through.

I turned and looked back. I could barely see Jeremiah and Beth through the trees.

Then I headed for the river. I'd be out of sight of the harpies as long as I stuck to the bank all the way to Saratoga West.

It took me about two and a half hours to work my way quietly down the river to Saratoga West, keeping to cover as much as I could the whole way. A few clouds rolled in, but otherwise the day was still. The closer I got to town, the fewer the trees, though here and there the bushes were thick enough to hide me if I stayed low.

When I got close, though, the cover came to an end. I made out about a dozen buildings scattered about a bit. The far ones looked normal. Some of the near ones were smashed like the Grand Lake town, but at least two nearby still stood. It looked like a small log house and barn, but from this distance, I couldn't make out much more than their shape. They were up a slope on the far side of the river and closer to me than they were to the wrecks.

I scanned the area. The wind kicked up some dirt and dust here and there, but otherwise there was nothing moving. I checked the skies as best I could, but saw nothing flying either. That was a relief, I had to say.

I tested my knee. It hurt a bit when I pushed down hard, but not too bad. I could lope, but probably not run.

Still ... with no cover, I had best get to that standing farmhouse as fast as I could.

To do that, I had to get across the river. I was beginning to curse the thing. It wasn't that it was very wide or deep, not this far up in the mountains, but it was wide enough and deep enough to be treacherous.

Except, I realized, there were buildings on both sides of the river here. That meant there had to be a bridge, somewhere. Even if it'd been destroyed, it was probably the best place to cross.

Nothing else to do but leave the bushes and move as fast as I could until I found a bridge.

With a deep breath, I took off at a trot.

I found the log and plank bridge before anything found me. Across the river on the far shore, I passed two horse-sized piles of bones the harpies had obviously eaten most of, but otherwise saw little sign of them.

To my surprise, the bridge was intact. I'd expected it to be smashed because, well, for no good reason other than that's how my luck had been running. I carefully, slowly, crossed it, keeping my eyes out in all directions.

Nothing but grass, wind, and sun lay between the end of the bridge and the remaining log cabin.

Nothing moved on the land, left, right, in front or behind.

But something did in the sky.

I saw it a ways off, back toward the way I'd come. It had wings, and it was rising up in the air.

My blood froze. We hadn't seen a single bird since we'd crossed the pass. I didn't know if the harpies were eating them or what, but I doubted that was a bird.

I raced as best I could toward the cabin.

It was a squat thing, maybe one room inside judging from the size of it. The walls were still rough hewn pine logs and the roof a slanted thatch over planks. The closed wooden door faced this way, along with a single window that was shuttered. There was a large pile of junk off to the cabin's side, but I didn't look at it close. I was too busy running.

Halfway there, the door flew open. Cassidy stepped out, rifle raised.

My heart skipped a beat in excitement.

"Hurry!" he yelled. He pointed his gun above and behind me.

I didn't look back. Instead, I lowered my head and ran harder.

Twenty feet from the door, shrieks rang out behind me.

I ran harder.

Cassidy stepped to the side. I threw myself through the doorway. He immediately followed, pulling it shut and latching it. I dropped to the ground, winded. I struggled hard to catch my breath.

"You okay?" he asked. His voice was hard, demanding. "You hurt?"

"Banged up my knee," I said, "but not bad."

"Good." He gave me one more quick glance before moving to the window and peeking out through the gap in the shutters.

"How's Beth?" McNab asked.

I blinked in the dimness before I saw him. The light from the cracks around the window shutters and door barely lit the room. McNab lay on a simple dirty straw pallet against the far wall. He looked pale, but he'd rolled on his side to face me. His shirt was off and bandages covered most of his right shoulder and upper arm.

"Um, fine," I said. "Well, we're out of medicine, but she's good other than that."

I glanced around the rest of the cabin. A rough wooden table and slat chair sat shoved against one wall, along with some low shelves with cans and bags on them.

"Where's Maria?" I asked. For a moment, I started to panic at her absence.

"In the barn," McNab said, "tending to our last horse."

"Last?"

"Mmm hmm," Cassidy said. He didn't turn from his observing post. "The harpies got all but Maria's."

"They got Jeremiah's."

"What?" McNab asked.

I briefly explained what'd happened in the harpy attack, with emphasis on his injuries and our hope that Maria would have something for them.

"Aye," McNab said, "she does. Used it on me." He pointed at his shoulder, where the bandages seemed thickest. "She should have enough for him, too."

"If we can get to him," Cassidy said. "They're back. At least four or five of them."

'That means there's still some near Jeremiah and Beth," I said.

"Probably," Cassidy replied. "But maybe not. We need to assume they could be anywhere."

"Them and the cyclops," I said.

That got Cassidy to turn and look at me. He raised an eyebrow and tilted his head, When I nodded, he turned back to his lookout post.

"Figures," McNab said. "The harpies didn't make sense otherwise. You sure you saw a cyclops?"

"Saw one? I killed one!"

"Really?" McNab said. He sat up a bit, as if he was trying to rise, but then winced.

"I did! But first, we had one chase us in Grand Lake …" I told them what had happened, including me dropping the paddle in the lake. Then I told them about Jeremiah finding us, and then us spotting the cyclops and me shooting it.

"Lucky shot," McNab grumbled.

I bristled, but I was too excited to argue with a wounded man.

"It was lucky," I said, "but sometimes you make your own luck."

"That you do," Cassidy said, "and with Billy here, maybe it's time to make some of our own."

He still stared out the window, but he'd furrowed his lips. I figured he had to be thinking hard.

"Lure 'em in?" McNab said.

"Mmmm hmmm," Cassidy said. He finally turned from the window to face me.

"Here's the problem, Billy," he said. "Those monsters may not be as smart as humans, but they're cunning. They've figured out what my rifle range is, and are staying just outside of it."

I swallowed hard. I hoped they weren't bright enough to figure out how to get at Beth and Jeremiah.

"And when I go out," Cassidy continued, "they either pull back, or they attack from behind."

"That's how they got me," McNab said. "Hit me from behind. They're fast."

"So here's where you come in," he said. "I want you to run for the barn. You should be able to make it just fine, but that should draw a couple of them into my range."

I nodded at first. It made sense. But then I started to breathe hard.

"But, uh," I said, "what if they come from behind the cabin?"

"Then you better duck and pray my aim's good."

I nodded, but that didn't stop me from shaking inside. I knew Cassidy was a good shot, but was he good enough?

Because a bad shot from Cassidy was definitely not the way I wanted to die.

TWENTY-ONE

WE STOOD THERE, in the gloom of the cabin, while McNab shuffled and coughed behind us.

"Uh," I said, "uh … how about if you run and I shoot?" I said. "With my knee and all, I'm not that fast."

Cassidy scowled. "Are you questioning me?" His voice was hard, cold.

"Uh, well, It makes sense …"

"No, it does not. You don't know where the harpies may come from. You don't know how to shoot them on the fly, and you certainly aren't going to be able to pull me back inside if the worst happens. You run, I shoot."

My face flushed, but that didn't stop the trembling in my legs. Could I actually make it to the barn?

"Well …," I began.

"Look, kid, you're not on my team. You don't get to question my orders."

That got rid of my shakes. Didn't get to question his orders? Jesus, anyone should be able to question bad orders.

And what was that about not being on his team? Hadn't I been a part of his team since we got to Grand Lake?

I got madder and madder the more I stood there.

Cassidy stared at me, his eyes narrow and steely.

"Fine," I spat. "Give me your Peacemaker, in case your aim isn't good enough."

He snorted and turned back to the window, peering out once again.

Not a word from him.

"Take mine," McNab said from his pallet. "I can't use it anyway." He sat all the way up, rummaged around his blankets, and then extended a Colt .45 toward me, butt first.

He probably could, I realized. He wasn't as hurt as I first thought. Still, I was grateful and took it.

"Thank you, Mr. McNab," I said with a nod of my head.

He waved me off.

Part of me didn't want to do this. It wanted to stay and argue with Cassidy. But part of me didn't see the point. We had to get Maria's medicines back to Beth and Jeremiah. No way we could do that with all the harpies. We had to take a couple of them out.

Had to.

Even if I didn't like how.

I moved to the door and cracked it a bit so I could peek out. I could just make out a couple of harpies flapping around on the ground, a ways away. They cawed and cackled and after a bit one took off and began to soar up into the blue heights, though not coming our direction.

"Ready?" I asked Cassidy.

"Get going, kid." He never looked my way.

I took a deep breath, tightened my grip on the Colt in my hand, threw open the door, and ran.

———

I ran like the wind, or at least like a new-foaled colt. I tried not to stumble. I ignored the shots of pain in my knee and focused on the barn door. I ran like fire.

A shriek ripped through the air behind me. I didn't look back. Instead, I kept running.

Another shriek, followed by the bark of Cassidy's rifle. Then a monstrous scream.

I pounded across the uneven sod to the barn door. It was a regular-sized wooden one. A small open window in it was covered by a flap of leather. More important it was cracked open.

It swung all the way in when I got close. I dashed through the narrow opening and Maria slammed the door shut behind me. She threw a latch, while I stumbled to my knees on the hard dirt floor.

I panted and gasped for air. Like the cabin, the barn was dim, but with a lot more light coming from a small fire in a crude stone ring at the mouth of one of the horse stalls. It smelled worse, though, of blood and musty straw and manure.

Maria peeked out the little window in the door. She still wore her yellow dress but it was streaked with black and grey mud. Her hair, which had been perfectly coiffed back in Golden City, was a long tangle with a half-hearted braid.

"Did he get it?" I asked.

"One," she said. "The others have stayed back." She watched for a minute more and then turned to me with a smile.

"Good to see you, Billy. How are you doing?"

"Banged up my knee a bit, but otherwise I'm okay. Jeremiah's hurt, though."

I filled her in on the harpy attack and how I'd left him and Beth. She nodded slowly as I talked, with emphasis when I mentioned Beth washing his wounds with boiling water.

"She remembered," she said quietly. "Good."

"Yeah," I said, "but I don't know how long the harpies will hold off."

"They can be persistent," she said with a wry smile.

"You've been trapped here the whole time?"

She shook her head. "They arrived at dawn." She turned back to the little window and didn't say more.

That gave me a chance to get up and look around. I pressed on my knee with my fingers, but while it hurt to the touch, it hadn't failed me. I made a silent prayer of thanks that it wasn't worse. I stood, shakily at first, but then just fine.

The cozy barn had two horse stalls, a small hay loft, with more hay and a few barrels piled along the wall across from the stalls. One stall had the small fire in it. Maria's horse snuffled and shifted around in the other.

One horse. Five of us. Six, if you counted Beth.

A canteen and Maria's medicine bag rested against a stall post near the fire. I looked closer and realized she had a small pot nestled into the coals a bit away from the actual flame. Wisps of steam rose from the top. It might have been homey if there weren't winged monsters lurking outside.

"Okay if I have some water?" I asked, suddenly well aware of my parched throat.

"Yes," she said. She pointed toward the canteen.

I drank greedily, and then wondered if I was taking too much. Did Maria need it for her medicines? We could get water from the river, if we could get there.

Maria seemed to sense my question because she left the window and came and knelt by her small fire. She gave the mixture a stir and then lifted the spoon and let it dribble back in. She gave a satisfied nod at whatever she'd seen and turned to me.

"Let me see your knee," she said.

"Uh … I'll have to take my pants off." For some reason the thought of being in front of Maria in just my unmentionables made me sweat harder than the sprint from the harpies.

She raised an eyebrow. Then she quietly turned her back. "Cover your lap with your trousers."

I did as she said, but then sat on some scattered dry straw feeling like a plucked chicken. Meanwhile, Maria looked unperturbed. At least from the back.

"Uh …ready," I said.

She turned back around and didn't seem to notice my red face or the way I clutched my trousers over my privates. Or maybe she noticed but did a good job of not caring.

Instead, she knelt next to me. She examined my knee and poked it a bit. The skin had turned an ugly shade of purple and blue and it had swollen up on one side.

"You will be fine," she said as she sat back. "Ice would help get the swelling down, but we don't have any."

"Thanks," I said.

"This will help." She pulled a small jar of ointment from a pouch near the fire and smeared it over my knee. Then she returned to her seat by the fire. Once again, she turned her back on me. I quickly got dressed.

Outside, somewhere, a harpy screeched. No gunshots, though.

"So, uh," I asked, "what happened here? In Saratoga West, I mean?"

She turned back to me with a small smile, but then stirred the medicine again.

"The ghost talked of winged monsters from the sky," she said. "They descended on the town several days ago at dawn. The people fought but there were many and the people were surprised. Many died."

I nodded. If the harpies had shown up just when folks were beginning their morning chores, it must've been awful.

"Then news came of Grand Lake, the ghost said." she continued. "The survivors fled, leaving everything behind. They did not even bury their dead.

I scratched my head. "Where were they going?"

"The ghost did not know."

"Okay." Talking to ghosts was way beyond something I'd even thought was possible a week ago.

"Is the ghost still ...?"

She shook her head. "He moved on once he'd told us what happened."

That was a relief.

"We buried the dead," Maria said. "Then last night a giant arrived. It did not stay and departed to the east. This morning, the harpies returned."

"So ... how'd they hurt McNab?" I asked.

"He had taken his and Cassidy's horse to the river to drink," she said, "when the harpies arrived."

I nodded, remembering the piles of bones I'd passed.

"Any survivors like Beth?" I asked.

"No," she said with a shake of her head. "We buried many and helped the ghost. Then the monsters returned."

"So what else do we need to do here, before we go?"

She gave me a wry smile. "You think we can leave?"

A loud caw from outside reinforced her point.

But it also reminded me of Jeremiah. He needed Maria's medicine soon. It was late afternoon and the cyclops had come at night to both Grand Lake and Saratoga West. They might not come back, but it would be a good idea to not be here in case another one did.

The problem was how to get rid of the harpies.

As much as I hated Cassidy using me as bait, he'd gotten one of the foul things. Would that work again?

I moved to the little window in the door and lifted the flap. I could see the cabin in the distance, but none of the harpies. They had to be off to the side, away from my view. I cracked open the door, but didn't hear much.

"Okay if I open this?" I asked Maria over my shoulder.

"If you can close it fast enough."

"I can."

I eased it open, until the opening was wide enough for me to step into. That gave me a full view of the yard, the far cabin and, yes, off toward the river about two hundred yards, a few harpies hopping around on the ground. They seemed to be eating something, and it took me a minute to realize it had to be the body of the one Cassidy'd shot.

I didn't see any on top of the cabin, or around it. It all looked peaceful and serene, with the warm sun on the wooden roof shingles making them shine.

"Hey Cassidy!" I called as loud as I could. After a pause. "Cassidy!"

The door on the cabin opened and Cassidy appeared.

"You wanna try it again?" I yelled.

He nodded and gave me a thumbs up. Then he quickly disappeared back into the cabin but returned to the doorway holding his rifle.

I took a deep breath and looked at the harpies. A couple of them seemed to be staring at me.

I lowered my head and ran.

I paced myself a little better, and watched my feet so I wouldn't trip. The harpies shrieked but I just focused on Cassidy when I wasn't watching the ground. He had his rifle shouldered and aimed, but didn't fire.

I ran. I ran hard.

Gasping for breath, I arrived at the cabin door. Cassidy stepped aside and I slid past him.

They hadn't gone for the bait.

TWENTY-TWO

INSIDE THE DARK CABIN, McNab had sat up. He grimaced and nodded when I came in, his face a white mask of pain. Cassidy slammed the door behind me and returned to the window where he stared out, muttering obscenities under his breath. The scents of blood and sweat and straw filled the air.

I took a deep breath and checked my knee. It throbbed, but I could stand just fine, and I'd run without any problems.

"That didn't work," I said.

"They're not stupid," McNab said with a dark chuckle. "They don't scare easy, either. We tried making a lot of noise like you do to drive birds away and they were having none of it."

"The way they squawk is loud enough to drive birds away on its own," I joked.

"Maybe," McNab acknowledged.

"The only thing we know drives them away is bullets," Cassidy said. His tone was stern, and I got the sense he was angry, though not at me.

I could understand that. When I imagined those beasts getting to Beth or Jeremiah, I got angry too. If the harpies were smart enough to stay out of rifle range, they were smart enough to figure out how to get under that tree, eventually.

We couldn't wait here until dark. We had to kill them or drive them off soon.

I had an idea. A bad idea, but it made sense.

Cassidy hadn't liked it when I'd balked about being bait. It had kinda worked though—we got one of them.

And Cassidy had made it clear I wasn't one of his team. He hadn't said it, but I was expendable.

I hated that thought, but I remembered the story of General Grant, and how he'd launched a suicide attack in the early days of the Giant War to give Lee's army time to escape.

My pulse started racing.

Grant had died, but Lee had been able to stop the Jotun from taking New York the next year.

The same had happened in the West, I realized. How many men had died on the barricades at Golden City, so us cannoneers could kill the giants?

We had to get the harpies into rifle range. That required bait. McNab couldn't do it, not with his injuries. We needed Maria to save Jeremiah and Beth. That left me and Cassidy.

We couldn't lose Cassidy. The West couldn't lose Cassidy. Heck, *humanity* couldn't lose Cassidy.

I started shaking out of fear. I didn't want to get hurt or die, and maybe I wouldn't, but I was still awful afraid.

McNab started coughing. He fumbled for a canteen near his bed and started drinking. Cassidy only briefly glanced back from his spying.

I looked at the man. His long black hair was greasy and tangled, much like Maria's. Dirt smothered his shirt and pants and he had a minor scratch across one unshaven cheek.

He still stood solid, though, like I'd first seen back in the Battle of Golden City. Powerful, in the way he held himself. Even though the shine had worn off my admiration these past few days, I still thought he was a hero.

What would a hero do?

I took a deep breath. I became aware of McNab's Colt pressing against my belly.

I drew it and went to the door. I started to pull it open, but stopped and turned to Cassidy.

"Cover me?" I asked.

He glanced my way and frowned. "Going back to the barn?"

"No."

I pushed open the door and walked out.

Cassidy didn't call after me and I didn't look back. With measured strides, I walked toward the harpies. I aimed the Colt, but I was well outside its range. After two dozen steps, the monsters noticed me. They looked up and shrieked that horrendous shriek.

Two stared at me, their horrid scowling faces and sharp beaks bathed in blood and entrails. They batted their greasy wings and hopped to face off with me. Two others kept eating a bit, and then lifted their heads to watch.

I kept walking.

The first two screamed in challenge, and then the other two joined them.

Then all four were aloft, going up to higher altitudes. They became evil shadows against the bright blue sky.

I planted my feet, braced myself, and raised the Colt.

They dived. Two in front, two behind.

Their screams deafened me!

Still, I found an inner calm. I aimed at the nearest one on the left.

Behind me, Cassidy's rifle barked. The harpy on the right spun and started to tumble.

I kept my eye on the one on the left, and when I could see its teats, I fired twice.

Then I threw myself to the ground and rolled to the side. I made sure to tuck the Colt into my chest so I wouldn't lose it.

I rolled hard and fast, my ears ringing from the cries of the harpies and more gunshots. Finally I thudded to my back and stared up at the sky.

High up, a lone harpy, shrieking like a devil from hell, flew away east.

I sat up. Three harpies lay on the ground near where I'd been standing. Two were still, but one still flopped its wings. I put a bullet in its body and it cried out one more time, and then the wings flailed twice more before it was still.

I checked myself. No scratches—the monsters hadn't touched me. I ached a bit from the roll, but that would pass.

Cassidy pounded across the grass toward me, still carrying his rifle. He slowed when he neared, and then came to a stop, just near my feet. His jaw remained set, but his eyes glowed.

"That was a foolish thing to do," he said.

"Yeah, but it worked."

"That it did." He broke into a grin, one of the first I'd seen in a long time. He extended his hand and I took it and he pulled me to my feet.

"Let's go get Jeremiah and Beth," he said.

"Let's."

I felt ten feet tall the entire walk back to the cabin.

McNab looked expectantly at us when we walked in. Despite the gloom, his eyes were bright with anticipation.

"Got three," Cassidy said. "The last one fled." He nodded to me. "Not a scratch."

McNab started chuckling but it turned into a full blown belly laugh. "We need to bottle the kid's luck, Cass," he said with a merry shake of his head. "He's one lucky son of a bitch."

"Language, McNab," Cassidy warned.

The older man scowled. "Sorry, kid. Didn't mean to call you that."

"I've been called worse." I shrugged as casually as I could.

"Besides," Cassidy said, "it wasn't all luck. He moved well out there and did a good job of getting out of the way." He looked at me. "You did good, Billy, even if it was a fool thing to do."

I nodded, trying to stay cool on the outside, but inside … I did good! I did good!

Cassidy extended a hand to McNab and helped him to his feet. McNab stood shaky, and with the open door and better light, I could now see how bad his shoulder was torn up. Even with the big bandages covering most everything, there was enough clotted blood and bare scarred flesh to be a fright. The harpies had gouged him good.

"Let's load up the wagon and go," Cassidy said.

"You have a wagon?" I blurted out.

"Behind the barn," McNab said. "We moved it out before the harpies showed up."

This was good. This was real good.

Cassidy pointed to a pile of saddlebags and told me to take them to the wagon. Then he headed out himself. McNab reached for his rifle which he'd propped against the wall by his pallet, but then winced in pain and pulled his arm back.

"You take it Billy," he said. "Might as well have it be used."

I blinked and gingerly picked up the gun. It was an 1860 Henry Rifle. I turned it over and studied it closely. Other than a few nicks in the handle, it was in great shape.

"Bullets are in the bag," McNab said as he pointed at a large leather pouch. "Can you hand me that canteen?"

I did so, and he took a long pull out of it. Meanwhile, I loaded up the rest of what I could carry. When McNab was done, he gestured for me to hold the door.

"Thank you, Billy," he said as he walked out. "I'm glad you're along."

He faced the other way and couldn't see how happy that made me feel.

In the bright sunshine of the late morning, Cassidy hitched up Maria's horse to the wagon while I loaded all the good supplies I could find into it. Besides the provisions the three of them had brought, the cabin held a supply of dried food and basic cooking stuff. I also added some blankets and an axe from the barn. Then Cassidy and I lifted a barrel of feed into the back. We hadn't had a lot of forage and he thought we might need it.

While we did that, Maria changed McNab's dressings, using some torn up shirts from the cabin as new bandages. I winced when I saw her doing that, in part because of the ugliness of the wound and in part because I couldn't help thinking about the person that must've owned those shirts before.

After we'd all gotten on the wagon, Cassidy drove us down to the bridge. He had me get out and make sure the wheels aligned where they needed to across the rough planks. On the far side, I got back on and sat next to Cassidy on the seat and we went down the road back toward Grand Lake.

We went slow, and I started to get more nervous as we did. There'd been a lot more harpies when they attacked Jeremiah than we'd seen since. I was sure some were still there, watching him and Beth.

I wanted to get there fast. But we were also taking Maria and McNab, with all his wounds, too. Was that smart? Headed into a battle?

Cassidy seemed as cool as ice. If he was worried, it didn't show.

We rode on. I got more nervous and more nervous.

Cassidy must've sensed it. He looked at me and raised one eyebrow. When I gave him a forced smile back, he looked a bit harder at me.

"You afraid?" he asked.

"No sir," I said, "just worried."

"It's reasonable to be worried. You just can't let it control you."

"I know. It's just … well, it's hard."

He nodded knowingly.

"At the Battle of Golden City," I said, "I was too young to

understand enough to be scared. I mean, I was scared, but not bad, you know?"

"Like my first battle," he said. "I was older than you were. Older than you are now. I couldn't sleep at all the night before. I kept wondering what to expect."

"Which battle was that?"

"Belmont," he said, "under Grant." He shook his head and swore softly. "We made so many mistakes, but we survived. That seems so long ago."

Fourteen years, I thought. It was hard to think Cassidy was once young like me, but he must've been.

We fell quiet for a while. Only the creak of the wagon wheels and the huffs and snorts of the horse could be heard. I glanced back and saw McNab was sleeping under a blanket while Maria had gotten out a needle and thread and was mending his shirt. Meanwhile, the sun shone, and the grass waved in the breeze.

It would've been downright peaceful if there hadn't been harpies up ahead.

"Let me know when we get close," Cassidy said.

"We're close," I said. I pointed to a distant lump on the road ahead of us. "I think that's what's left of Jeremiah's horse."

Cassidy pulled up on the reins and yanked the wagon brake. He turned to me.

"Get your rifle, kid. From here in, we walk." He turned to Maria. "You still have the Peacemaker if worst comes to worst?"

She nodded.

Cassidy and I dismounted from the wagon. I hefted McNab's Henry in front of me, and held it at the ready. Cassidy did the same with his own rifle.

Then side by side, we started walking toward the monsters.

TWENTY-THREE

I STRAINED to see the horse corpse in the distance. Nothing moved around it, not that I could tell. It looked picked clean, like the piles of bones back by the bridge. I kinda hoped that meant the harpies had decided to go somewhere else, but I was sure they hadn't.

Cassidy didn't break his stride.

My legs were shorter, so I had to quickstep to keep up. Cassidy noticed and slowed, but only a little bit.

Slowly, we closed on the horse, and then we could see the trees where I'd left Beth and Jeremiah.

In front of the trees, several harpies tore into a body. My blood chilled for a moment before I realized it was the one I'd shot earlier. Cannibalism was not a problem for these beasts.

Off to the side, one faced the tree. It flapped its wings and shrieked.

Cassidy and I broke into a trot.

When we got to about fifty yards away, the harpies dining on the corpse looked up at us. Cassidy skidded to a halt and raised his rifle to his shoulder I followed suit.

"I'll take the ones on the right," he said. "You aim for the left."

I didn't even bother to nod. I just picked out one that was looking hard at me. She hadn't taken wing yet, but I suspected that was just a matter of time. I sighted down the barrel at her chest, aiming right between her breasts.

Cassidy fired. Then so did I.

Mine flopped back. With shrieks and screams, the others took wing.

I followed one as it rose up, shooting into the sky. A long way up, it paused and turned to dive. I fired and missed.

Cassidy's rifle rang out with his second shot. I was too busy taking a bead on the diving harpy to see what he'd done.

I fired.

The harpy shrieked and spun to the side, but kept flapping one wing.

I kept my sights on it and fired again. It cried and plummeted toward the ground.

"Down!"

I dropped to the dirt and rolled as soon as I heard Cassidy's command.

Wide wings shot through the air where I'd just stood, followed by a scream of frustration.

More shots followed, and then another inhuman scream.

The ground jarred the rifle out of my hands. I clutched for it while also looking around wildly. Then I remembered the Colt and pulled it out.

All was eerily quiet. All I could hear was the fading ringing in my ears.

I sat up. Cassidy knelt on one knee a few feet away. He had his rifle pointed up towards the east. There, two harpies flew away, getting smaller in the distance.

Around us and near the trees, five more bodies lay.

"Woo-we!" The loud shout came from the tree. Jeremiah stepped out from under the branches waving his hat. "That was some fine shooting!"

I smiled at Cassidy, who returned the grin.

"I'm surprised it was so easy," I said.

"You showed me how, earlier." He rose and came over and offered his hand.

"Huh?" I said as he pulled me to my feet.

"They hunt by diving," he said, "like a hawk. That's how they tried to get you earlier. I figured that meant we'd have time to get a couple of them first if we could see them coming."

I nodded. It made sense, and suddenly walking straight toward them didn't seem so foolish.

We made our way over to Jeremiah. Despite standing earlier, he'd taken a squat on the ground. He didn't get up when we approached.

"How are you doing?" Cassidy asked.

"I'll live," Jeremiah said. "Probably. My back's pretty hurt, and I can't use my arm." He nodded his head to the right to indicate which one. "I may be infected, too."

"Maria's still got some of her mold medicine left after taking care of McNab," Cassidy said.

"What happened to McNab?" Jeremiah asked.

"Harpies got him while he was watering the horses. But he'll live, too."

"How's Beth?" I asked.

"In pain," Jeremiah said, "but otherwise fine. The harpies didn't attack. I think they were too full from their meals." He gestured toward the piles of bones that had been living creatures only that morning.

Cassidy said, "take me to her." He looked at me. "You go get the wagon."

"You have a wagon?" Jeremiah said. He turned and he and Cassidy headed under the tree and the rest of the conversation faded so I couldn't hear.

Instead, I took a deep breath and looked around at the harpy bodies. My blood raced and part of me felt downright giddy.

My first big battle.

No, my second. But this one I was in the middle of instead of watching from the hills.

I'd survived them both, which was what really mattered.

I started back up the road for the wagon and the rest of our team.

Beth cried out in delight when she saw Maria. The older woman checked the girl's ankle, smeared some ointment on it and rebandaged it, and gave her some medicine to drink. Then she did the same with Jeremiah's wounds. She also had him drink the tea she'd prepared back in the barn.

The rest of us loaded their bags and gear into the wagon. Cassidy and I were able to carefully lift Beth up into it without hurting her. Cassidy took the reins again and motioned for me to join him on the front seat. The rest clambered on board and we set off toward Grand Lake.

"So what now?" I asked once we were on the way.

"It depends," Cassidy said, "on what I find in Grand Lake."

"We searched it pretty good," I said. "Is there something you're looking for?"

"I want to see if anything's changed, for one. Then we'll see."

He paused a moment, as if lost in thought. Meanwhile, the wagon bumped along the rough dirt road as the shadows from the setting sun grew longer. Behind us in the wagon, McNab told Jeremiah about the ghosts.

"The harpies flew east when they fled," Cassidy finally said. "So their nest should be east near Grand Lake, or beyond it. Maybe north or south of it a bit."

"Jeremiah didn't find anything," I said, "except empty camps."

"Yes, I want to look at those myself."

"What are you looking for?"

He let out a long breath and stared ahead for a bit. The horse kept tromping along as the wagon wheels squeaked.

"Do you know how rifts get made?" he asked.

"No," I said. "Until a few days ago, I thought there was only one, ever."

"There've been others," he said. "We're pretty sure Maria's

people had some open when Cortez arrived. Good thing he shut them down."

I tried to recall who Cortez was. He'd conquered Mexico for the Spanish, but that was all I could remember.

"Rifts come from human sacrifice," Cassidy said.

"Not necessarily," Jeremiah chimed in, from behind us. "Natural deaths can create them, too, under the right circumstances."

"Which are circumstances a skilled witch can create," Cassidy said.

"Witch?" I asked.

"Mmm hmm," Cassidy said. "Someone who can see and interact with souls."

Jeremiah added, "Lots of people can see souls after they've left the body. We call them ghosts.

But not everyone can help them move out of this world."

Maria could, I thought. Is she a witch?

"An *evil* witch can halt the soul's final passage, so they move halfway out, and only halfway," Cassidy said, "which creates the rift."

"Like propping a door open," Jeremiah said, "with the poor soul as both the key to open the door and the stop to keep it from closing."

Oh, God. I shuddered at the thought. Not only not going to heaven, but not staying on Earth?

It was horrible. Completely horrible.

"There has to be a witch around for there to be cyclopses and harpies," Jeremiah said. "We need to find her."

Cassidy snorted. "You seen your wounds, Jer? There's no 'we' here. You're going back to Empire."

"Is that safe?" I asked.

"It should be," Cassidy said. "If there was trouble that way, Luke would've come back instead of going on to Golden City."

"If he could," I said morosely.

"Luke's one of the best scouts in the country," Cassidy said. "He's fine."

I thought about that for a bit. Some harpies might've flown

south, the way he was going, but we'd have seen any cyclopses. Besides, he had a big head start. He'd probably already crossed the pass into Empire and was headed down to Golden City for reinforcements.

But what if he wasn't?

"So, if I can't come with you," Jeremiah said, "where do you want me to send the cavalry to save your sorry rear?"

Cassidy chuckled, but didn't answer.

Daylight faded and Cassidy had us stop near some cottonwoods that looked like they might offer a bit of protection, should the harpies return. We set up camp and Maria, Cassidy, and I took watch shifts. The wounded all slept. Fortunately, nothing happened during the night and we pushed on as soon as it was light.

We stopped when we got to the spot where I'd killed the cyclops. Cassidy wanted to examine the body, but the harpies had gotten to it. All that was left was torn tunic, sandals, and bones. Jeremiah showed the others the medallion we'd found, but no one had any good ideas about the writing on it.

We arrived where the road forked, one branch going north to Grand Lake and the other south to Empire, around noon. We stopped for a break and Cassidy told me to catch us some fish in the river nearby while he talked to Maria and Jeremiah. I only caught one, but it tasted real nice mixed with the hardtack and dried fruit we'd taken from the cabin in Saratoga West.

After our meal, Cassidy had us all get back into the wagon. We shifted all the tools and supplies we'd scavenged earlier around so there was room for all of the wounded to lie down, though not comfortably like. They were tight packed. Then Maria climbed in as well.

"Think you can drive the wagon, Billy?" Cassidy asked.

"Uh, yeah," I said.

"Good," he said. "Jeremiah may be able to spell you for short times, but only in the flat where he could use one arm."

I nodded, but then the implications sunk in.

"But ... what about you?" I asked. "Why aren't you driving it?"

"I'm going to look for the witch," he said. "Also see if I can find the giants' camp and harpies' nest."

"Don't forget the rift!" Jeremiah called from the wagon.

Cassidy snorted and shook his head as if that was a dumb comment.

"By yourself?" I asked.

"Who else could come?" he said. He gestured toward the wagon. "We can't wait. More monsters could come through every day. And most of my team is injured. Maria needs to take care of them. And I need you civilians safe and out of the way."

I bristled hard. Civilians! Maybe Beth, but ... I killed a cyclops!

Cassidy sensed my mood. He reached out at patted me on the shoulder.

"You've done well, Billy," he said, "and you'll make a fine sharpshooter for the army some day. But right now, I need you to drive these folks to safety. Understand?"

It was all I could do not to throw a punch. For the army? A sharpshooter? I was a giant hunter!

"Go on," he said. He stepped back and gestured toward the wagon.

I bit my lip hard to keep from saying anything. Then I turned and stomped off in the other direction.

Everyone in the wagon watched me go. Conscious of their eyes, I slowed and turned. McNab had a tired smirk on his face. Jeremiah was shaking his head sadly, and Maria was inscrutable as ever.

Beth, though, stared at me with wide eyes and an open mouth.

TWENTY-FOUR

I STORMED off until my temper fell, and then slowed as the embarrassment rose. I'd behaved like a little kid in front of everyone! In front of Cassidy, worst of all.

What he'd said made sense. I just hadn't liked the way he'd said it.

I'd done great things the past few days. *Amazing* things. Killed a cyclops. Killed a bunch of harpies. I'd even walked into the face of danger at Cassidy's side.

And I'd been dismissed.

Cassidy didn't want me. Not on his team, at least. He just wanted me to keep Beth safe.

My feet had carried me down the road a ways, to the edge of the river. I pulled out of my head and gazed across the bubbling water. The bright sun glinted off it here and there. I remembered how peaceful the lake had looked the morning after I'd taken Beth out in the canoe.

I glanced around. I'd hooked the fish for lunch along a shore like this one. Some bugs buzzed around some nearby white flowers that I didn't remember. I must not have been paying attention.

Beth had wanted to know what it was like to be on Cassidy's team. Now I'd never really know.

Worse, I'd lied to Beth about being on his team. She'd never look at me the same again.

But at least she could, I realized. She was alive, and I'd had a lot to do with that.

That's what matters, I told myself. I could almost hear Ma's voice, telling me to do what was right. She'd even whooped me once, not long after the Battle, when I'd hidden a book from Tom 'cause I wanted to read it so bad. It'd been his book, and she'd not only tanned my hide but made me apologize to him and promise to never do it again.

I sucked in a deep breath. I needed to apologize to Beth. And to Cassidy. And to all of them, really.

And as much as I hated to admit it, someone needed to drive the wagon over the pass. Me or Cassidy, and I was a much better choice.

It took all my will, but I turned and trudged back to the others.

They hadn't waited.

They hadn't gone far. I could see the wagon in the distance on the road south, slowly rolling along. But they hadn't stayed.

My face burned with shame once again. I jogged after them not sure what I'd say when I caught up.

It took me maybe half an hour to get close. Cassidy slowed the wagon, and then stopped it and hopped off when I was nearly to it. He walked around the side and stood, feet apart, one hand on his hip, staring at me.

I pulled up a few yards away. Everyone else was looking at me from the back of the wagon. I took a minute to catch my breath.

"I'm sorry," I said. "I shouldn't have stormed off like a little boy. I'll drive the wagon like you asked."

Cassidy nodded. I couldn't tell how mad he was. His jaw was fixed and his eyes hard but he didn't say anything.

"I'm sorry," I said again.

"People die," he said, harsh but slow, "when other people don't do as they're ordered."

Sometimes they die anyway, I thought. But I didn't say it. Instead I just nodded agreement.

Cassidy went back to the wagon and grabbed his rifle and a pack. With them both slung over his shoulders, he walked toward me, clearly intending to keep going past me and into Grand Lake.

But he stopped right in front of me and gave me a stern look.

"Billy," he said, "you're a good kid. But you're still just a kid. You've been lucky, but in the long run luck kills people. You need to grow up."

"Yes, sir," I said. I lowered my head because I couldn't meet his eyes.

He let out a long, frustrated breath, and then walked on.

I don't think either of us looked back.

No one said anything as I took my seat on the wagon. I gave the reins a shake and we started moving down the bumpy road. Slowly. Too slowly, frankly.

After a while, Jeremiah broke the silence by asking McNab more details about Saratoga West. He asked McNab to repeat himself a couple of times, so I glanced back to see what was going on. Jeremiah had gotten out a pen and a bound tome of paper and was taking notes.

Great, I thought. I'll be immortalized as the kid kicked off Cassidy's team.

Except I was never really on it.

I brooded and tried not to dwell on the way I was being sent home.

We didn't make much speed and stopped mid-day by a stream to let the horse graze and all of us eat a bit ourselves. Maria insisted McNab and Jeremiah stretch their legs a bit and she herself went to look for some medicinal flowers she knew grew in the meadows here.

Beth sat glumly in the back of the wagon. I brought her some water and sank to the wagon slats beside her. She gave me a sullen glare.

"You're not on Cassidy's team," she said.

"Nope." My gut knotted, but I didn't want to say more than that.

"You told me you were."

"Yep." I wasn't sure I actually had, but I'd led her to believe it, which was just as much a lie.

"Why?"

I let out a long ragged breath.

"Because," I said, "it's what I've wanted, more than anything in the world. And for a while, I thought I had it."

"Why'd you think that?"

"I was traveling with them," I said. "I was fighting with them. I figured, you know." I made a dismissive gesture with my hand. "I figured that made me one of them, even though Cassidy hadn't said so."

"That was dumb," she said with a snort.

"I know."

"So," she said, "stop being dumb."

I couldn't help but laugh at her tone. I was being lectured by an eight-year-old!

She just rolled her eyes and dramatically huffed.

"You must be feeling better," I teased.

She nodded. "My legs still hurt, but Maria says I'm getting better."

"I'm sure in no time you'll be as good as new."

Her face fell, and she hunched her shoulders. She took a deep breath.

"No," she said raggedly, "not as good as new."

Tears filled her eyes. She started to sob softly.

"Ma and Pa are gone. I don't think Cassidy can get them back!"

I put an arm around her to comfort her. She leaned into my chest and started to wail. I didn't know what to do, so I just held her.

Somehow all my worries about Cassidy, and all my fears about not being on his team seemed small.

I felt small.

But at least I could hold Beth.

I tucked my head down over hers and closed my eyes. Pulling her as close as I could, I rocked her while she soaked my shirt with her tears. Some of mine might've joined hers.

Sometime, a long time or a short time or a medium time I didn't know which, the others shuffled back onto the wagon around me. They talked low and I didn't quite make out what they said. Beth's sobs were too loud in my ears.

Someone lightly touched my shoulder. When I looked up, Jeremiah's calm eyes met mine.

"We need to go, Billy," he said. "Want me to drive?"

I nodded and wiped my face. My nose had begun to run, somehow. Thankfully, Beth's sadness seemed to have run its course. She still snuggled into me, as best she could, but the cries had turned to sniffles.

Beth pulled back and looked around. "Water?" she said plaintively to no one particular.

"Here," Maria said, reaching over my shoulder with a canteen.

Everyone was clustered around. It was starting to feel tight.

"I'll drive," I said, letting my hands slip from Beth. "You need to take care of our girl." I gave her a warm smile, which she partially returned, and then scrambled back up to the driver's seat.

There was a whole lot of hurt in the world, and most of it was worse than mine.

A rainstorm blew in about mid-afternoon. The sky clouded up and roiled in blacks and ominous blues. The wind's whoosh made it hard to hear much and the chill seemed to seep through every stitch of my clothes. Twice I had to grab my hat before it went flying off.

When the rain itself started, it fell in large plops. First a few that spattered here and there on me and the seat. Then they started falling harder and bigger. One smacked me on the wrist and it nearly stung.

I looked for some trees or any sort of cover, but we were in the high moraine meadow and there wasn't anything. I spotted some low bushes far from the road, but they wouldn't help. Meanwhile, the drops of rain turned to streams.

I pulled up the wagon break and turned to the others. "Under the wagon!"

They were already moving before I'd even spoke.

Beth winced in pain when we lifted her down, but by then the rain was solid sheets and the wind was fierce. It did snatch my hat when I was trying to help slide Beth's feet under the wagon but I didn't have more than a moment to glance where it was tumbling. We all got underneath, leaving the horse and our gear to their fates.

Beth and Maria huddled together as the wind tried to whip around and under the wagon to where we were. Jeremiah looked pale and was holding his bad arm and rocking. I figured he must've hurt it when we were scrambling but didn't want to say anything. McNab had his eyes closed and his lips were moving, but I couldn't hear what he was saying.

We were a sad lot.

We'd run from the rain. Just as we were running from the cyclops.

Because it was the smart thing to do.

I hated that. Some heroes we were.

But what were we really?

I was a seventeen year old kid, good with a rifle, and not much else. Beth was a real kid, who'd had some bad stuff happen to her. Maria was a witch. I hated the word, and it didn't really seem to fit the quiet serene woman, but she had to be. She didn't show up in any of Jeremiah's books, but I began to wonder if that was intentional. Ghosts didn't show up in the books either, but McNab and the others were real familiar with them.

I started to wonder how much Jeremiah left out of the tales. He himself wasn't in the books, but he had to have been along. The books were just all about Cassidy, and how great he was.

He *was* great.

Maybe the books exaggerated, though.

McNab coughed and shuddered. He leaned against the inside of a wheel and ignored the splashes ricocheting off the rim.

At least McNab was in the books, as quartermaster, gunfighter, and the man who always worked with the army. Jeremiah had written him gruff, too, so at least that was real.

Luke was in some of the books too, now that I thought about it. He'd appeared in the last two, though not in a big role. He'd replaced a scout who'd gotten killed in an earlier tale.

Was that what it took to get on the team? Someone else dying?

That could work.

I immediately felt ashamed of the thought. There was enough misery in the world to not be wishing for the death of some other man.

I sat, with my shoulders hunched, and let the thoughts of the books and how they matched what we'd done run through my mind. I was sure Jeremiah would write a heckuva yarn when this was over. "Cassidy and the Giants of Colorado" or something like that.

Maybe I'd even be in it.

I snorted. I'd be in it. The question was whether he'd write me as a fool or not. What kind of fool sets off to join a fighting band that doesn't want him, and doesn't even bring a gun?

I looked over at McNab's Henry rifle. I'd have to give that back when we got to Empire, along with the Colt revolver at my waist. Then I could slink back down to Golden City with my tail between my legs.

The rain continued to beat down on the wagon above our heads.

At least I could get everyone out safe, I figured. Jeremiah wouldn't write me as a fool in his book if I did that.

We just still had a long way to go.

TWENTY-FIVE

THE RAIN itself lasted just long enough to chill us and thoroughly soak all the supplies we'd left in the wagon. Puddles had formed at the edges of our shelter in the dirt, but not flowed inward in any significant way. Beth didn't get any wetter and the rest of us at least didn't get much worse.

We clambered out and did our best to sluice the water from the wagon. Maria's medicines had stayed dried but the barrel of feed had leaked. We still had a few mostly dry blankets and Maria insisted on wrapping Beth and McNab with them. I gave Jeremiah my coat. The horse wasn't too happy, but at least he'd behaved during the storm. I made a silent prayer of thanks that Maria's gentle mount had been the survivor instead of Cassidy's fiery stallion. He'd have taken off on his own to escape the storm, certainly upsetting us all.

The fading afternoon light never recovered from the storm. The clouds filled the skies and even the mountain peaks around us in gloom. At least the wind had faded a bit. It still bit at us, icy cold, but it didn't seem likely to gust.

It took us a while, but we did manage to trudge on. The storm hadn't been long enough to turn the road ruts into deep mud, but it still dragged on the wagon. We passed the fork that led to Rollins Pass and kept going south towards Berthoud Pass and Empire.

About dusk, we spotted a building in the distance, all by itself, in the grass not far from the river.

"What's that?" I asked Jeremiah, who now rode beside me.

"Looks like a homestead," he said.

We continued toward it as the daylight faded. When we got close, to my surprise, there was light coming from a window. It wasn't too bright as it flickered, probably from a fire.

I halted the wagon while we were still a ways away and looked back at my passengers. McNab huddled under a blanket while Maria held Beth's hand and the little girl lay still with her eyes closed. Jeremiah leaned against the side and his head turned my way.

"Someone's home," I said, pointing toward the house.

He nodded. "Be careful."

"I'm not worried," I said. "Harpies don't use lights."

Jeremiah chuckled and waved me on.

Still, I approached slow, with my rifle across my chest. Well, McNab's rifle, but still. I got up to the house without much changing. The light sneaking out from around the door and the window blinds flickered, but I couldn't hear anything above the breeze. So I knocked on the door and stepped back three paces.

A wild-eyed woman with unkempt dark brown hair threw open the door and stared at me.

"Evening ma'am," I said.

"You're human!" she said. Her eyes darted from me to the wagon and back again.

She stood strong there in the doorway. Her brown wool dress was crinkled and splattered with something, and her skin pale with fright.

"Yes, ma'am," I said. I gestured toward the wagon. "There are five of us, but three are wounded. We were hoping to take shelter for the night. But first ... are you all right?"

She let out a long shudder. "No, we're not all right."

A boy, maybe thirteen, appeared behind her. He held a Henry

rifle, but wasn't pointing it at me. He leveled a steely gaze at me instead.

I smiled back.

"Let 'em in, Ma," he said. "Maybe they can help Pa."

"He hurt?" I asked.

Both the boy and his mother nodded.

"We've got someone who knows medicines. Let me bring the wagon up."

I turned, but before I could take three paces, the cabin door erupted in merry chaos. Two younger girls came tumbling out, all talking at once, shouting happily, followed by the boy. The girls quickly scampered past me toward the wagon in a tumult of noise and shouts.

"That's Beth, Ma!"

"It's Beth!"

"You can help?"

The last one was the boy talking to me, loping along by my side.

"Hope so," I said. "What happened?"

"Pa was attacked by some big bird," he said, "when he was bringing in the cattle. He's hurt bad."

I nodded. "So are two of our men, by the same birds."

The girls reached the wagon before us, where Maria was just starting to stand. She smiled warmly at them. Beth had sat up and was waving excitedly and calling the girls' names. I picked out "Sarah" and "Mary" but couldn't put the name with the girl.

The boy and I picked up our pace a bit and made our way to the front of the wagon.

"Will Cozens," he said, introducing himself.

"Billy McCarty."

"You running from the giants?"

"Uh, yeah. What do you know about giants?"

"A man came through a few days ago. He warned us about giants and told us to get out. But Pa's been too sick to move."

"A man? Did he give his name?"

Will shook his head.

"Tall? Brown hat and coat?"

"That was him."

Luke. That felt good. He'd made it this far, which meant he probably made it all the way to Empire.

We got settled on the wagon and drove it up to the cabin door. It took a bit to unload, especially to get Beth moved, but the boy and I managed to get her down and then Jeremiah and McNab said they could help her the rest of the way with her crutches. The boy said he'd take care of the horse so I gathered up our things and went inside.

The cabin turned out to be more of a small house. The door opened into a small hall with a sitting room to the left and the kitchen to the right. A larger room was at the end of the hall and the girls were hustling back and forth bringing ceramic mugs and a pitcher of water down to it, so I followed them. There, McNab and Jeremiah had settled onto sturdy pine wood chairs at a plank table, both looking weary. The girls turned and quickly dashed back to the kitchen.

"Where's Beth and Maria?"

"Beth's in the sitting room," Jeremiah said, "lying on the couch. Maria's attending to Mr. Cozens in his bedroom."

I nodded. I decided to pile our gear in along a wall that was free of shelves and went back for another load.

On the way back in, I stopped in the sitting room. Beth had stretched out with her head on a pillow. She grimaced, which meant the move hadn't been pain free, but one of the girls, the younger one, was talking to her excitedly and holding her hand.

I went over to the Beth. "You okay?" I asked. "Need anything?"

"Willow bark, please?" she asked. Then her eyes darted to the girl. "This is Sarah Cozens. We'd play together when they came to Grand Lake. Her brother's Will and her sister's Mary."

"Nice to meet you, Sarah," I said with a tip of my hat. "I'm Billy McCarty."

"Good to meet you, Mr. McCarty. My Pa's named Billy, too." She pointed toward a door to the right, that apparently led to the bedroom. Mrs. Cozens stood in the entryway, rubbing her hands together and leaning forward, as if hanging on every word that was being said in the room beyond.

"Your Pa was attacked by a bird?" I asked.

Sarah's eyes went wide. "It was huge! It just flew down and hit him!"

"Did you see it?"

She nodded slowly, her eyes still as big as saucers. "It scared me bad, but Ma came out screaming at it and shaking her broom and it flew away."

"Where'd it go?" I asked.

"Down to the river where the cattle ran."

"I see." It'd gone for easier prey. "Have you seen it since?"

"No, sir," she said with a shake of her head.

"We saw them!" Beth said to Sarah. She started to tell the Cozens girl about our own adventures.

I drifted over to Mrs. Cozens's side.

Beyond her, the small room contained an ornate double bed with a carved pine headboard, a cushioned sitting chair, and a dark wood dresser and nightstand. A man Cassidy's age lay on the bed under several thick blankets, facing the wall. Maria stood next to him, speaking softly while touching him gently on the upper forearm.

The blankets were folded back below his shoulders. A ragged shirt peeked out, along with exposed bandages caked with blood. Slowly Maria peeled back the top one.

I sucked in my breath. The wounds looked all too familiar. Deep scratch wounds from harpy claws. Mr. Cozens's were red and inflamed, with his entire flesh looking like it was on fire, but otherwise they were the same as McNab's and Jeremiah's.

Mrs. Cozens put her hand to her mouth, but didn't cry or weep.

"Hot water," Maria said.

Mrs. Cozens hustled away to the kitchen. A moment later she returned with a kettle. Maria took a rag, dipped it in the water, and started sponging the wounds. One of them broke open, oozing yellow green pus and dark red blood.

I couldn't watch anymore.

I still had a job to do.

Maria's medicine bag sat on the little nightstand, partially unpacked.

"Maria?" I said. "May I get some willow bark?"

She nodded and tilted her head toward the bag.

Mr. Cozens groaned, loud and long.

I flinched and lowered my head as I walked by. Fortunately, after a bit of fumbling, I found the powder. When I returned to the sitting room, Sarah Cozens got me a mug of water and I took it to Beth. She gulped it and the medicine down quickly.

Mr. Cozens screamed.

Beth and Sarah clutched each others' hands. A tear ran down Sarah's cheek.

I glanced back at the bedroom. Mrs. Cozens still stood at the door, watching.

"You need anything else?" I asked Beth.

She shook her head.

I didn't know what else to do, so I went outside to look for Will.

I headed into the barn. Like the homestead, it was small, but the barn felt more utilitarian. The thick log walls kept it warm, and the flickering light of Will's lantern filled the space with an inviting feel. With only a few stalls and some space for feed and hay, that wasn't hard. Of course, the smell of horses beat the smell of pus and blood by quite a bit.

Will had been brushing down Maria's horse in a far stall, while a roan fed in the near one. He came out, his face drawn with worry.

"How's Pa?" he asked.

"Not good," I said, "but if anyone can fix him up, it's Maria."

"What is she? Some kind of doctor?"

"Kinda," I said. "She knows a lot about healing. Other stuff, too."

"Huh."

"He made it this far along. What four, five days? He's tough."

"Yeah," Will said with a nod. "He is."

He fell quiet, focused on the horse and whatever was on his mind.

"Need some help?" I asked.

"Sure," he said. "Check her feet? There's a pick over there if you need it." He nodded toward the far wall.

I got the pick and started on the mare's back hooves. I found a couple of small stones in among the mud and cleared them out.

Will and I worked quietly for a while. Both of us concentrated on doing our jobs with the mare, who shuffled and snorted a bit but was otherwise well behaved. When we finished, we both walked out of the stall. Will looked at me.

"You headed to Empire?" he asked.

"Yeah," I said with a nod. "Get the wounded out of the way and bring in reinforcements."

"Reinforcements?" he said, "For who?"

"Cassidy," I said. He'd heard of Cassidy, but didn't seem enamored. I wondered if he'd read the books.

Anyway, I briefly explained what we'd found in Grand Lake and Saratoga West, leaving out the gory parts. He grumbled when he heard about the empty towns, and asked a few questions about the harpies and the cyclops, but otherwise let me ramble.

"So what's he looking for?" Will asked.

"The person who created the new rift," I said. "We know that it's a new one. The one in Andersonville was to Jotunheim. This one's to somewhere Greek."

"Oh," he said. "Greek, huh. Do you suppose the Pappas sisters might be able to help?"

My chin nearly dropped. "Pappas sisters?"

"Yeah," he said. "They came through here last fall with the older sister's husband. He was from New York, though. Not Greek. He was gonna try mining."

My heart was hammering. I couldn't be sure, of course, but I *knew* the witch had to be one of them.

"Let's go tell Maria and Jeremiah," I said. "They'll know." I hustled toward the barn door. "C'mon."

Will was right on my heels.

TWENTY-SIX

INSIDE THE HOUSE, Mrs. Cozens had started serving the evening meal. Smells of warm beef stew mixed with the smoke from the stove along with a hint of sage. Oil lamps in the kitchen and parlor gave it a homey feel. Will ushered me toward the back room. On the way, I glanced into the sitting room. Beth was asleep on the couch.

We found the rest clustered around the table. Sarah and Mary sat at one end with stoneware bowls and little metal spoons, sipping quietly from little white cups. The others all had their own bowls and what looked like crusty wheat bread. Mrs. Cozens immediately began filling two more bowls from a large tureen when she saw us.

"Thank you, Ma'am," I said. I went to tip my hat, but of course it wasn't there, having blown off in the rain.

She nodded, her face too drawn and tired to even attempt a smile.

There weren't any more chairs, so after we got our stew, Sarah and Mary took their bowls to the other room. Will and I sat in their chairs and I looked at him.

"Tell them about the Greek sisters," I said.

Jeremiah, McNab, and Maria immediately perked up and looked at Will expectantly.

"Well," he said, "there's not much to say. They were sisters. One of them was married and they were traveling with her husband. They stopped here in October."

"Late September," Mrs. Cozens said. "And they weren't married. His name was Mr. Bartholomew. She was just Miss Pappas." She looked at Maria apologetically. "I didn't think it was proper, but my husband said to let them be."

"The sister didn't look too happy," Will said. "They stayed just the one night. Paid Pa thirty cents."

McNab and Jeremiah shared a meaningful look, but I had no idea what about.

"Where were they headed?" Jeremiah asked.

"The mining camps north of Grand Lake," Will said. He shrugged. "I don't know which one."

"Did either woman have a special necklace or amulet?" Maria asked. "At least that you saw?"

Will and his mom exchanged furrowed looks.

"Well," Mrs. Cozens said, "her sister wore this gold ring with an inscription on it. She said it was an old family heirloom."

"What did it say?" Jeremiah asked.

"I couldn't read it."

Jeremiah turned to me. "Billy, can you fetch my notebook, please? I think it's in my bag by the front door."

I nodded and went to find the bag. Behind me, Jeremiah continued asking questions about the sisters. What did they look like? How old were they? Did they have any unusual luggage?

I found a smooth leather-bound book underneath Jeremiah's shirt inside his bag. I flipped through it once—about a third of the pages were filled with scrawled notes, sometimes with hand drawn pictures. One was a map of the area, showing everywhere we'd been. It was obviously the right book, so I took it to him. He smiled when I returned to the back room.

"Ah," Jeremiah said. "Good." He flipped through it and motioned for Mrs. Cozens to come look over his shoulder. Maria, sitting nearby, and I both crowded around as well.

Jeremiah folded the book open flat on a page with a large sketch of the medallion we'd found on the Cyclops. "Did the inscription on the ring look like this?"

"I reckon so," Mrs. Cozens said. "Not exactly, but close. That one." She put her finger on a symbol I didn't recognize.

"Well, well, well," McNab said with a chuckle, "we have our witch."

Maria and Jeremiah nodded in agreement.

I nodded too, though I wasn't completely sure why.

"Witch?" Mrs. Cozens said with alarm. "There was a witch in my house?"

"Don't worry, Mrs. Cozens," Jeremiah said. He turned and met her eyes. "Witches can't harm you, at least not directly."

"But what about curses? She could've—"

He slowly shook his head, never looking away from her eyes.

"You're safe," he said. "As safe as can be, given the circumstances."

"But Pa—," Will interjected. His voice cracked. "Is he gonna be …?"

"He has a good chance," Maria said. "He needs rest, and broth, and to stay warm."

Will's face flooded with relief.

"When will he be good to move?" McNab asked Maria.

"The morning," she said, "though another day of rest would be better."

"Move?" Mrs. Cozens asked in alarm. "Move where?"

"Empire," McNab said. "Or maybe all the way to Golden City. It's dangerous to stay here with more of those monsters about."

She grimaced, but nodded. There was a fire in her eyes.

"We can figure it out in the morning," Jeremiah said. "We all need rest."

With that, people turned back to their stew.

After dinner, we moved the table so we could stretch out some bedrolls on the floor. The girls would sleep with Mrs. Cozens and Beth in the sitting room. The men would stay in the back.

Except Will announced he'd sleep in the barn. I decided to join him. So after we'd helped Mrs. Cozens clean up the remains of the meal, we took some blankets and headed over to it. Will checked on both horses, but they seemed to be fine. He set the lamp near the place he claimed for himself and proceeded to lay out his blankets.

I spread out my own blanket in the small space next to the hay, with my coat as a pillow. I probed my knee, and it only hurt when I touched it, which was good. The smell and sounds of the horses shuffling around was comforting, too. It reminded me of the times I'd bedded down in the stables back at the Astor House, way back when.

My mind wandered to Mr. Lake and then to Tom. He'd given me all that money for supplies, and there was no way I could pay him back. Not now. I was headed back to Golden City with less than I'd had when I'd left.

I let out a deep sigh.

Will lifted his head and looked at me. The lamp burned low near his head.

"What?" he said.

"Just thinking about a friend," I said.

"Good friend?"

"Best I ever had," I said. "He's back in Golden City. He gave me money to come on this trip."

"You didn't get it from the Government?"

I turned and looked at him. Shadows danced on his face from the flickering lamp. His eyes were wide and earnest.

"I …," I let out a deep breath. "I'm not on Cassidy's team," I said. "I kinda followed them."

"Oh." He propped his head on on his arm, his elbow to the ground. "Why'd you do that?"

"I wanted to be on the team."

"So you just followed them?"

I didn't know what to say. That's what I'd done. Was that really a bad thing?

"Yeah … yeah, that's what I did," I said. "But I still helped." I briefly told him about the cyclops and the harpies and me keeping Beth safe.

"Wow," he said when I was done. "You did all that?"

"Cassidy did most of it."

"Sounds like you did," he said. "You shot the cyclops and about half the harpies and got Beth into that boat. That's more than he did."

I blinked. Could that be true?

"He mighta been in charge, but you did your share."

I lay there, thinking about what he'd said. I knew he was right, but I'd never thought about it like that.

"So do you think he'll find the witch?" Will asked.

"Sure," I said. "He's going to the mining camps. That's where she was headed."

"What'll he do when he finds her? Kill her?"

"I suppose," I said. "I don't actually know. He didn't say."

"Oh." Will's face fell and he looked like he wanted to talk more, but didn't know what to say.

"Let's get some sleep," I said. "We need to get moving early."

Will nodded and blew out the lamp.

We were up at dawn, when the dim light snuck through the edges of the barn doors and the occasional knothole. We groggily got ourselves up, stretching and shaking off the rest of the sleepies. Inside, we found the whole homestead was also up and moving, at least those that weren't hurt. Maria passed the word that they were to sleep as much as they could.

Mrs. Cozens had decided they were going with us, so there was a lot to do to get ready. They had a wagon of their own, so Will and I spent the morning loading up their chickens and feed and tools and keepsakes that Mrs. Cozens didn't want left behind. Meanwhile she and her girls cooked food for the trip and dug out smoked and salted meats and vegetables that could sustain us all for days.

Maria tended to the wounded nearly non-stop. She was a whirl-wind of medicines and bandages and comforting touches. When Beth woke up, she changed her splints and suggested that Beth try walking with assistance or crutches when she could. McNab she told to drink plenty of water and rest. Mr. Cozens she disturbed as little as possible.

To my surprise, Jeremiah seemed the best off. The harpies hadn't gouged him as deep as McNab or Mr. Cozens and he'd gotten less infection. He sat at the table nursing a cup of water when I took a mid-morning break. The chair next to him was empty so I eased into it.

"How do you think Cassidy's doing?" I asked.

"Just fine," Jeremiah said. "I'm sure he's well on the trail of that witch by now."

"He gonna kill her?"

"That depends," Jeremiah said. "Cassidy doesn't like killing humans and he'll try to avoid it if he can. But if he has to, he'll do it. We have to stop her from expanding the rift."

"Expanding it?"

"The size of the rift depends on the number of souls used to prop it open, so to speak,"

"Must be a lot," I said, "to let a cyclops through."

"Just think how big the one that let the Jotun army through was."

I swallowed. We'd only seen one cyclops. How many were there?

Will came into the room with a pitcher of water and a glass. He offered it to me and then pulled up a chair.

I thought a bit more about the size of the rift. "So ... how many souls does it take to make a rift big enough for a cyclops?"

"Plenty," Jeremiah said. "Which is a bit of a puzzle. We know they had it wide enough for the cyclops to come through before they attacked Grand Lake. So where did they get the souls?"

"The miners?" I suggested.

"It'd be hard for a witch to capture of bunch of them to sacrifice," Jeremiah replied.

"What about the ghosts in the lake?" Will said.

Jeremiah and I stopped and stared at him.

"Some mornings, you can see them over the lake, floating there," he said. "It's haunted, you know."

"No," Jeremiah said, his tone even and measured. "We don't. Who's haunting it?"

"The Indians that died." When he saw our looks of confusion, he frowned before continuing.

"Legend is, the Utes, they were camped on the shores of the lake when, uh, a war party of Arapaho attacked. They, that is the Utes, put the women and children on rafts while the warriors fought, but a storm came up and drowned 'em all before the battle was done. Anyway, you can see their ghosts some mornings. Or at least I can."

Jeremiah's eyes were wide. "Where was the Ute camp?"

"East side of the lake," Will replied.

"The mining camps are north," I said. "Cassidy's looking in the wrong place."

Jeremiah nodded.

I thought about the missing townspeople and shuddered at the obvious conclusion.

"She took the townspeople to make a bigger rift," I said. "She'll kill them all by the time Cassidy figures out he's looking in the wrong place."

"You're right," Jeremiah said grimly. "We have to stop her. Now."

TWENTY-SEVEN

THE ROOM FELT stuffy and eerily quiet. None of us moved much, or even spoke. We could hear Mrs. Cozens bustling around back gathering up chickens, but that was it. Jeremiah, Will, and I just all looked at each other as we all considered what to do.

My heart hammered heavy. I didn't like our choices, and it seemed there was only one.

"I can go," I said, finally breaking the silence. "Mrs. Cozens or Will can drive the wagon. I'll take Maria's horse. Maybe I can catch up to Cassidy before he gets too far north."

"I'll go with you," Jeremiah said.

"No." Maria stood in the doorway. From her expression, she'd heard the entire conversation.

"Why?" he said. He threw up his hands in disbelief. "I'm feeling fine."

"You've been resting," she said. "You can't ride. You can't fight."

"I can ride!"

She nodded toward the door. "Go help Mrs. Cozens finish loading the wagon. Then tell us how you feel."

Jeremiah sagged back in his chair with a defeated sigh.

"Should I go, too?" Will asked. "I can show you were I saw the ghosts."

"No," I said with a shake of my head. "Your Ma needs you. Besides, we don't know for sure there's no giants or harpies between here and Empire. Somebody's got to keep everybody safe. I think you're man enough for the job."

The thirteen year old boy stood straighter and blinked, his eyes eager at my compliment.

"He's right," Jeremiah said, "for another reason, too. If Luke did get through, he's bringing the militia from Golden City. They'll need someone to guide them and that's going to have to be you."

Will nodded eagerly in agreement. I wasn't so sure about Jeremiah's logic, but if it made Will happy, I was all for it.

"Perhaps you can draw Billy a map?" Jeremiah suggested. He reached for his journal and a pencil that lay nearby on the table.

"Sure!"

Will quickly sketched out the lake, with the town on the west and the place he'd spotted the ghosts on the eastern shore. Jeremiah then carefully tore the page out of his book, flipped it over, and started copying the amulet symbols onto the back.

"I don't know if these will be useful," he said as he drew, "but you might as well have them."

"Thanks," I said. "So if I don't find Cassidy, how do I stop the witch?"

"There will be an anchor," Jeremiah said, "where she sacrifices her victims. It'll be some sort of altar or temple."

"We think they used trees at Andersonville," Maria added.

"That's right," Jeremiah said. "But these are Greek, so I think they'll have a stone table of some sort like they do in the mythology books. Anyway, you need to stop her from putting anyone on it."

"Can I destroy it?" I asked.

"You should. It won't close the rift, but it should slow her down."

"How do I close the rift?" I asked.

"You don't," Jeremiah said. "You stop the witch and you watch the rift until Maria and the militia can arrive."

I stared at Maria for a moment as the implications sunk in. She's a witch!

A good witch, thank God.

"Uh ...," Will said, "then shouldn't she go with him now?"

"It's not that simple," Jeremiah said.

"If I go," Maria said, "your father dies."

Will's face went white.

"We also don't know what's out there," Jeremiah said. "If Billy runs into trouble he can't handle when he's alone, that's bad. But if Maria does ..."

...there's no one to close the rift.

I let out a deep breath. No one else spoke either.

"So," I said, "my job is to find Cassidy if I can. If not, I'm to find the witch and slow her down until Will can lead the militia and Maria to the rift."

Jeremiah and Maria nodded.

"By any means necessary," I added solemnly.

"Welcome to the hero business." Jeremiah said. His expression was more ironic than happy.

That didn't comfort me a bit.

I stayed long enough to get the wounded loaded up. Mr. Cozens moaned the whole time and shrieked in pain when we lifted him into the wagon. Maria quickly put a spoon at his lips with medicine that he slurped down and that seemed to calm him. Beth looked tired, but on the mend. She gave me a hug.

"You take care of yourself, you hear?"

I grinned. The ten year old had chastised me enough. What was one more time?

McNab told me to keep his Colt and his Henry Rifle. Jeremiah added his own spare ammunition and a few pages of his notebook, torn out, along with a pencil.

"Take notes," he said. "Cassidy never remembers everything when it's over and I suspect you won't either."

Dumbly, I clutched the paper and looked at him. He only smiled back.

Maria's mare seemed pretty easygoing. She said her name was Daisy, which just seemed wrong for a horse, but I didn't say anything. Maria gave me a little powdered willow bark in case I needed it, but I told her to keep it for the wounded.

"We have enough," she said. "You may need it more."

Somehow that didn't comfort me.

I took a few days' supply of food and a canteen. Will gave me his Pa's broad brimmed hat, saying he wouldn't be needing it as much as me. After that, it was just a matter of saying my goodbyes.

Everyone wished me luck, and the little Cozen girls gave me big hugs. But from the worried looks in everyone's eyes, I kinda got concerned myself. No one was sure I'd make it back.

Not even me.

I rode to Grand Lake under cloudy skies. A light rain fell in the afternoon, but after it cleared the air was still, without even the usual breeze. Still, it felt ominous, like it could break at any minute. I wished I could hear birds, at least. It was just too quiet.

I arrived in the town just as the sun set and the grey gloom turned to black. I found our old camp, but nothing had changed in it. My note was still in the fire pit, though the rain the night before had made the paper ragged and shriveled. I couldn't see any sign that Cassidy had stopped for any meaningful length of time.

I briefly considered spending the night in the same spot, but decided against it. A cyclops had found it before, and I couldn't set a watch when there was just me. I pushed on north around the curve of the lake.

The trees on the north shore grew all the way to the edge of the lake, with thick underbrush beneath them. Mountains rose up on all sides, cradling the lake like a teacup. I stared at the far shore, but couldn't see any fires, which I wasn't sure whether was good or bad. I decided to head a little further north, along the road to the mining camps. After about a half hour, it was too dark to really continue. I moved off the road a distance—close enough to see it, but far enough to make it hard to see me. If I didn't have a fire myself, I figured I'd be fine.

But as I bedded down, my mind started wandering. All the doubts set in. All the worries.

I kept coming back to the books. They didn't show the bugs or the problems finding water or how awful the wounds were. You couldn't smell the blood in the stories.

You couldn't feel the fear.

And, I realized, you knew that however thrilling the story might be, Cassidy was gonna win in the end.

This was real life. I had no idea if we were gonna win. The thought of dying scared me.

But, I realized, the thought of all those people from the town dying—Beth's Ma and Pa, the other folks—because I didn't do something, well that scared me worse.

Maria said we didn't know where souls went, but they went somewhere. Maybe Heaven was real. I hoped so.

I just knew I didn't want to get there and have to face people I'd failed.

I was scared, thinking of what was ahead.

But I wasn't a coward.

I just hoped my best would be enough.

After a while, exhaustion caught up with me. Despite the racings of my mind, I fell asleep.

I awoke to the quiet whir of insects and streaks of the orange sunrise across the sky. Nothing had disturbed me during the night. At dawn, I ate just a bit, checked on my horse, and then headed back down to the lake. It looked to be a clear day—only a few thin clouds floated here and there. I didn't see anything of note. It all looked the same as it had the night before—the lake reflected the sky and only the destroyed town marred the otherwise pretty picture.

The track headed north to the mining camps wasn't a road really —just some ruts in the ground from wagons. The way headed around the lake to the east didn't even have that. I might be able to find a trail, but otherwise, I'd have to bushwhack through the woods.

And now, I realized. I had to make the hard choice. Follow Cassidy and try to find him? Or go investigate where Will said the ghosts were?

Cassidy would be fine without me. And I ... I'd be fine without him.

It took a moment for that to sink in.

Then I mounted Maria's horse and headed east.

I rode a little ways back from the shore. I didn't want anyone to see me across the water, just in case. After I'd gone halfway along the length of the lake, I decided to check on what I could see again. I tied the horse up to a nearby pine, put out enough feed to keep it happy, and crept over to the lake on foot.

I couldn't see much. There might've been something over at the far east edge, but I couldn't make it out.

I decided to try the same thing a bit further down.

This time I found a small grassy clearing, maybe twenty feet across. I staked my horse to one side and gave her enough rope so she could graze. I worried a bit about water—I didn't want to lead the animal to the lake edge where it could be seen, but we hadn't passed any streams feeding the lake yet. I'd have to figure something out.

With the horse tied up, I once again carefully crept up to the shore of the lake. There was something moving in the trees, just off the shore of the southeastern corner of the lake, but I couldn't make out what.

Something big.

I hunkered down under some small scraggly firs and watched.

I was far enough away to make it hard to see anything but the trees. The mountain on the south side of the lake dropped steep to the shores and trees filled the slope, creating a crag of pines. On the eastern side, the ground was more forgiving, though still rough and tumble. It looked like that was where the stream from the mountains fed into the lake. The corner where the two regions met sat in deep shade, aided by the general cloudiness of the morning.

But something still moved there.

A screech broke the stillness.

A harpy circled high up in the sky over the lake. It soared in wide loops, appearing to scan the area.

It screeched again, and then a second one launched from the far peak. It flapped its powerful wings to gain height, and then joined its sister. I watched them for a bit as their circles moved from over the lake to directly overhead.

Nervously, I quickly glanced across the lake again.

On the far shore stood a cyclops—as tall as the trees he'd been in a bit before. I couldn't make out much other than the brown tunic and lighter skin against the green background, but he appeared to be watching the harpies.

Who shrieked and dove.

I shuddered for an instant, before realizing they weren't after me, but diving at something further from the shore. I gave a quick breath of relief and then froze.

My horse.

TWENTY-EIGHT

I SCRAMBLED to my feet and dashed through the woods. I tripped once and went sprawling, but other than banging my shoulder and elbow, I was fine. I shook off the pain and kept going.

I burst into the clearing not ten feet from the harpies. It was too late. They perched on the corpse of the horse, ripping strips of flesh out with their teeth. They gulped them down and only looked around now and then.

I seethed.

My horse!

I raised my rifle. At this distance, I couldn't miss. I steadied my breathing and braced my feet. I took aim ...

...and fired.

The crack of the rifle echoed off the hills.

The harpy I'd aimed at flopped over and fell off the horse.

Just like a prairie dog.

The second one immediately squawked and rose into the air. I didn't give it a chance. It rose maybe ten feet before I put a bullet in its chest. With a scream, it tumbled to the ground.

I stood there, breathing heavy, as the fury flowed out of me.

The horse was a bloody, awful mess of torn flesh and gaping

wounds. It smelled awful, and flies already surrounded it. My stomach surged, but I swore I wasn't gonna get sick over this. I'd seen dead men before. What was a horse?

I walked around to where I could get to my saddle bags. I was able to free the ones on top, but the poor horse had fallen on the others. I tugged at them, but wasn't able to pull them out. I tried lifting the horse, but it weighed too much. Finally I got down on my hands and worked at them, lifting and tugging and shifting, and was able to pull them out.

I backed up into the trees far enough to get away from the smell. Then I inspected my bags. They were squashed, but most of the stuff in them could take it. My blanket didn't care how much weight had been on it.

Unfortunately, my canteen had been under the horse. It was banged up and leaking around the cap.

That was bad, real bad.

I tried to wrap it in my spare shirt, but that wouldn't plug the leak. If I could carry it upright, I could keep some water in it, but how was I gonna do that, when I had to scramble over the slope?

A shriek sounded high above. Four harpies circled high in the air. Another took off from the peak.

How many of them were there?

I readied my rifle and found a spot where I could see through the treetops.

The monsters made wide soaring loops, as if they hadn't a care in the world. Except they kept circling lower and lower. Their cries were only every now and then, more of a call to the others than an attack shriek.

They were looking for me, I figured. They hadn't spotted me yet, but they surely knew where the horse was.

I decided to hold my fire until they got closer.

But then one of them pulled up and let out an sharp cry. It sounded more of alarm than anything, and all four turned and flapped back to the mountain.

Something had scared them off.

I swallowed hard. Anything that could scare the harpies should scare *me*.

Something was coming, which meant I needed to be *leaving*.

I hoisted the saddlebags onto my shoulders as best I could and started hustling south toward the lake, simply because that was the way I'd come. But when I got almost to the shore, I stopped.

What about the cyclops?

I carefully edged my way forward to the edge of the trees.

The cyclops strode along the shoreline, coming toward me. He carried a large spear and was looking ahead.

The gunshots drew it, I realized.

I swore, and pulled back into the trees. As fast as I could, I started running west, away from the approaching monster. I could only hope he hadn't seen me and even if he hadn't, I needed to get as much distance as I could between me and the dead horse, which he'd almost surely find.

In my haste, I banged into fallen logs and brushed through trees where the branches whipped back and slapped my side.

I kept running.

After a bit, I had to slow. Gasping for breath, I stopped and put my hands on my knees as I tried to recover. The saddle bags had been thumping against me something fierce and I briefly considered stashing them somewhere so I could run faster. I decided against it simply because with the luck I'd been having, they almost certainly would've been destroyed or lost forever if I parted with them.

I checked behind me and couldn't hear or see anything of the cyclops.

So what now?

I decided I needed a better way to carry my gear. The destroyed town of Grand Lake wasn't too far away, so I decided to go see what I could find.

When I got to the northernmost destroyed building, on the opposite side of town from where we'd made our camp, I decided to get bold and check on the cyclops. I crept back to the lakeshore and peeked out from behind some juniper bushes.

I got lucky. I spotted him on the northeast shore, almost as far away as I could see. He was striding east, back towards the end he'd come from.

Apparently he'd given up on finding me.

At least for now.

I sat by the lake and watched for a bit. The heavy scattered clouds continued to provide more shade than sun, but the lake remained still and smooth. The lack of bird noises still perturbed me a bit, but enough insects buzzed around to keep it from being too quiet. If it hadn't been for the distant figure on the shore, it would've been a truly peaceful day.

I continued to watch the cyclops until it turned and disappeared into the trees, just about at the far southeast corner of the lake. Nothing else moved over there. I glanced up, but couldn't see any harpies either.

I figured that gave me the break I needed to look for supplies.

The closest destroyed cabin was much like the others. The log walls had been pushed over on one side and a cyclops had clearly walked through it smashing the rest. This cabin had been a two room affair with a separate small bedroom, but the roof had smashed that bed flat.

Still, I checked underneath it, but didn't find anything of note except some breeches and shirts.

In what was left of the kitchen, I did find two burlap sacks on the bottom of a destroyed shelf. I also found stale bread and honest to goodness cans of sauerkraut. I didn't quite know what to make of those, but I did find a knife I could use to open them if I needed to.

I realized the breeches from the bedroom had cords for tying them around the waist that I could use. I removed them and used them with the burlap bags to fasten shoulder packs. I managed to transfer all of the supplies from the saddle bags to my new packs except for my blanket, which just wouldn't fit. I decided to leave it behind safely tucked in a sheltered corner in the wrecked building. If I needed it, I knew where to find it.

But where exactly was I going?

I didn't want to hug the lakeshore too closely or I'd risk getting spotted by the cyclops. The sight lines were just too good across the lake, and it was clear he was a lookout of some sort.

If I went around the south end of the lake, I'd have to climb the steep mountain that the harpies were nesting on top of. I looked up at the peak and grimaced. The trees that ran up the sides weren't thick the entire way. I could do it, but there'd be stretches where I'd be pretty exposed. Crossing those did not look like a good idea. Even if I could stay out of sight of the cyclops, there'd be no telling when the harpies might take wing and spot me there.

That left north. If I went a few thousand yards away from the lake, I should be able to work my way east and then drop back down and come up behind the likely cyclops camp. There was one ridge in the way, but it looked climbable.

Even better, it had no harpies on it.

I decided to follow the trail toward the mining camps for a ways, simply because it was easier than bushwhacking. I made one last check across the lake, but couldn't see the giant. I just hoped he'd hunkered down and wasn't still out looking for me.

So with a deep breath, I set out.

The sun was high overhead when I decided I'd gone far enough north. Enough clouds had scattered to make it hot out of the shade, so I stopped for a long sip of water.

And found my canteen mostly empty. It'd leaked into my pack, though fortunately not everything was soaked. A lot must've dripped out without my noticing.

So how was I going to hike over the ridge and hide out behind the cyclops camp without any water?

I had food. I had matches. I had just about everything else I needed, but water was a problem.

I realized I should've searched the buildings for another canteen.

I cursed myself for missing something so obvious. I'd been dumb. It was something no one on Cassidy's team would've missed. Jeremiah, McNab, Luke, Maria—they would've replaced the canteen first thing. Heck, McNab would've spent an hour making sure he had every provision necessary.

I'd been dumb.

Except … what did it matter?

Cassidy's team made mistakes. They'd completely overlooked Beth, and that was a big one. They hadn't thoroughly searched the town either, though to be fair, Cassidy was in a hurry to get to Saratoga West and warn the people there.

There were even examples of mistakes in the books, now that I thought about it. Cassidy had almost killed a man in *The Battle of Cincinnati*. The scout before Luke took over had gotten them completely lost in Indiana once.

Heck, Cassidy and Jeremiah had spent time arguing about mistakes of famous generals, just a few days ago. You could be a famous general, or a hero, and still make mistakes.

Besides, no one was here to know I'd made a mistake.

So I figured to rest a bit and then return to the town, find a canteen or bottle I could use for water, and then try again.

I put everything in my makeshift pack, making sure to put the wet stuff on the outside where it might dry. I hoisted it to my shoulders and froze.

I could hear something coming down the trail from the north.

It was close, so I barely had time to slip into the trees before I could see it.

A man with a rifle, walking slowly.

Cassidy.

TWENTY-NINE

CASSIDY LOOKED WORN. He walked slow, almost at an amble, though his eyes continued to dart back and forth. His hat sat crooked on his head and didn't shade his face. Mud splattered his boots, but he walked quiet, without a branch snap or a kicked rock to his name.

"Cassidy!" I called as I stepped out of the trees.

He blinked and pulled up short. "Billy? What're you doing here?"

"Looking for you! And the witch. But we know where to look and who she is!"

His brow furrowed. "We do?" He quickly walked close enough for us to talk without shouting.

"We do! We stopped by the Cozens Homestead and they told us about the witch and the ghosts in the lake."

"Ghosts in the lake? Wait, tell it from the beginning."

So I started with our arrival at the Cozens ranch and told him about Luke's visit and Mr. Cozens's injuries and then about the Greek sisters. His face darkened when I mentioned the symbol on the ring but he just frowned. When I got to the part about the ghosts in the lake he interrupted me.

"Did Will say how many ghosts he saw?"

"No. I didn't think to ask."

He gestured for me to go on.

He nodded when I told him how we'd decided the witches were trying to expand the rift and how we realized he was looking in the wrong place.

"Mostly," Cassidy said. "The big camps were abandoned like Jeremiah reported. The miners had taken their things, orderly like. But I found two small camps where they hadn't. One had signs of a struggle."

"Maybe the townspeople weren't enough."

"No, I think it was the other way around. We heard rumors about giants near the mines first, remember? It'd be easier to grab a man off by himself than an entire town."

"So grab a few miners. Use their souls to expand the rift big enough for a cyclops, then have the cyclops attack the town."

"That's right," he said.

"Well, they did a good job of staying out of sight," I said. "We never noticed them across the lake."

"We weren't exactly on the shores either. These trees can be pretty thick."

I nodded. We hadn't made any noise and kept our fire small. It hadn't been until the second night that the first giant had come to investigate.

"So we know where they are," I said. I briefly described seeing the cyclops walk the shore after I'd shot the harpies.

"That's why I came back," Cassidy said. "I heard the gunshots."

I grimaced. "I wasn't thinking. Sorry."

He shrugged it off. "I've done worse, and you killed them both. That's two fewer of those beasts."

I nodded as the relief at his approval flowed through me.

"So let's go," he nodded toward the east, "and see what the rest of those monsters are up to."

A ridge ran down from the northeast fairly close to the lake, creating a narrow neck between it and the water. Our path put us far enough north to keep it between us and where I'd seen the cyclops. A small stream ran along the bottom and that reminded me I'd been headed back to town to get a new canteen.

I cursed under my breath, but Cassidy caught it.

"Is there a problem?" he asked. He looked at me with a raised eyebrow.

"I forgot. I need a new canteen." I got it out and explained how the horse had crushed it. "I was gonna go back to town, but then I met you …"

He frowned, and his eyes scanned the ridge above us, and then the path back to Grand Lake. He looked up at the sun, still high up, but clearly starting its descent.

"We can share," he said. "We need to scout their camp before it gets dark."

"Well, let me get a good drink with my own here before we go."

After I'd finished, we started clambering up the ridge. The slope shot up enough to take the wind out of us as we climbed. More than once, I thought I'd have to use my hands to scramble up steep parts, but we usually found a way to work sideways to a shallower grade.

Fortunately, the pines and the junipers and the stickery bushes were sparse enough for us to pick our way through. It was still hot, sweaty work and more than once we had to stop and catch our breath and take some water. My canteen held out about halfway up, before it'd leaked too much to be of use.

Near the top of the ridge, Cassidy suggested we go slow and stay under cover. We crept over the ridge's summit near a cluster of small pines and stared down into the small tight valley below. Packed with trees, the mountains sharply fell on the east, to our left, and then opened up into a small grassy meadow where the stream meandered through and then plunged back into trees before it got to the lake.

Several large animals moved around in the meadow. It looked like a small herd of shaggy brown cattle standing there—some drinking at the main stream and another intake steam, some grazing. Maybe thirty animals in all.

I squinted and let out a long breath.

Buffaloes.

A herd had come close to the ruins of Denver City once, and Tom and I'd gone over to see 'em. Some of the men from Golden City rode out and shot a few and shared the meat.

But I'd never thought about them in the mountains. I suppose it made sense, being summer, that they might migrate into the area.

I took the time to slowly look over the entire herd, from one side to the other and then back again. I did it a second time. That's when I spotted a cyclops standing near some pine trees on the right side edge of the herd. The buffaloes came up to his thighs, making him look like a shepherd among fuzzy dogs. He held a long spear and seemed to be facing the other way.

I nudged Cassidy and pointed. He got out his spyglass and took a good look. After a bit, he passed it to me.

"Notice anything funny?" he asked after I'd taken a spell.

"He's looking up," I said, "and toward the mountain with the harpies."

"Uh huh. He's not scanning the tree line."

"Gotta protect their meals," I joked.

His chuckle was most unsavory.

"Something to keep in mind," he said. "But we need to find the townsfolk."

"They'll be down there." I pointed to where the tree tops appeared a little sparser, about a hundred yards in from the lake.

"Think you can move quietly enough for us to sneak up?"

It was my turn to chuckle. "Not a problem. Not a problem at all."

Cassidy gave me an amused look, but didn't say anything. Instead, he started slowly and quietly creeping down toward the place I'd pointed.

We worked our way down the hill slowly, making sure to be both silent and out of sight. It wasn't hard to avoid the shepherd cyclops, but we didn't know where the others were.

Neither of us made much noise. It helped that there wasn't a lot of dry twigs and such on the ground. As long as we went slow and stepped careful like, we could be quiet.

We didn't speak. When we stopped briefly for water or a bite of food, we used gestures to communicate what we wanted. It didn't take long before a simple nod of Cassidy's head was enough for me to know which way he wanted to go, or if he wanted to hold up a spell.

It felt a lot like when we'd walked into the fight with the harpies, side by side. We weren't quite side by side, but he wasn't sending me away either.

We made our way down to a rocky area, with the stream below us noisily tumbling over some small falls. The water wasn't wide— I could've easily jumped across it, but the drop was steep, forcing us to turn aside. Talking by gestures, we agreed to head toward the lake.

Meanwhile the sky clouded up. We didn't have much choice but to keep walking when the drizzle started. It didn't come down hard, but the tiny track we'd been following soon became muddy and slippery. After Cassidy almost lost his footing, he gestured toward a large tree over a rock outcropping. It wasn't a perfect shelter but it was better than keeping on.

We stood close, so as to both be under the branches as best we could. The rain pattered all around us, muffling sounds of the bugs and anything else. Cassidy leaned close.

"We can talk if we keep our voices low," he said. "Did Jeremiah ever figure out those symbols?"

I shook my head and he frowned.

A gusty breeze blew through our little nook. It shook the branches and sprayed us with the water from them. I got a drop in my eye, despite wearing a hat. It stung bad and just reminded me how soaked I was.

"Jeremiah doesn't put this part in the books," I grumbled as I wiped my face.

"No one wants to read this part," he said.

"Yeah, it's not heroic." I gestured to the storm and the valley beyond. "None of this is heroic. Not like the books at all."

"No," he said. "It's just necessary."

His flat, defeated tone hit me like a brick. I looked at him with disbelief.

"Then why write the books?" I snapped. "Why make it all out to be so glorious, when it's bloody, and scary, and downright miserable?"

He sighed and curled his lip. His eyes were full of pity as he regarded me, but then I realized it wasn't pity for me. His mind was somewhere else.

He turned and looked out into the drizzle. It still fell steadily, giving a grey blanket to the forest ahead of us. He fished out his canteen and took a long swig.

"When we get to San Francisco," he finally drawled, "*if* we get to San Francisco, those idiots in Congress aren't going to listen to Joe Nobody. They barely listen to the generals."

He spat. His eyes never turned my way.

"But Jeremiah," he continued, "Jeremiah was right. They listen to 'Cassidy the Giant Killer.'" He snorted. "Good old Cassidy the Giant Killer. Not Captain Cassidy, or Mr. Cassidy, and, God forbid, not Robert Cassidy. They only listen to 'Cassidy the Giant Killer.'"

He took another long drag of water.

"Don't become a hero, kid," he said. "You wanna fight giants? Be an army sharpshooter."

He ran his finger around the lip of his canteen. His voice dropped to almost a whisper.

"It's a better life."

I just stared at him, my mouth half open. What could I possibly say?

Instead, I let the silence drag on. Cassidy did too.

But my mind raced. I had a million questions I wanted to ask him, and not a single nerve to make my voice work.

So we stood there and watched the rain. The breeze kicked up a couple of times, and I learned to duck my head when it did. After a bit, it tailed off. It hadn't quite stopped, when Cassidy motioned to me.

"C'mon," he said. "It's gonna be dark soon." He strode off toward the lake.

I hustled to keep up with him, but I needn't have bothered. We went maybe four hundred yards and the trees parted into a small sandy meadow. On the far side, a row of trees screened the lake and the setting sun beyond it. To the right, the ridge we'd crossed came down to the shore not more than a thousand yards away.

And to the left, through some trees, a small fire flickered.

THIRTY

CASSIDY PUSHED his hat up and stared at the distant flames. His eyes narrowed, serious-like. We couldn't make out the fire itself, but the light was unmistakable in the lengthened shadows. A whole bank of firs and pines separated the fire from the lake, but from where we were, it was a beacon.

Cassidy unslung his rifle from his shoulder and motioned for me to do the same.

He leaned in. "If we get separated," he said quietly, "meet back at the cliff over the stream, understand?"

I nodded in reply.

Sticking to the trees around the edge of the sandy meadow, we slowly crept forward. The bugs were out in force, with their chirps and whirrs, but that just made our footsteps all the more quiet.

As we approached, we could see figures near the fire. One, human sized, stood nearby it. Another, cyclops sized, suddenly walked in front of it and then off toward the buffalo herd. We froze, and watched its head bob through the smaller trees until it disappeared.

Then we continued our slow, silent walk forward.

After a bit, we got close enough to see more. Beyond a thin line of trees sat another clearing—much larger than the first, with higher trees. There appeared to be a solid wall or something on the far side, but it was too dark to make out details, especially with the fire blinding our night vision.

Even so, my eyes were on the human. A raggedy woman with messed hair and a torn skirt turned a large spit with a huge haunch of meat on it. She struggled with getting it to turn, often leaning her whole weight into it.

On the other side of the fire, a young girl, maybe six, equally dirty and ragged, tugged large logs up to the edge of the fire and then shoved them in. She jumped back to avoid the flames and then trundled off into the dark.

We slowly, carefully, quietly continued forward, until we were nearly on the edge of the fire's clearing. The woman now stood maybe twenty yards away, but she didn't look our way. Neither did the girl when she returned, dragging another log.

Cassidy froze and went tense. His eyes were up, looking beyond the woman.

Leaning against the log wall on the far side stood another cyclops with a spear. This one idly watched the woman and girl, but from time to time he looked all around as well.

My heart pounded in my chest so hard I was sure the cyclops would hear it. I had a nearly uncontrollable need to raise my rifle, to aim at the monster, but I fought it down.

Beside me, Cassidy didn't twitch a muscle.

We stood, as still as we could, watching.

A minute.

Two minutes.

Five minutes.

An eternity.

Another cyclops came out of the shadows to the right of the wall. This one, shorter than the other and with a fatter belly, said something to the first that I couldn't understand. As they talked, Cassidy gestured for us to back up.

Slowly, quietly, we made our way back to the far end of the sandy clearing where we'd first seen the fire.

"What do we do?" I asked in hushed tones.

"We need to know more," Cassidy said. "Where's the witch? Where's the rift?"

"The woman will know. We could rescue her."

He frowned. "If she goes missing, they'll know we're here. We need to work our way around their camp to the other side."

"We have to go by the lake then. Otherwise we run into that buffalo shepherd."

"Yeah. The rift's probably by the lake shore anyway, if what you say about those ghosts is true."

I nodded. I figured it had to be as true as anything. Of course, I hadn't believed in ghosts at all just a few days ago, but a lot had happened in that time.

With a nod of his head for me to follow him, Cassidy crept along the north side of the sandy clearing. Like before, we moved slowly so we could stay quiet, though not as slow as before. We knew where the cyclopses were, or at least where most of them were.

Still don't want to get surprised by one wandering around, though, I thought.

Cassidy pulled up when we reached the lake. The sun had fully set and blackness covered the far shore. Even the mountain to the south was pure dark. We couldn't see the fire the woman tended, or much of anything besides the silhouettes of the trees against the lighter sky. The water lapped the shore with barely a sound, but in the stillness, it was enough to remind me of how quiet we needed to be.

We walked on the shore, which kept the thin screen of trees between us and the cyclops camp. My boot sunk into the mud at one point, which forced me to keep a closer eye on where I was stepping.

We went slow. Eventually, though, we saw a light through the trees opposite the lake. We crept on until we were squarely between the lights and the lake and then paused.

I took a deep breath. Cassidy did the same. Then he motioned for us to go into the woods.

The light ahead sat high, at head level, not like the fire we'd seen before. We went maybe ten yards before the trees thinned enough for us to see.

I sucked in my breath. We'd found the altar.

A dozen torches rimmed another small clearing. Their smoke curled and slowly floated up, only tossed a bit in the breeze. The ring of trees had a gap to the far left, back toward where I guessed the building we'd seen earlier must be.

In the center sat a stone slab. Waist-high, it had to be the altar.

Cassidy leaned in close. "To the right. The rift." He nodded with his head toward the general region.

At first, I couldn't see anything. In the dark, it all looked the same. But then I realized the shadows weren't all the same. One area didn't have tree outlines—it was just a large black blob. The top was about thirty feet up and peeked above the trees. It blocked the stars beyond. Down lower, it didn't appear to be nearly as wide, but I couldn't tell for sure. I couldn't see where the black jagged edges of the rift ended and the dark shadows beyond began. Not everywhere at least.

I just sat and stared. My heart hammered wildly and my brain raced, but I didn't know what to think.

The rift. A real gosh darn rift!

Cassidy stiffened. A moment later, I realized why. Something was coming down from the gap to the left.

More than one something.

We raised our rifles and waited.

A cyclops approached. Ahead of it walked a human in long dark robes carrying a lantern, which swung back and forth.

The woman, and I shouldn't have been surprised it was a woman, had long black hair framing her face. She walked with steady slow strides, as if she was precessing down a church aisle. She looked straight ahead, though it was hard to see her expression.

The cyclops carried something.

Oh, God, it was a boy!

The monster held the boy, maybe nine or so, to his chest, with one meaty hand across his shoulders and arms and the other across his legs. The boy's eyes bugged out but he didn't cry.

The procession went all the way to the altar. The woman set the lantern down on one end of the cold stone and stepped back.

I shuddered. With the new light, we could see ropes at the four corners of the altar.

The cyclops moved to the side of the altar opposite the woman. He stood facing her.

"Nooo!" the boy cried. He started to kick and struggle, but the cyclops held him tight.

"Shoot the cyclops!" Cassidy hissed in my ear.

I nodded and took aim at its head.

Cassidy's rifle barked. A moment later, mine did, too.

The cyclops howled and slapped its cheek.

The boy slithered out of its loosened grip and dropped to the ground. The witch ducked behind the altar and the cyclops turned to face us with a roar.

I fired again, but it moved its head at the last moment and I missed.

The cyclops charged.

"Run!" Cassidy yelled.

I didn't need prompting. I turned and dashed through the underbrush as best I could without tripping. I skidded to a stop at the edge of the lake.

The cyclops smashed through the trees, still roaring unintelligible words.

Then it screamed. I could see some thrashing, but the few remaining trees obscured my view. It screamed again, a half cry, a half yell.

Run away, I thought. Back to the cliff, like Cassidy said.

Instead, I charged toward the cry.

The monster thrashed on the ground. Cassidy circled around its legs, stabbing and slicing at it with his saber. The cyclops flung its arms back but couldn't reach him.

Cassidy paused when he saw me.

"Run!" he yelled.

"Not without you!"

The boy burst into sight through the underbrush behind Cassidy. He quickly looked from one of us to the other.

Loud deep guttural shouts came from the altar clearing.

"Follow him!" Cassidy shouted to the boy as he pointed at me.

The boy startled. Cassidy sheathed his saber and grabbed the boy's arm. They circled the fallen giant at a safe distance. Cassidy tugged the boy forward so fast he seemed to slip at times.

The cyclops lifted its head. It looked my way. Blood covered the side of its face and its teeth gleamed in the low light, as did its massive eye.

A perfect target.

I shot it.

Then Cassidy and the boy were beside me. I slung my rifle over my shoulder and the three of us ran back to the lake. We followed the shore back to the sandy clearing. Behind us, bellows and angry cries continued.

We ran.

As we entered the sandy clearing, we saw something disappear into the woods on the far side. One human sized figure and a second much smaller.

The woman and the girl, making a break for it, I realized.

They were following the lake shore instead of turning toward the safety of the ravine Cassidy and I'd sheltered in earlier. It was an easy but obvious path.

Cassidy figured it out, too. He swore.

"Take the boy," he said. "I'll get them."

He was off too fast for me to reply.

I grabbed the boy's arm. "This way. It's safer."

How much safer, I didn't know, but the boy followed me anyway. We didn't speak, but as soon as we were a little ways into the woods, I slowed down. Then I paused and gasped for air. Every muscle in my body screamed from exertion.

"We go quietly now," I said. "If they can't find us, we'll be safe."

He nodded, and I saw he was gasping for air himself.

"You hurt?" I asked.

"I'll be okay." His voice was ragged and full of pain, but he'd been able to run, so I figured he could make it the rest of the way.

We went slow, though, as much to be quiet as anything, but I checked on him from time to time. He seemed to be all right, though he winced once when a tree branch jabbed his shoulder. Most of the time, he let his right arm hang by his side.

We reached the waterfall and the rocks without any sounds of pursuit. I told the boy to sit by a scraggly tall pine with missing lower branches while I refilled my broken canteen. Then we both drank, and I broke out some jerky from my pack. He wolfed it down hungrily.

"So what's your name?" I asked.

"Matthew," he said.

"I'm Billy. Your shoulder okay?"

He shook his head.

I gently touched it and he winced. It didn't look right, more like it was dislocated. That was something I didn't quite know how to fix.

"I'm afraid it's gonna hurt for a while," I said, "but if you can stand it, we'll be safe for now." I remembered the willow bark. "I've got some medicine if you want it."

He nodded.

I squatted next to him and fished through my pack by feel until I found the powder pouch. I poured a little into the canteen and had him drink it. He quickly gulped it all down.

I went back to the stream for a refill. When I returned, Matthew was asleep.

THIRTY-ONE

DAWN FOUND me bleary-eyed and exhausted. I'd stayed awake the whole night waiting for Cassidy and listening as best I could for giants. Neither came. Still the forest came alive with the buzz of insects and the swaying of pine branches in the gentle breeze.

Matthew stirred. After a bit, he sat up. In the light, I could see how dirt-encrusted his face and clothes were, and how purple bruises covered one cheek and his neck. He winced every time he moved his shoulder and he looked as exhausted as I must've been.

We shared some dried fruit and more jerky before he looked like he was recovered enough to talk.

"How are you feeling this morning?" I asked.

"Better. "

"Good." I smiled reassuringly and was rewarded with a smile in return.

"So what happened?" I asked.

"Well," he said, "a few nights ago, Miss Pappas showed up in town with two giants." He looked at me. "You've seen 'em."

I nodded.

"One of them smashed up a house. Then ..." His voice cracked.

"Then she said if we didn't go with her, they'd kill us! But they're killing us anyway!"

He burst into tears. I put my arm around him and shushed him. "Quiet," I said. "We don't want to be heard."

He nodded and stifled the sobs, but the tears kept coming. I wanted to ask more questions, but it didn't seem like he could answer. So I did my best to comfort him until the tears slowed. When he took a big gasp and sighed, I gave him another comforting squeeze.

"How many people are left?" I asked quietly.

"Two dozen. All women and kids." He scrunched his face up and the tears began to fall again. "They took Pa the second night!" He buried his head in my chest as the sobs started.

I held him, like I'd seen Cassidy do with Beth, and made what comforting noises I could.

Cassidy found us there, mid-morning. Matthew had sobbed himself to sleep once again, and I'd let myself doze a bit as well. The warm sun filtered through the branches just enough to make it a bit too comfy. My eyelids had grown heavy and I'd only managed to lift them from time to time.

Still, I wasn't completely asleep and saw Cassidy coming through the trees before he saw me. I shook myself and sat up straighter, but if he noticed, he didn't react.

A ragged dark haired woman and dirty little girl trailed behind him.

"You found them!" I struggled to my feet. Matthew slumped off my side, then rubbed his eyes and sat up.

Cassidy nodded and stumbled closer. He looked as exhausted as I felt. His hat was gone and scratches covered his cheeks.

"You okay?" I asked in alarm.

"Ran into a tree." He sagged to the ground nearby.

The woman and girl approached, slowly but not timidly. The woman had a fire in her eyes, but stood thin and gaunt. Her torn dress had been tied in places, neatly so. The girl clung to her, but also lacked fear in her eyes.

"Billy," Cassidy said with a gesture towards the woman and girl, "meet Mrs. Smith and Laura Jenkins. Ladies, this is Billy the Kid."

"Pleased to meet you," Mrs. Smith said with a dip of her head.

Cassidy gave an unsavory chuckle. "Manners," he said, "at a time like this."

I blinked, but figured why *not* a time like this?

"This is Matthew," I said and gestured toward the boy who now sat on his haunches. "Matthew, meet Cassidy."

Matthew scrambled to his feet and extended his hand. Cassidy shook it.

"So you got away," I said.

"It wasn't easy," Cassidy said. He briefly told of catching up with the woman and girl not too far down the shore, but then a cyclops spotted them and gave chase. They'd played hide and seek until the sun rose and it turned back. Then they'd slowly crept back to the falls and us.

"Mrs. Smith says there's only eight cyclopses," Cassidy concluded, "and the witch. They're holding about twenty people though."

"Seven," I said. "I killed the one you took down."

He gave a weary bark of laughter. "At least that works the same for a cyclops as for a Jotun." He saw Matthew's look of confusion. "You cut their knees from behind. They drop like a rock."

"But that still begs the question," Mrs. Smith said. "How do we get away?"

"We don't," Cassidy said. "At least not right now. The only safe path for you," he gestured to the three townspeople, "is west around the lake and then south to Berthoud Pass. That's a little difficult right now." He turned to me. "When the cyclops gave up trying to find us, he set himself between us and the town. It's going to be hard to sneak past him."

"Maybe he'll give up."

"I hope so," Cassidy said. "In the meantime—Billy, can you take first watch?"

I nodded. I *thought* I could stay awake.

"Good." He turned to the others. "Get some rest while you can. We'll see if he's still there this afternoon."

With that, Cassidy stretched out on the ground near the tree. In a few moments, he was asleep.

It didn't take long for Mrs. Smith, Matthew, and Laura Jenkins to drop off to sleep themselves. Before they did, I asked them if they knew Beth Armstrong. They did and said Beth's mother was still alive, to my relief, though a prisoner. I told them about finding Beth and Mrs. Smith winced when I described Beth's injuries.

I sat on a nearby sharp rock where I could keep an eye on the most likely approach. It also forced me to stay awake, as there was nothing to lean against or any way to get comfortable. My eyelids dipped a few times, but the dozing earlier must've helped because I just felt tired and not like I was about to collapse.

Cassidy slept rough. He rolled over constantly, and shifted around, but appeared to be asleep the whole time. At one point, his breathing quickened, and I figured he must be dreaming, but he didn't wake or cry out.

A little after noon, he slowly sat up, while the others slept on. He dusted off his pants as he stood and came over to me.

"Anything?" he asked.

I shook my head. "Some harpies circled high up for a bit, but then went back to their mountain."

He nodded. His eyes grew focused and he curled his lip.

"You prepared to lead these three to safety?"

"No."

He looked at me with a raised eyebrow. His gaze seemed to pierce me through.

I met his eyes, and for a moment, my heart pounded in fear. But I forced myself to draw a deep breath.

"There are twenty more people to rescue," I said. "I'm not leaving without them."

"And if I order you to?"

"I'm not on your team, remember? You can't order me to do anything. I'm staying."

His gaze turned to a glare. I watched him fight the anger down. I almost started to shake. This was Cassidy! The man I'd wanted to ride with for years!

He seemed to read my mind.

"You could be," he said quietly but still firmly. "Get these people to safety. Lead Luke and the rest back here and then we could work something out."

Yes! Yes! Yes!

I let out a long deep breath. "No."

"If you stay, you could die."

"So could you."

We stared hard at each other. Outside, I was as mad as spit. Inside, I couldn't stop quaking. To my surprise, it was Cassidy who broke the stare contest first.

"Fine," he said without looking back at me. "What do you suggest?"

"Attack the buffalo," I said. "It's their food, right? They'd have to come defend them."

His jaw slowly unclenched, and then he made a slight nod of his head.

"It could work. It'd have to be a big attack."

"Draw the harpies down. That's why the shepherd is there—to keep the harpies away."

"Mmm. That might work."

"If it doesn't," I pointed out, "we're no worse off than we are now."

"True." He looked at me, and for a moment I thought I saw respect in his eyes. "Think you can do it?"

"Yeah," I said confidently, "it's just a question of how long it takes."

"Cocky kid, aren't you?" He smiled and the knots in my gut finally untangled.

"I've killed two cyclopses," I said with a smirk. "More than anyone else, I think."

Cassidy just shook his head and waved me off. "You take the buffalo. I'll get the other townsfolk out. We'll meet back here when we're done."

Then he walked away.

———

I thought about our talk the whole time I crept toward the buffalo herd. I'd stood up to Cassidy! I couldn't believe it!

But he'd been wrong, and the more I thought about it the more sure I was. It wasn't like I was the only one who could drive a wagon. Mrs. Smith and the kids could walk just fine and would be fine once they were away. Mrs. Smith struck me as one tough woman. Anyone who'd been the cyclopses' cook had to be.

The only reason for me to go with them was to get me out of the way. I was sure that's what Cassidy wanted.

But why?

My first thought was that he didn't like me, but that was silly. Maybe he didn't trust me, but he'd asked me to walk with him to kill the harpies. He also trusted me to help him scout the camp. We'd been side by side. Heck, I'd *been* his sidekick in all but name.

But as soon as some townsfolk showed up, he tried to send me away again.

Why?

I'd have to ask him. If I dared.

But first, I had a job to do.

I came upon the buffalo clearing a little to the west of where Cassidy and I had seen it before. I'd moved quietly, which meant slowly, and so it was mid-afternoon already. Scattered clouds had moved in and the wind had picked up, but it hadn't yet begun to rain. Enough tree branches swayed in the wind to make me less worried about getting seen. But still, I needed to be careful.

It took a bit to spot the cyclops shepherd. He'd moved, assuming it was the same one. He now sat on the ground on the far eastern side of the herd. HIs head and shoulders still stuck up above the backs of the buffalo. He held a spear and his head was tilted towards the herd and not the sky.

There wasn't a hint of the harpies.

That wasn't good.

Still, maybe I could do something.

I needed to get closer to the shepherd.

I slowly snuck through the trees around to the north. I stayed near to the clearing so I could keep an eye on the cyclops and also on the sky.

Where were those harpies when I wanted them?

I thought I saw something move up at the top of their mountain. I stepped around a tree for a better view. Something had moved, but it didn't look like it was coming this way.

The nearest buffaloes snuffled and shuffled. They were still a ways away, but I jerked my head to see.

The cyclops shepherd strode through the small herd. He'd raised his spear and held it back, ready to throw.

And he was walking straight toward me.

Oh, no!

I quickly raised my rifle and took sight at his head. He'd lowered it, making his eye a smaller target. Still …

I fired.

And missed.

THIRTY-TWO

THE CYCLOPS ROARED AND CHARGED. Fury contorted his face, and he cocked his arm back even further.

I fired again. This time I hit the side of his head and left a streak of red blood. It didn't slow him at all.

He hurled his spear.

I threw myself to the ground.

The deadly shaft flew through the space I'd just been in and smashed into a tree behind me, blasting it to splinters. My ears rang between the gunshots and the tree's explosion. I covered my head as branches landed around me. One slammed into the back of my leg, but then rolled off.

When I looked up, the cyclops still ran through the herd, the buffaloes practically stampeding out of its way. His head was still down.

So I shot the buffalo in front of him.

It collapsed. The cyclops stumbled over it and fell.

I scrambled to my feet and took off running up the nearest slope. I didn't dare lead the cyclops back to our camp.

At first I ran like a madman. I plunged through bushes. I wove through trees and ducked under branches. I leapt over rocks and fell more than once, only to pick myself up and run further up the mountainside.

Fortunately, it was the same ridge Cassidy and I had crossed when we'd arrived. It didn't take long for me to reach a height where I felt safe turning and looking back. Of course, I was also completely winded and had to catch my breath as well.

Below, two cyclopses were rounding up the buffalo that had scattered across the small meadow. One cyclops came out of the trees carrying one of the animals, and a fourth stood off to one side and watched the skies.

Which was a good thing for them. Under the scattered white clouds, three harpies soared in wide loops. They screeched and called, but didn't dive.

Now they're here! I fumed.

I checked my stuff. I hadn't lost anything in my mad dash, which was good. My leg hurt a bit where the branch had landed on it, but I'd been able to move fine, which meant it was just a bruise.

I watched a bit longer, but nothing much happened. The harpies returned to their mountain and two of the cyclopses left in the direction of the building and the rift. From time to time, one of the remaining ones scanned the mountainside where I sat. He didn't react, so I assumed he never saw me.

There was nothing for me to do. Carefully I crept through the trees and bushes along the ridge and made my way back to the waterfall.

———

Cassidy sat under the large pine when I returned. He held his canteen in one hand and his rifle and saber lay nearby. He looked as grim as I felt.

"How'd it go?" he asked.

"Not good," I said with a shake of my head. "The shepherd spotted me first. I didn't get him."

He nodded. "They left too many behind. I couldn't get close to the building."

"Where's Mrs. Smith and the kids?" I asked as I sagged onto the ground next to him.

Cassidy passed me the bottle and a small smile cracked his lips.

"Got away," he said. "At least the sentry came back. Mrs. Smith said they could make it on their own if I gave her my Colt."

"She did, did she?" I gestured for the canteen, which he passed me.

"Strong woman. She'll survive, I'm sure, and keep both those kids safe."

I drank some water, and we both fell silent for a bit.

"So what now?" I finally asked.

"We rest. We wait until dark. Then we try again."

"Are you gonna try to send me away again?"

He looked at me with a raised eyebrow, but didn't say anything. Instead he reached for the canteen. I passed it to him and waited. He took a long swallow and then a second before passing it back.

"Would you go if I did?" he asked.

"Only if I had to," I said. "I'd rather stay here and save those people."

"You've really got it, don't you?" he said with a snort. "You've got it bad."

I furrowed my brow in confusion. "Got what?"

"The Hero Dream."

"The what?" I'd heard those capital letters, and I didn't have an idea of what he meant.

He just shook his head and stared off into the distance. I looked out that way, but there wasn't anything to see. Just sky and clouds growing grey in the evening light and the tops of trees.

After a long pause, he spoke. "When the War started, a bunch of boys wanted to go be heroes. Beat Johnny Reb in a glorious fight. Earn ribbons and medals and kisses from the lasses. Most of those boys are dead now.

"Some of us survived."

He flicked something off his sleeve, I couldn't see what.

"The thing is," he continued, "some of those heroes got a great many other people killed. Custer, for one. If he hadn't been so eager for glory the good people of St. Louis would still be alive."

He snorted softly and looked at me, his eyes sad with irony.

"I know Jeremiah doesn't see it that way," he said, "and if you ask him, he'll give you all sorts of reasons why Custer's charge didn't matter. But it did. It mattered a whole lot."

"Oh." It sounded so small coming from my lips, but I didn't know what else to say.

Cassidy sat up straighter and stared out into space once more.

"You know who the real hero was? Grant. Yeah, he led a suicide charge, but it gave Lee time. Without Grant's charge. Lee and his army don't survive. Washington doesn't get evacuated in time. Or Baltimore. Or Philadelphia."

With a sigh, he shook his head.

"Nobody writes books about Grant, but he's the biggest hero we've ever had. The Hero Dreamers don't see that though. They just see a general who marched off and never returned."

He closed his eyes for a bit. Finally he looked at me, but without any heat. More with … sadness.

"That's what a real hero is," Cassidy said. "Someone who does what needs to be done without flinching. Even if it means they're going to die."

He looked away once again.

"I've flinched too many times," he said softly. Without looking at me, he waved his hand dismissively. "Go find someone more worthy of being your hero."

I walked down to the stream. I told myself it was to get a drink of water, but I knew better. I needed to think about what Cassidy'd said.

A Hero Dreamer, he'd called me. It stung, because I couldn't deny it. I'd dreamed big since I was ten.

But the real thing? It wasn't at all what I'd dreamed about. It was miserable and confusing and downright scary at times. I'd seen good people hurt—Beth, McNab, Jeremiah, Mr. Cozens. I'd barely escaped serious injury myself.

All the bruises on my own body ached, but I shook off the pain. I was fine. More than fine. I was alive and more or less unhurt.

That was better than the men of Grand Lake. They'd been killed —no, foully murdered!—and for what?

To bring monsters into the world.

Heroes defeated evil like that, didn't they?

But what did Hero Dreamers do?

According to Cassidy, they died. I believed that, and I didn't want to die. I was pretty sure Cassidy didn't want me to die either.

Which is why Cassidy wanted to send me away.

I snorted softly. It made too much sense. He'd been happy to have me at his side when it was—what was his phrase?—"what had to be done." But when that was over? And he thought he didn't need me?

I shook my head and started walking downstream, toward the lake. My mind still whirled.

As I strode on, I got angry. Not at Cassidy for calling me a Dreamer, but at Jeremiah. The books had *lied!* They'd been nothing like the truth! I'd been fooled!

But after a bit of vigorous stomping, I started to calm down. I hadn't been entirely fooled. I'd seen Cassidy at the Battle of Golden City. I'd seen him fight the harpies. I'd seen him take care of Beth.

He might not have been a hero like in the books, but he was still a hero.

All too soon, my feet carried me to the sandy clearing near the lake. I paused and hung back in the trees, but didn't see anything. No fire peeked through the settling gloom to the south, like the night before. Everything was quiet, except the sound of the wind.

Maybe Cassidy was right in sending me away. I'd saved a bunch of people, and I could do a lot of good as an army sharpshooter, like he said. I'd live, and I'd probably kill a lot more giants before I was through.

Except ... except I didn't see how Cassidy could save the rest of the people without my help. That Greek witch was going to keep killing them if we didn't stop her. The cyclopses were too much for Cassidy to handle on his own. There might be only seven, but—

Why were there only seven?

The thought was like a lightning bolt pinning my feet to the ground. When the Rebels opened the Andersonville rift, a huge army of Jotun had poured through, followed by trolls, wights, and even a dragon or two. But here, we had less than a dozen cyclopses and maybe two dozen harpies.

Why?

I had to talk to Cassidy.

He was asleep under the tree when I returned. I hesitated at first. He looked so worn and exhausted I didn't want to wake him. But he'd said we'd try again when it grew dark, and I guessed we didn't have much time before the witch tried her next sacrifice.

I knelt and gently shook Cassidy's shoulder.

He jerked and his eyes flew wide. A moment later he yanked himself up to sitting.

I rocked back. "You said we'd try again when it got dark."

He glanced around at the gloom which had turned to blackness. Then he nodded.

"But first," I said, "why are there only seven cyclopses? Why not more?"

"That must be all there is on the other side. At least near the rift in that world."

"I don't understand."

He gestured towards the canteen, which sat nearby. I passed it to him and he took a long drink before continuing.

"The rift is a door," he said, "but that doesn't mean it opens into a busy place in the other world. There probably aren't many cyclopses wherever it is."

"Unlike Jotunheim."

"Right," he said. "We think the Andersonville Rift led straight to the heart of Jotunheim. This one … who knows? Thank God it wasn't the heart of whatever Greek realm it connected to."

"Or we'd have a huge army, too."

"Maybe," he said with a shrug. "If the Rebels hadn't made such a large rift, they might've been able to stop the Jotun army. It's a door, remember? You can defend a small door against an army because they can only come through one at a time."

"Instead, they let a whole bunch of Jotun through at the same time."

"Exactly."

"Huh." I paused and let that sink in a bit. It made sense, and now I understood why Cassidy had been in such a hurry to get here. The sooner we could control our side of the rift, the sooner we could prevent more cyclopses from coming through.

Except …

"Um, Cassidy?"

"Yeah?" He'd gotten up and gone to his pack and was rummaging in it.

"This rift's been here for what, ten days, two weeks?"

He sat back on his haunches, smoked meat in his hands, and looked at me. "Something like that, why?"

"And only seven cyclopses have come through. Well, nine if you count the two I killed."

"Yeah. What are you driving at?"

"There's no cyclops army on the other side to come through, because if there was, they'd've had plenty of time to get here. So … why is the witch trying to widen the rift? It's big enough for a cyclops. Why is she trying to make it bigger?"

His eyes went wide. He stood quickly and started swearing. He put his hands on his hips and stared out into the dark, toward where the rift sat.

I waited.

"She's trying to bring something else through," he said at last. "Something bigger, nastier, and almost certainly more evil."

"Uh huh," I said. "But what?"

"I wish I knew."

THIRTY-THREE

THERE IN THE dark under the tree, with the small bubbling waterfall just down the steep rocks, we ate a quick meal of dried fruit and smoked meats and checked our gear. Cassidy strapped his saber across one hip and I put McNab's Colt in a similar place. We both slung our rifles over our backs.

"Take our packs?" I said with a gesture toward the stuff that still lay piled under the trees.

He shook his head.

"We need to move fast and light," he said. "If we can't get back by morning, we're not coming back."

I swallowed and nodded. The thought that we might not come back was sobering.

"So what's the plan?" I asked.

"They know we're out here, so they'll be on guard. But there's only seven of them, and they have to protect three different areas."

"The altar, the prisoners, and the buffalo."

"Correct," he said with a nod. "So, what's left?"

"Umm … I think that's everything."

"No. Water. Just like food, they need water. We take away their water supply and they're easy pickings."

I stared at him like he was crazy. "And just how are we supposed to do that? There's a *lake* here."

"And if they go down to the lake, you can shoot them. From the canoe if needed. The shoreline's too exposed."

"Okay," I said, granting him the point, even though the thought of getting back into the canoe made me shudder. "But they've got the stream. We'd be hard pressed to dam it, and even if we could, they'd just break the dam."

"We don't dam it, we foul it. We make it too polluted and disgusting to drink."

"And how do we do that?"

He grinned, viciously, and even in the night his face seemed alight with anticipation.

"With harpy corpses," he said. "With diseased harpy corpses."

I couldn't suppress my own unsavory chuckle at the thought.

———

We moved fast. When we came to the narrow stretch of woods between the Greek altar and the lake, we stuck to the shore and hustled across as fast as we could, even wading through the water at spots. I was half afraid the cyclopses would hear us and come running, but we made it through without seeing them.

The mountain on the far side rose achingly steep. We scrambled up as best we could, with frequent breaks to catch our breath and share the canteen. My leg muscles screamed with every step, until I just started ignoring them.

About halfway up, we turned and looked back down. We could see small fires where the altar sat, which I guessed to be torches. Cassidy grumbled that he should've brought his spy glass, but not in any serious way. It'd been his idea to travel light after all.

We made it to the summit sometime around midnight. I'd worried that we'd have trouble finding the harpies' nest, but needlessly. While there were still scattered trees obscuring the view, the smell was unmistakeable.

Putrid, decaying flesh. An awful, rotten stench that was worse than anything I'd ever smelled in my life. I fought to keep from vomiting until Cassidy took a kerchief and put it over his nose. I did the same and it only helped a little, but I was able to get my innards back under control.

We followed our noses past a few scraggly pines to a large bowl-shaped rock outcropping. Offal and bird skeletons caked the ground around it. The ridge of a harpy wing peeked out over the top. It moved only slightly and rhythmically.

They were asleep.

Cassidy held up a hand for us to stop. He unslung his rifle and handed it to me, before leaning in close.

"We don't want to wake them," he said quietly. "Cover me with your Colt in case something goes wrong."

I nodded and slung his rifle over my shoulder next to mine. Then I drew my revolver. Cassidy unsheathed his saber and crept toward the nest. I followed three steps behind. We stepped carefully, checking each spot before we put our foot down, so as not to step on something that crunched. Like a sparrow corpse.

Slowly, slowly, we crested the rim of the outcropping. Inside, four harpies huddled, heads under wings, all asleep. The fearsome daytime hunters looked like overgrown geese in the night.

Cassidy picked his way down the steep rock into the nest. More than once, he had to reach down and brace himself with his hand.

The harpies stirred, but didn't wake.

Cassidy moved to the side of the nearest one, close to where its head was, and raised his sword.

He struck.

The harpy jerked and flailed. Its wings shot out, but to my surprise, it didn't make a cry. Before it had even started to stiffen, Cassidy turned and slashed the next one.

This one did squawk, and Cassidy stabbed it again. It flailed and one of its wings almost knocked him off his feet, but he was able to dodge in time.

The other two raised their heads and screeched.

Cassidy lunged at the one on the right. Its wing batted his sword and knocked it to the side. He slashed down into the feathers.

I fired at the one on the left, and then fired again. Both shots caught it in the breast and it flew backwards with a scream.

Cassidy stabbed at the one in front of him. I tried to get a shot, but Cassidy was in the way. The harpy lunged forward and bit his right arm. Cassidy tossed the saber to his left hand and chopped downward. He took the harpy's head off.

And like that it was over, and quiet once again. Other than the pounding of my heart and heavy breathing, of course.

Cassidy stumbled backward and dropped his saber. He clutched his arm. I scrambled down the rocky slope to his side.

"You're hurt!" I said.

"I'll live." His grimace betrayed how much pain he was in. "Get their talons. I'll bind this."

He clambered out of the nest, holding his arm the entire time. I picked up his saber and started butchering the corpses.

We'd decided to take the talons and teeth to use for our creek poisoning, as we figured the whole bodies would be too hard to carry. In cutting them up, I found some fluid filled sacs near their cheeks, that reminded me of rattlesnake poison glands. I took those as well. We'd brought one empty bag and the harpy parts almost overflowed it, but it closed, which was what mattered to me.

When I climbed out, I found Cassidy sitting on the ground, his back against a fallen log. He'd bound a kerchief around the wound on his arm, but looked pale in the low moonlight.

"Are you going to be okay?" I asked.

He chuckled. "I'd better be."

"I've got some willow bark in my pack," I said, "but none of Maria's mold mixture."

"We just have to get to your pack," he said with a touch of irony in his voice. "First, you have your scarf? Let's bind my upper arm."

"Why?"

"We want to constrict things. Maria says it makes it harder for poisons to flow."

Well, if Maria said it …

I did as Cassidy asked, There wasn't too much blood soaking through where the wound itself was, which gave me hope that it wasn't too bad. The poison was probably the real problem.

We made our way down the mountain, a little less quietly and a lot faster than we'd been during the climb. By the time we reached the lake, the torches near the altar were out. We crept by and heard and saw nothing.

They probably killed someone during the night, I thought.

I shuddered and guilt coursed through me. Whoever it was, we hadn't even tried to save them!

My mind went to Matthew, in the giant's arms, about to be lowered onto the altar. My blood went cold. At least we'd saved him.

But after a moment, I reminded myself that if we'd saved the person last night, we wouldn't have been able to kill the harpies. Surely that would save others down the line.

Cassidy stumbled. He'd brushed a tree with his right arm and now clutched it in pain. He shot a quick glance my way and kept walking.

We made it back to our camp near the cliffs and small waterfall just as dawn arrived. Cassidy sank to the ground as I rummaged through my pack for the willow bark. I had to fill his canteen in the creek before he could take it, but he was grateful and drank it down quickly. We split the last of our dried fruit and jerky while we sat there under the tree.

"You get some sleep," Cassidy said when we were done. "I'll poison the creek and keep watch."

"But you're hurt! You need the rest more than me."

He shook his head and then raised his arm. It shook despite his efforts to hold it steady.

"I can't shoot," he said. "You're going to have to deal with the cyclopses that come to the lake. But it'll take a while for the poison to get downstream. Get some sleep so you can aim straight."

A bunch of arguments leapt to my lips, but I bit them back. As far as I could see, he was right.

"I'll be fine," Cassidy said. "I'll sleep while you watch the lake."

His eyes didn't match his words, but there was nothing I could say.

I awoke with the noon sun on my face. I'd rolled to a spot where the overhead branches didn't quite block it out. The pines waved just enough in the breeze to make the light dance. When I sat up, I didn't see Cassidy at first. He was over on the rocks above the stream, out in the open.

I stretched and then went over to him.

"Your turn to sleep," I said.

"After you get down to the lake," he said. He nodded his head toward the bubbling water. "It should've reached them by now. The poison turns the water black, which means they won't miss it."

"Too bad," I said. "If they drank it, there'd be fewer of them."

"And if they gave it to the humans first?"

My cheeks pinkened, but Cassidy waved me on.

"Go," he said. "Do what you can. I'll be here when you get back. And take my saber."

"I don't know how to use it," I said.

"It's just a big knife," he said with a grin. "Aim for their knees."

I found a good sharpshooter's spot about a hundred yards around the curve of the shore from where the altar was. Two pines grew close together, with a leafy bush between them. I stretched out and pointed the rifle barrel through the lower branches of the bush. I could lay on my stomach and watch the entire area without being seen.

I waited for a while. The sun crept to the west, and the afternoon clouds began to cluster. Meanwhile, other than the breeze coming and going, nothing moved, except me from time to time as I shook off the stiffness of lying in wait.

Finally, finally, the trees on the far shore swayed. Something big pushed through them. I made sure I was comfortable and stretched out so I could sight down my rifle barrel. I'd have to hit the cyclops's eye, and at this distance it'd be tougher than a sparrow on a log. I'd done that in the past, but just as often I'd missed.

The branches on the last trees parted and the cyclops stepped into view. As massively tall as the others, this one wore a metal helm and leather jerkin over its tunic. In one hand, it held a massive wooden bucket and in the other, the ends of two thick ropes. They led to—

Oh, God. Two half naked women stumbled out of the woods behind the cyclops.The other ends of the ropes formed nooses around their necks.

THIRTY-FOUR

I NEARLY FROZE in paralysis as I watched. The leaves of the bush fluttered in front of me, but I ignored them. I eased my finger off the trigger just a bit, and resisted the urge to poke my head up for a better view.

The women's clothes were in tatters, exposing legs and arms and one woman's side. They bowed their dark heads and carried smaller, human-sized wooden buckets. They half-ran, half-stumbled to keep up with the cyclops as its longer strides carried it the last few feet to the shore, and then into the water a ways.

The monster stopped when it was knee deep in the lake and bent to fill the big bucket. The women, much closer to shore, did the same.

The rope between them and the cyclops hung slack.

I hunkered down again and aimed my rifle at the giant's head. I needed it to turn my way, just for an instant. I needed a good shot at the eye.

The cyclops finished filling its bucket and trod back to shore.

My heart raced. He'd never turned my way! I pulled back and glanced around for something, anything to throw.

Nearby lay a small rock, maybe the size of an egg. I grabbed it in my left hand and quickly returned to sighting down the rifle.

The cyclops stood on the shore, with water dripping from the bottom of its tunic. It set the bucket down in the mud and reeled in some of the rope slack.

Blindly, I threw the rock to my left. It clattered through the trees.

The cyclops spun at the noise. It looked squarely in my direction, its eye wide with surprise.

I fired.

With a howl, the cyclops fell backwards. The women dodged to the side, and one barely missed being crushed. Her rope went taut, pinned under the cyclops, and pulled her down.

I dropped my rifle, jumped to my feet, and dashed forward. The giant twitched and its arm reached up before flopping back and going still.

The woman still standing tugged at her noose and pulled it off just as I arrived. I ran past the cyclops's body to where the other lay, choking and clutching at the rope around her neck. I pulled out Cassidy's saber and in a few slashes she was free.

Guttural yells came from the direction of the altar.

The unhurt woman knelt and helped the other up. They both looked gaunt and worn with wild shocked eyes that went wide when they met mine.

"Can you run?" I urgently asked.

They shared a look and nodded.

"Go!" I said and I pointed east. "Go along the shore back to town. You should be able to find some food in the destroyed buildings. Then go south to Empire. Understand? The militia's coming and you should meet them on the way."

My words seemed to sink in, at least for the unhurt woman. She stood and pulled the other to her feet.

The yells turned to bellows and the nearby trees shook.

"Run!" I yelled.

The women took off as best they were able, half-running, half-loping.

I didn't have time to watch.

I quickly cursed myself for leaving my rifle at my shooting blind. I drew my Colt just as another cyclops burst through the trees with a spear.

Just ten yards away, the monster towered above me. It roared and looked down.

I fired twice at its face.

It howled and charged forward. I turned and dashed along the shore as best I could. I ran in the water for a bit and glanced over my shoulder as I did. The cyclops stabbed its spear where I'd been a few moments before, but hit only air. It swung its head, side to side, but didn't seem able to see me.

I ran for my rifle. As I slid to the ground behind the covering trees, I heard another bellow. Panting for breath, I looked back.

The cyclops I'd wounded stood holding a bloody hand to its face while the other hand held his spear aloft. A second in a tunic stood next to it, also clutching a spear. The two giants were talking in a language I couldn't make out. They ignored the cyclops body sprawled nearby.

The new cyclops clutched his spear and slowly turned, scanning the area.

He's looking for me, I realized.

It also meant that his eye was soon looking my way.

I fired.

This time, I didn't miss.

But as the giant collapsed to its knees, the wounded one whipped around and threw its spear my direction. I reflexively ducked, but the huge shaft smashed into the trees twenty feet to my right.

The trees between the lake and the cyclops camp rustled once again. The wounded one crouched and started wiping its face with the hem of its tunic, but as it did it kept looking my way.

He doesn't know exactly where I am, but he's got an idea, I realized.

And when he got reinforcements, I'd be done for.

I rose to my feet and retreated as fast as I could without making a lot of noise.

I stopped to catch my breath about twenty minutes later. I'd jogged through the pines along the shore, hoping to find the women, but never saw them. I decided they had to be safe, or at least if they weren't there wasn't much I could do.

It was still two more people freed, I reminded myself. Only eighteen or twenty to go!

That made me pause. If the cyclopses were looking for me at the lake, could I circle around and free the rest of the townsfolk?

It was worth a try.

But it took a while to get to the sandy clearing, and then to creep past it to where we'd seen the cooking fire. I had maybe an hour of daylight left by the time I got there. The area wasn't deserted, though. Two young boys were butchering a buffalo under the watchful eyes of another cyclops. It wore an iron helm and kept looking this way and that.

I didn't see any way to approach close enough for a good shot. Reluctantly, I slowly pulled back.

I considered working my way over to the buffalo herd and seeing if I could attack the shepherd there, but decided it would take too long. Instead, I made my way back to Cassidy.

I found Cassidy lying on his side under the broad branched tree that had become our camp. He looked at me with glazed tired eyes and struggled up to a sitting position. As I knelt by him, I realized he'd rolled the sleeve of his shirt up and changed the bandage over the harpy bite. Still, streaky black lines ran through his arm, radiating out from the wound.

"You okay?" I asked in alarm.

"I'm fine," he said. "Get me some water?"

I found his canteen and saw it was empty. "Be right back." I hustled down to the creek, a good distance above where he'd poisoned it of course, and quickly returned. By then he'd composed himself a bit and the gleam was back in his eye.

"How'd it go?" he asked.

"Good, I think." I filled him in on what had happened. He nodded approvingly as I described freeing the women and then again when I told him of my decision to retreat.

"You might've been able to shoot one or two more," he said, "but it would've foolishly exposed you."

"It felt like a Custer Move," I said.

He laughed, a sharp ironic bark, and then looked at me, and then chuckled some more.

"A Custer Move," he said. "I like that. I do."

I felt my cheeks redden, but I didn't look away.

"Well," he said, "I reckon Miss Pappas is going to be feeling a tad panicked tonight. She's down to five cyclopses, and they haven't been able to stop you. They know we're out here, but they don't know what we're going to do next."

"What *are* we doing next?"

"Well," he said, "I figure we have a day, maybe two, before Luke and the militia get here. At that point, it shouldn't be hard to finish off the cyclopses and rescue the rest of the folks from Grand Lake."

"And close the rift," I added.

"That ... that won't be easy." His face grew somber for a minute. "But we can deal with that later. First we stop the sacrifices.That's for you and me."

"How?" I asked. "Kill the witch?"

"If we have to. I'd rather take her prisoner. There's so much we don't know."

I nodded. *Why?* was the big question. Where exactly this rift connected to was another, and what else was she trying to bring through.

But why here? Why in the Colorado mountains? It seemed a long way to come to open a rift. I thought a bit about the long journey the Pappas sisters must have taken to get here. That gave me an idea.

"If we kill her," I said, "we could ask her sister. I mean, she's gotta be around here someplace too."

Cassidy's eyebrows shot up in surprise. "Um, Billy ... didn't Jeremiah or Maria explain to you how rifts are created?"

I shook my head. "I always assumed it was a spell or something."

"No. There's no such thing as magic. Witches can't cast spells any more than you or I can."

Cassidy started struggling to his feet. He was shaky, far more shaky than I'd ever seen him, but that just made how driven he was more apparent. I stared at him, open-mouthed.

"There's not?" I said. "But all the stories about spells and potions—"

"Just stories," he said. "You've seen Maria's 'potions.' They're mostly medicines, though she can mix up a few other things. No, what witches can do is see and talk to disembodied souls, or ghosts, and sometimes make them go places, though Maria's never been able to explain how in a way that makes sense to me or Jeremiah."

"So, uh, our witch kills someone and guides their soul into the rift."

"Exactly," he said with a nod. "Where her sister's soul traps it. To make it wider, remember?"

"But ... that means her sister ..."

"Was the first sacrifice, yes."

"She killed her sister?" I exclaimed. It'd been a long time since my brother had died, but I still missed him bad when I thought of him. I couldn't imagine killing someone you loved.

"It's a bit more complicated." Cassidy reached down next to him and grabbed his pack with his left hand. He winced as he threw it over his shoulder. "You see, her sister had to agree to it."

"She killed her sister and her sister *wanted* it?"

"Yeah. That's pretty much it. It's why there aren't too many rifts. How many people are willing to die just to open a passage to another world?"

I just stared at him in shock.

"Let me have that," he said. He gestured toward his saber at my waist, so I unbuckled the sheath and passed it to him. "Make sure your rifle and Peacemaker are ready."

I nodded, but my mind was still a blank, trying to grasp what he'd just said.

Cassidy stepped next to me and clasped me on the shoulder with his good hand.

"Relax, Billy," he said. "What's done is done. What matters now is stopping Miss Pappas and saving as many people as we can."

In the fading light, he looked as sincere as could be.

"We can do it," he said. "You and me. Together."

That shook me out of my shock.

"Yeah," I said. "Together." I put my hand on his good shoulder in return.

"Let's go."

We turned and strode off for the lake to go and do what we could.

THIRTY-FIVE

WE STRODE QUICKLY through the woods, past the sandy clearing, to the lake. My eyes quickly adjusted to the gloom. The unclouded sky gave plenty of moonlight outside of the deep shadows of the trees. We paused once we'd reached the water's shore to drink some water. I unshouldered my rifle and held it in front of me.

A woman's scream rent the night.

Without a word we both ran south along the shore toward the altar.

We'd gone halfway there when a large shadowy lump ahead of us moved.

Cassidy drew his saber and charged. I pulled up near a tall pine and raised my rifle. I sighted down the barrel at the lump, trying to determine exactly what it was.

The lump stretched and rose—a cyclops! It stood from behind the low cluster of firs that had only partially concealed it. I tried to get a shot at its eye, but I could barely make out its head.

A cyclops roar sounded to my left.

With a loud crack, the tall pine next to me crashed down on me.

A trap!

I tried to scramble forward, but the heavy wooden branches slammed into my head and shoulders and drove me to the ground.

I lay there, stunned, for I don't know how long.

When my brain started to work again, I realized I was flat in the dirt. My knee hurt badly, as did my hip and my lower back. My left arm was trapped under my chest and the right flung forward, where rough pine needles scraped the back of my hand.

I flexed my fingers. They moved on both hands. I did the same with my toes. They moved within my boots.

That was good. My spine wasn't broken.

I rose up, but the weight of the branches pressed me back down. I squirmed until I could free my left arm from under me. In doing so, I brought my right arm back and rose on my elbows.

Something heavy and thick lay across the back of my thighs. A higher branch bounced just above my back, with its smaller offshoots stabbing my side and the ground next to me. They kept most of the weight off, which I appreciated, but scraped and scratched my back every time I moved.

At least nothing was in my face.

I dug my elbows into the ground and pulled myself forward. The branch in my back dug into me and I gasped with pain. But I could move. I pulled forward again, a bit slower, and tried to wiggle as I did. It hurt a little less, but still sent sharp stabs into my body. I flattened myself and reached back with one hand, grasping for it. After a bit, I was able to wrap my left hand about the slim branch, as long as I ignored the pine needles jabbing my palm and fingers.

The branch wasn't too thick. Mostly it appeared to be at the wrong angle. I moved my hand up to the top and winced as one dried needle jabbed the fleshy web between my thumb and forefinger. I pushed the pain aside and twisted the branch until it broke. I let out a long relieved breath as the pain and pressure lessened.

Then I started slithering forward again. The big weight on my legs was just that—weight. The bark and branches shredded my pants and in some spots my skin, but I grimaced and kept pulling myself forward. Finally, finally, the large branch was below my knees and I could crawl. A few more small branches loomed in front of my face, but I was able to bend them back and forth until they broke.

I rose to my knees and paused. I could finally see out from this mess of a tree.

Cassidy crouched at the lake's edge with his back to the water. He held his saber in his left hand in front of him and waved it back and forth slowly.

Two cyclopses stood twenty feet in front on him, both with leveled spears. They jabbed them in his general direction, but not with any seriousness. It seemed to be a stand-off of some sort.

Why didn't they charge?

I scanned the area and the answer became obvious. A cyclops corpse sprawled face down in the water a dozen feet behind Cassidy. The huge monster *had* charged—and paid the price.

The farther cyclops took a few steps forward and stabbed with his spear. Cassidy jumped to the side and the huge pointed head missed him. The cyclops jabbed again and Cassidy dropped down, under it, and then dashed forward. The monster tried to slam his spear down on Cassidy's head, but only succeeded in smashing the tip into the dirt.

Meanwhile, with a yell, Cassidy raced by the cyclops's leg, slashing as he went. The monster kicked at him and missed, and Cassidy's blade caught the monster on one toe.

It roared, but he was into the woods before it could turn.

The cyclops turned and started smashing trees with its spear, sending logs and huge splinters every which way. The second cyclops quickly joined his side.

I pulled the rest of my legs out from under the branch and stood. I shook as I did so. Pain screamed through my body, from the wound in my back and all the scrapes and scratches on my hands, arms, and legs. My right knee felt ready to collapse. I reached down and steadied it and took a deep breath.

I hurt, but I was alive.

Cassidy dashed out of the woods and past the cyclopses. They swung at him with their spears, but once again he was too close to them too quickly, and then he was beyond, back at the lakeshore.

I needed to help him! Where was my rifle?

I dropped to my knees and started feeling around for the Henry. I tried to keep an eye on Cassidy, but it was hard to do both. Every time my left hand brushed against something, the cuts stung like a billion bees all at once.

Then I found it! My hand brushed the stock, and I was able to yank it out from underneath the morass of broken branches and needles. I struggled back to my feet with it firmly in my grip.

Once again, Cassidy stood with his back to the water while the cyclopses probed at him with their spears. They spread further apart this time, slowly circling to his left and his right simultaneously. They continued to jab at him, but now the stabs were coming from opposite directions. He barely dodged a thrust at his back by dropping to his knees and then bounding back up before the second could jab his stomach. As he leapt to his feet, one of the spears grazed his upper left arm.

Cassidy fell to the ground.

I gasped and started forward, but stopped. I couldn't get there in time! I raised the rifle instead. I pushed aside the stabbing pain in my hand and the aches in my arms. As best I could, I aimed at the back of the nearest cyclops's head.

But then Cassidy got up! He dashed forward—toward me!—and around the surprised cyclops. It whirled around to give chase.

And gave me a clean view of its face and its big, beautiful eye.

I fired.

The cyclops howled and collapsed forward. It fell to its knees and dropped the spear. Then it pitched forward onto its face.

Cassidy dodged the falling body and kept running my direction. He'd dropped his saber and clutched his left arm with his right.

The second cyclops roared and pulled back its spear arm.

"Down!" I yelled.

Cassidy threw himself flat. The thrown spear whistled through the space where he'd just been and hit the ground in front of him. It didn't stick, and instead bounced and flipped end over end.

I reflexively ducked, even though it came nowhere near me. When I looked up, the cyclops stared at us, his fists on his hips. He seemed to be looking at Cassidy, who writhed on the ground. The giant's mouth gaped in an evil grin. He took a step forward.

No!

In anger, I fired two shots at his head. I didn't aim. I was just too mad.

He howled and clapped his hands over his mouth. Then he turned and ran into the woods, smashing trees aside as he went.

I dashed to Cassidy's side.

He was on his back, clutching the spear wound on his left arm, which almost matched the harpy bite wound on his right. It spurted blood in almost a steady stream. His face was white as he gritted his teeth.

I didn't wait. I whipped off my belt, looped it around his arm above the wound as a tourniquet, and pulled it tight. I pressed directly on the wound with my other hand, almost willing the blood to stop. For an agonizing long minute, it looked like it wouldn't, but finally, finally it began to slow.

Cassidy watched, his eyes glazed and his breath short.

"Can you hold this?" I said. I pointed to the makeshift tourniquet.

He nodded and reached across and pulled it tight with his right hand. That gave me the chance to yank my shirt off and wrap it around his arm as a bandage. Doing so stung like mad from all the little cuts, but I ignored both them and the cool air on my bare skin. Instead, I focused on Cassidy.

I was able to make the bandage work, mostly. It took some careful wrapping to get it so it would hold. The whole time, I worried that Cassidy would go into battle shock, but somehow his eyes stayed with me and slowly his breathing settled. Once I had the bandage secured I rocked back on my haunches and studied his arm. The wound was both deep and wide, and that meant it was likely to open up again if I took the tourniquet off.

Cassidy seemed to know that, too. "Leave it on," he said. "Help me stand."

"If we leave it, you'll lose the arm."

"It's okay—"

His words were cut off by a loud human scream. Both our heads whipped toward the altar area it had come from.

"Help me up," he said.

I stood and grasped his right hand. He grimaced in pain as I pulled him to his feet, but he managed to stand. I glanced around but couldn't see his saber in the dark.

"Give me your Colt," Cassidy said. He took a deep breath as I passed it to him. His arm shook when he held it, so he clasped it to his chest.

"Maybe I should go by myself," I said.

He shook his head. "We're a team. We go together."

I swallowed hard at what he'd said. By the look in his eyes, I knew he meant it.

Another human wail filled the air.

"C'mon," he said, "let's go do what has to be done."

THIRTY-SIX

WE DIDN'T TRY to be quiet as we stormed through the thin woods between the lake and the altar. We moved as fast as we could, though between my knee and Cassidy's general weakness, that wasn't very fast. Still, we stumbled through the trees without slowing up. As we burst through the last bit of cover, we skidded to a halt.

The witch stood with a knife poised over a woman tied to the altar. Behind them, another cyclops stood with a teen girl in his arms. Both the witch and the cyclops glared at us.

"One more step, and they both die." The witch slowly twisted the knife to make her threat completely clear.

Cassidy raised his Colt and pointed it at her. "They die, you die."

I shouldered my rifle and aimed it at the cyclops. I didn't have a great shot at its eye, but I hoped the threat would suffice.

"I die and the dragon kills you." She tilted her head toward the rift.

Dragon?

I glanced over at the rift. It swirled grey instead of the black I'd seen before. Now as wide as it was tall, it blocked the sky and the trees for dozens of feet.

"Maybe it does," Cassidy drawled. "But you'll still be dead."

The witch laughed, long and deep. She held the knife steady as she did, though the woman on the altar whimpered quietly.

I studied the witch. Her black hair and long robes made her look like a dark priestess against the flickering light of the torches ringing the clearing. Fury filled her face, even as she twisted the long thin knife back and forth in her hand.

The thin brown-haired girl in the cyclops's arms squirmed. She didn't cry out, though she trembled with eyes wide. The monster held her tight, its huge meaty paws covering her entire body. His grip tightened as I waved my rifle barrel and the girl peeped once as he squeezed her.

We all stared at each other, none daring to move.

Meanwhile, the torches flickered and the smell of blood and dung reached my nose. It reminded me of the corpse of my horse. Though I didn't dare look away from the cyclops long enough to search for bodies in the area.

The witch loudly called out something in a language I didn't understand. The cyclops echoed her, repeating some of the words in its booming voice. Neither looked away from us.

Sweat beaded on my forehead. I sensed Cassidy starting to slump next to me. I quickly glanced his way. His face was pale and his right arm with the gun shook. His left arm hung uselessly at his side, but blood once again oozed out of his bandage. The tourniquet had come loose.

Oh, God.

But I kept my rifle up and trained on the cyclops. I tried not to think about Cassidy. I did my best not to think about Cassidy. I blinked but forced myself to sight down the barrel at the monster's eye. I would not think about Cassidy.

Cassidy's breath grew labored and ragged.

Something lumbered up the path from far building. It didn't take long to realize what. The last cyclops, a skinny one, marched in, its spear held across its chest and a mean grimace on its face.

Both the witch and the first cyclops turned their heads to look at the newcomer.

"Now!" Cassidy yelled. Two shots rang out from his revolver.

The cyclops with the woman whipped its head back around to face us. My rifle hadn't wavered, and that big beautiful eye came cleanly into view.

I fired and watched the bullet slam home.

The cyclops I'd shot roared and toppled backward.

The witch was down too, but I didn't have time to look close because the last cyclops pulled back his spear.

I threw myself down and to the side and the huge shaft slammed into the trees behind me. Wood exploded everywhere.

I clambered back to my feet. I'd dropped my rifle and my right arm bled from a shallow gash. Not fatal—it hadn't hit the artery! But it hurt bad, overwhelming all other cuts.

I couldn't see Cassidy. The cyclops stomped around its fallen companion and scanned the area. When it saw me, it roared and charged.

I ran.

Not back into the woods, but sideways. I put the altar and the fallen giant between me and it. The one chasing me roared and stomped, but picked its footing carefully. That bought me a little time.

Then, suddenly, I was next to the rift. The cyclops paused and I quickly glanced around. Cassidy had risen to one knee, but the giant hadn't noticed him.

The giant was intent on me. It roared and lunged forward.

I turned and dove through the rift.

Flashes of light filled my eyes and my skin crackled and buzzed like it was covered with bees. My stomach lurched, and then I was falling. I put my hands out and smashed into the ground. My head slammed into a rock and my knees and elbows scraped through scrabbled gravel before I came to a stop.

I lay there, stunned and gasping for breath. Wherever I was, it was night, judging by the dimness and the stars I could just barely see. The tufts of grass and pebbles jamming into my side were all too familiar as well.

Slowly, I pulled myself to my knees.

I was on a rough pebble beach with red sand. Waves lapped the shore not far from me, mostly behind the rift. Ahead, a rolling hill lead up to what looked like leafy woods. Beyond the woods, another hill rose up, steep against the sky.

The far hill moved.

My chin dropped.

Slowly, the black patch uncoiled and a huge snake's head rose up. The head itself was easily as big as a cyclops and the sinuous body stretched further than I could see. Two golden eyes opened and a forked tongue licked the air.

Oh God, Oh God, Oh God, Oh God.

Trembling, I rose to my feet. The snake-dragon-whatever-it-was hissed and slithered forward.

A crackling came from the rift behind me. I ran to the side just as the cyclops that'd been chasing me stepped through. It had its spear again, clutched firmly in one hand. It immediately looked at the dragon, not seeing me at all.

The cyclops braced itself, studying the dragon.

I saw no point in sticking around.

I dashed past the cyclops and jumped through the rift once more.

My skin buzzed and my eyes filled with blobby bright lights once again. I managed to avoid vomiting, but I was still dizzy and fell as soon as I was through the rift.

Cassidy stood by the altar. He was cutting the ropes that bound the townswoman with the witch's knife. Her body lay on the ground nearby. He turned and his eyes went wide when he saw me.

"Dragon!" I yelled. "Dragon coming!"

He nodded before turning back to the ropes.

I stood. My right knee screamed in pain and my right arm throbbed. I tried to run, but the best I could do was lope. I got to the altar just as Cassidy finished freeing the woman's arms. She sat up while he worked on freeing her feet.

Cassidy could barely hold the knife. He shook and grimaced. The bandage on his left arm was once again soaked with blood.

"Let me," I said.

He handed me the knife and I went to work on the ropes. He turned to the woman. "Go," he said, "free the others. Go back to the town. The militia will be there soon."

The woman nodded. Frightened and filthy, she didn't look hurt. Once she was free, she ran off toward the building.

Cassidy sagged against the altar.

"You okay?" I asked.

He shook his head.

"Dragon coming. We have to run."

He shook his head again. "We have to close the rift."

"We can't. Maria's not here." I tugged on his arm. "Let's go."

He pushed my hand away. "No. We don't need Maria." With a groan of pain, he lifted himself up and sat on the side of the altar. "And we don't have time."

"What?" I snapped.

"We close the rift. Now. Before the dragon comes through."

"How?" I demanded.

"Same way they're made. Someone dies and their soul undoes what the witch created." He took a deep breath and laid back on the altar.

"But ... but ...!" I stared at him, my eyes wide. My heart pounded.

"I'm dead in a few hours anyway," he said. His calm eyes stared at me.

"We can fix the tourniquet!"

"But not the poison." He held out the dagger toward me and then tilted his head toward the rift. "I think my soul can find that."

"But ... but ... but ...!"

He gestured for me to take the dagger again. With shocked, trembling hands I did. My mind and my blood raced.

"No ...," I said softly as it all sunk in. "No ... we need you. The West needs you."

The rift crackled behind me. I turned just as a huge disembodied arm flew through and bounced on the ground. I stared it for a moment and briefly wondered about the rest of the cyclops.

"It needs to be done," Cassidy said calmly.

"No." I was on the edge of crying.

"Do it."

"No." Tears filled my eyes.

Once again, the rift hummed and sparked.

"Do it!"

I squeezed the knife and raised it above Cassidy's chest. Something thumped behind me, but I didn't turn. I took a deep breath instead.

I closed my eyes.

I plunged the dagger down.

I killed Cassidy.

THIRTY-SEVEN

I COLLAPSED in a sobbing heap by the side of the altar. Slowly, I turned and put my back against it. I wiped my eyes free of tears and looked up at the rift.

It swirled now, a mix of black and white and greys. The colors split and mixed and splashed, like coffee poured into a swirling whitecapped river. For a moment, it looked like it would all turn dark, but then it brightened and the white expanded. The rift glowed as the white expanded from the center to the edges.

And then the rift was gone.

I cried, deep chest-filled cries, as much from relief as grief.

It was over. It was finally over.

I sobbed until my tears ran dry, and then I sobbed some more. Great dry heaves that threatened to turn my guts inside out.

"Are you all right?"

I turned my head. Not five feet away stood the blonde girl the cyclops had been holding. She stood nervous, half turned with one foot back, as if to dash off like a deer at a moment's fear.

"Are you all right?" she repeated.

"No," I said as I wiped my face with the back of my hand. The cuts there stung with the sweat and the tears. "No, but I will be. You?"

"We're safe," she said, bobbing her head up and down quickly. "Safe. All six of us."

I shuddered. There were twenty only two days ago!

"Are there any ...?" She bit her lip.

"No," I said. "No more cyclopses. None. No more harpies, too, and no more damned witch."

She recoiled at the venom of my tone.

"No more Cassidy," I said quietly. I stifled a sob simply because I didn't have the energy.

"Uh ... well ... we're going to try for the town tonight. We know it's ruined, but none of us want to stay here. Will you come with us?"

"Sure," I said. I didn't want to stay here either, not with all the death around. But I wasn't truly done, I realized.

"There's a sandy clearing north of here," I said. "I'll meet you there in a little bit."

"Uh, good. Good!" She dashed off out of sight. Toward the others, I presumed, but I didn't watch her go.

Shakily, I stood. I closed my eyes but then forced myself to open them. I didn't want to turn around but I had to. I made myself look at Cassidy.

His open eyes stared up and his mouth formed an O. The dagger remained in his chest. I quickly seized it and pulled it out, and then dropped it to the side. With a quick pass of my hand, I closed his eyes. I wanted to cover his face, but didn't see anything immediately that would serve.

Instead I closed my eyes and said a little prayer. There had to be a God, right? If souls were real, then maybe Heaven was too. I prayed that Cassidy's soul would get there.

After that, there was nothing left to do, at least not until the militia arrived. I left to go find the other survivors.

They'd waited for me. Three grown women, the blonde girl, and two babies. Filth covered all of them, though they'd managed to wash their faces. The woman from the altar looked strongest of the lot. While her dress was torn so badly it barely covered her breasts, she strode forward to meet me with purpose.

"Thank you," she said. To my surprise, she reached for my hand to shake it and didn't recoil when she saw it was covered in blood.

"Wasn't anything, ma'am," I said.

"It was to us." She smiled warmly and deeply.

I felt my cheeks pinken a bit at her praise.

"Let's go," I said. "We have a lot of walking to do."

I was bone weary tired as we made our way to the destroyed town of Grand Lake. We stopped a couple of times to rest as we went, and on one of those breaks the blonde girl, Jane, washed and bandaged the wound on my back. The bleeding had long since stopped, but it still felt better once she'd tended to it.

When we arrived, the women bustled off to check their own homes. Cries of sorrow and surprise echoed through night as they found what had survived and what had not.

Me, I just stumbled on until I found my bedroll where I'd stashed it after I'd lost my horse. Was that yesterday? Two days ago? Three? In my exhausted state, I couldn't tell.

Jane stuck by my side as we made our way through town to our old camp. She offered to get water as I slumped against a log. I nodded and she was off toward the lake.

In the nearest house, a tall woman poked through the ruins, looking here and there. I watched her for a while before my brain finally kicked in. Beth's house.

"Are you Mrs. Armstrong?" I called.

Startled, she turned and looked at me. "Why yes, yes I am."

"We found Beth," I said, "she was hurt, but she's gonna live."

Mrs. Armstrong burst into tears of relief. She quickly climbed out of the ruins and ran to my side. About then, Jane returned with a full jug of water.

"What happened?" Mrs. Armstrong asked. "How bad is she hurt?"

"Broken ankle," I said, "but otherwise in good spirits."

"She survived the cyclops?" Jane asked.

"She survived a lot more than that."

The two women sat on the ground nearby as I told them about finding Beth. I had to back up and explain how me and Cassidy and the rest had come to Grand Lake, and Mrs. Armstrong smirked when I told them how I wasn't really on Cassidy's team. She didn't interrupt, though, so I told them about paddling the canoe and the trip to Saratoga West and the harpies. The other women drifted over just as I got to the part where Cassidy and I had walked down the road to save Jeremiah and Beth.

"You were very brave," Jane said. Her eyes shone in the growing dawn.

"I just did what had to be done," I said. I turned to Mrs. Armstrong, "but Beth helped out, too. She took care of Jeremiah, even though she wasn't so sure about him, him being a Negro and all."

"Good," Mrs. Armstrong said. "She did what Jesus would've wanted her to do."

I snorted softly. Jesus? Where was He in all this? I'd have to talk to Jeremiah about Jesus sometime, I promised myself.

"So what then?" Jane asked. She sat up and when I smiled indulgently at her, she lowered her eyes and blushed.

But she had a right to know, so I told them about the Cozens ranch and my trip back and finding Cassidy. Then about rescuing Mrs. Smith and Laura and Matthew.

My audience expressed relieved happiness at that news. So many had died that word of survivors seemed a blessing.

The last part was … hard. I talked about killing the harpies and poisoning the stream and Cassidy's wound. I told them how I killed the cyclopses—was it really that many cyclopses?—and that I regretted not getting the name of the women who'd escaped.

"Mrs. Stidham and Miss Evelyn," Jane said quietly. "They were the ones taken to get water. We'd feared the worst."

"I hope they're safe," I said, "but I don't know."

"They're fine," Mrs. Armstrong said firmly. "Mrs. Stidham has a good head on her shoulders. I'm sure they made their way to the militia."

"The militia should be here soon." Despite my best efforts to stifle it, I yawned.

"And then what?" Jane prompted.

"Not much to tell," I said. "Cassidy and I came back at night. We fought three cyclopses on the lake shore and killed two. The last one ran away. Then we found the rift," I looked at Jane, "and you know the rest."

She didn't, given as how she'd fled before the very end, but I didn't feel like enlightening her.

I yawned again.

"We should sleep," I said. "I know it's almost morning, but we all could use it."

The ladies murmured in agreement and then started discussing how best to arrange things, between all of them and the babies. I decided I didn't care. I stretched out on the ground and closed my eyes and soon enough oblivion took me.

My arm started to hurt, which woke me up. It throbbed, and then felt like it had been twisted, though I knew it hadn't. I opened my eyes to see an excited Tom Folliard kneeling next to me. He wore an oversized blue army uniform and cap and held an old Enfield rifle in one hand.

"Tom!" I exclaimed. "You're here!"

"We're all here," he said. "Well, except the Colonel and Cassidy's man, Luke something-or-other. They rode over to the other side of the lake with a squad."

"Good," I said. "They can take care of things there. Oh, there's still a cyclops running around—"

"We know," Tom said. "The women told us all about it."

I slowly sat up. The overhead sun made it clear how long I'd slept. Up near the collapsed town, dozens of men pulled and poked and prodded at the wreckage.

Tom followed my gaze. "We're setting up the militia camp on the other end of town. The Colonel said it was a better spot."

I rubbed the sleep out of my eyes. "Colonel? I don't remember any Colonel."

"Colonel Mosby, come back from the front. He was looking for Cassidy when Luke showed up in town."

I nodded. Mosby's raiders were legends themselves. According to Jeremiah's books, Cassidy had ridden with them several times.

"There's also a Mexican woman in camp," Tom said, "a healer. She said we should let you sleep but to bring you to her as soon as you were awake."

"Well, I'm awake," I said. "Take me to her."

I extended my hand and he pulled me to my feet. My knee and my arm and all the little cuts decided to remind me that I was alive all at once, and I gasped in pain.

"You all right?" Tom asked, his face full of alarm.

"I'm alive," I said with an unsavory chuckle. "And right now I suppose that's a lot."

"I'm glad you are, Billy." He squeezed my hand tight. "I'm really glad you are."

I smiled back at my oldest, dearest friend. "I am, too. Now let's go find Maria."

Maria sat next to a small fire near a utilitarian canvas army tent. She wore a blue dress this time, and her hair was neatly combed. A pot of dark liquid bubbled on the flames and she stirred it from time to time. She smiled when she saw me and reached for a small nearby bottle.

"Willow bark," she said as she passed it to me.

I nodded thanks and drank deeply.

"Let me check your wounds." She pointed to the tent. "Lie down in there. Clothes off if you can. Under the blanket."

I nodded again. I briefly thought about my modesty but threw the thought aside. If Maria needed my clothes off, she needed my clothes off. I had to just do what needed to be done.

So inside the tent I stripped down to my unmentionables and stretched out under the blanket. I'd nearly fallen asleep again when Maria came in. She carried the pot that had been in the fire and several clean cotton bandages.

"Roll on your stomach," she said.

Once I'd done so, she started attending to the wound on my back. It hurt bad when she pulled the old bandages off, but better once she'd smeared the ointment from the pot on it. Then she did the same with all the scrapes and scratches she found, working up around my arms, including the gash there, before adjusting the blanket and doing my legs. She paused when she got to my knee.

"Red sand?" she asked.

"I went through the rift," I said. My chest tightened at the memories of the strange beach and the dragon. I turned my head to meet her eyes.

"But it is closed."

"Yeah," I said. Sobs rose in my chest but I fought them back. "Cassidy did it. After I killed him."

"Oh." She raised an eyebrow, but that was about it.

"Did you hear me? I killed him!"

She put a calming hand on my shoulder.

"Only someone who wants to die can close a rift," she said. "What you did was a mercy."

"A mercy?" I choked on the words.

"Yes," she said. "We will miss him, but now he is at peace."

I stared at her, not understanding at all.

THIRTY-EIGHT

MARIA IGNORED MY LOOK. Instead, the Mexican angel bustled about with her normal calm efficiency. She continued to treat my scratches and cuts. When she'd finished, she stepped back. "Roll over." She turned her back.

I did so and pulled the blanket up around me again. When Maria turned around, she started with my legs, again smearing the ointment over anywhere my skin was broken, no matter how small a cut. She paused when she reached my right knee.

"You could walk on this?"

"I learned to ignore the pain," I said.

"Good." She pressed on it and moved the kneecap a bit.

I winced as I was now aware of the daggers of agony it was sending out. But mostly I was still staring at her, waiting for her to explain what she'd said about Cassidy. She gave me another enigmatic smile and I sucked in my breath, ready to ask.

She showed mercy and spoke first. "Cassidy learned to ignore his pain." She moved to my right arm. "He hid it, too. He didn't want anyone to see."

I didn't know what to say. I hadn't noticed at all. I also didn't know how to ask. Not that I thought Maria would tell me anyway.

Instead, I laid back and let her finish taking care of me. She washed the scratches on my arms and hands and dabbed ointment on the bigger ones. Then she did the same, delicately, to the ones on my neck. Fortunately, I hadn't gotten any on my face, but she still gave me a warm wet cloth and let me rub the dirt off.

"I will bring you some broth," she said. "After that, you rest. You've been through much."

That I could agree with. I closed my eyes as she left the tent.

Colonel Mosby returned at dusk. He found me sitting with Tom near the fire, sipping more broth that Maria had prepared. She'd gone looking for herbs with a promise to return quickly, so we'd been talking quietly. Mostly, I was enjoying the hot meal, which was a first in several days. Meanwhile, Tom wanted to hear all about what had happened.

Colonel Mosby surprised me—shorter and more slight than I'd expected. His piercing eyes above a full bushy beard studied me before he spoke.

"Mr. McCarty, I presume."

I nodded and started to salute, but he waved me off.

"I understand you're responsible for saving the people of Grand Lake. I'd like to thank you on behalf of the Army of the West."

"I didn't save enough," I said. I avoided meeting his eyes.

"If I understand correctly, you stopped something that could have been far worse."

"Cassidy did it," I said with a sour snort. "I just helped."

"Still." He waited and when it was clear I didn't have anything else to say, he continued. "We're going to bring Captain Cassidy's body back to Golden City for burial with full honors. I would like a full report from you at that time."

"Yes, sir," I said.

Colonel Mosby seemed to sense the hollowness in my voice. He turned and left without another word.

We stayed another day in Grand Lake while the militia scoured the hills for the last cyclops, the one I'd wounded in the mouth but not killed. They also gave proper burials to the townsfolk with Maria attending each ceremony. There weren't any ghosts, but we knew there wouldn't be. Every soul had gone into the rift.

Meanwhile, the rest of the militia milled around. They were mostly the men from Golden City and Empire pressed into service by the small corps of permanent soldiers stationed in the barracks out in the ruins of Denver City. Without a battle, they didn't know what to do, but Colonel Mosby promised they could leave after twenty-four hours and so most were willing to stay. Several fished, and a few hunted. Some climbed what they now called Harpy's Peak to look at the bodies there, though none dared touch them. Later, Colonel Mosby ordered the harpy bodies burned.

But along with the fighting men, the militia had brought supply wagons and two cooks. We enjoyed some real stew and coffee and even some fresh johnny cakes, which Tom scarfed down so quick that I gave him one of mine.

I just stayed by the fire and tent. Maria checked on me between funerals, but said I'd be fine after a bit. Mr. Lake and Boggs had joined the militia in Golden City, and they also stopped by to see me. Mr. Lake said my money was no good the next time I came around for a drink, which would be the first time, really. Boggs offered to sell me back my Winchester at a discounted price. Good old Boggs. I was sure his 'discounted price' was still gonna be more than was at all reasonable.

They didn't stay long, though. They didn't ask many questions, either. By now the stories told by Jane and the others had spread throughout the camp. Mr. Lake and Boggs seemed to have heard some versions that weren't complete exaggerations. So they mostly seemed to be stopping by just to pay their respects.

They weren't the only ones. Men I'd been acquainted with for years found a reason to come shake my hand. So did men I really didn't know, but had seen around Golden City. One scrawny boy, who was actually younger than me but wore a private's uniform and carried a bugle, said he was proud to have met a true hero.

He didn't know how to react to my unsavory chuckle.

Still, I knew he meant well, so I shook his hand and asked if he'd been the one playing Taps. He had, so I told him he was very good. He blushed and nodded a dozen times before he said he had to go.

Tom looked at me like I'd grown a second head after the boy left.

"Are you okay, Billy?" he asked. "You haven't been right, this past day. Did you get hurt in the head?"

I let out a deep sigh and smiled at my oldest, best friend. "No … no. I just learned a whole lot."

"I just thought you'd be happier. You're a hero! You got to ride with Cassidy! I mean, I'm sorry …"

"Sorry I killed him?" I said with a snort.

Tom's eyes narrowed. "Maria said he was gonna die anyway. Why don't you believe her?"

"Cassidy said the same thing. I didn't believe him. Why should I believe her?"

With a snort of disgust, Tom stood. "I gotta take a piss." He strode off, leaving me to stew in my own misery.

Will Cozens came by before Tom returned. He was tired, but his face glowed with satisfaction. He'd ridden with Luke in the vanguard and he told me about their hard ride and the search for the cyclops and about all the things they'd found in the cyclopses' camp. He seemed especially pleased at having been right about the location, but disappointed he hadn't seen any ghosts.

I just listened, and to my surprise, couldn't avoid smiling. His enthusiasm was just too infectious.

When he started telling parts of the tale again, I almost laughed. He mentioned the ghosts again and I suggested he go talk to Maria.

"She's seen ghosts, too?" he asked.

"Seen?" I said. "She's talked to 'em."

"Really?" His eyebrows went sky high.

"Really," I said with a nod.

"Well, if *you* say so ... I think I'll go find her."

I couldn't help chuckling once he'd scampered off.

That left me alone for a bit, alone with just my thoughts. Not being in as much pain as before I could actually think, too.

I spent a lot of time thinking about all that had happened, and what we might've done different. I came up with a few things, but most of them I knew was just a function of looking back. *If* we'd known the harpy's bite was so poisonous, we might've attacked the nest differently. *If* we'd known about the trap, Cassidy might not have been mortally wounded in the fight.

All "ifs."

The only truly stupid thing I'd done was forget to get a new water bottle and in the end that had barely mattered.

And in the end, we'd *had* to close the rift. I had no doubts what that dragon would've done to us, or to anyone, if it had come through.

So what choice did we have? The witch was dead, Cassidy was badly wounded—

—Cassidy shot the witch.

My blood froze with the revelation.

Any chance of closing the rift without sacrificing Cassidy had died with her. Jeremiah and Maria had said that one could persuade the witch that created a rift to close it, and I didn't know if they were right, but we'd never had the chance to find out. Cassidy had killed her and taken away that choice.

I didn't know if Cassidy had wanted to die, like Maria said, but he'd made the choice.

It wasn't my fault.

I sat there, letting it all sink in, for quite some time.

When Tom did turn up, I apologized. I didn't explain more than it'd been unfair of me and must've been the wounds talking. He accepted it. Then I asked about what had been happening in Golden City and he was glad to tell it.

Maria joined us just before supper. She brought more willow bark for me, and afterward I slept harder than I had in days.

In the morning, Colonel Mosby gave the order for all but a couple of patrols to head home. He and Luke stayed behind to keep looking for the last cyclops. Tom, Maria, and I rode together, with me on a horse loaned by the Colonel. The rest of the militia surrounded us but kept a polite distance as we went.

We took two days to ride to Empire, but the weather was fair and pleasant. We had a few afternoon rainstorms, but nothing that soaked us to the bone. The sun was high and bright as we crossed Berthoud Pass. I'd hoped to find Jeremiah and McNab in Empire, but they'd already pushed on. We camped just south of Empire along the river and by the night of the next day arrived in Golden City.

Coming 'home' felt strange.

For one, I didn't have to figure out where to sleep. Mr. Lake insisted I take the best room at The Astor. I also didn't worry about food. All sorts of folks stopped by with treats for "you and the brave militia boys." Everyone looked at me like I'd done something amazing.

I started to think that maybe I had.

But then I'd remember the knife in my hand, and the emptiness in Cassidy's eyes after he'd died.

So I learned to just mind my manners and smile and say thank you and let people go off with whatever impressions of me they had.

It wasn't home anymore, but at least it could be peaceful.

THIRTY-NINE

LATE THE NEXT AFTERNOON, I got a moment of true quiet in The Astor's parlor. By then the really curious had gotten their peek or good word with me. Mr. Lake had to see about a shipment from Santa Fe and his cook had started on the evening meal. For once, I had the place to myself.

I leaned back in my wooden chair at the small table in the far corner of the warm room. I nursed the whiskey Mr. Lake had left me with, slowly sipping it between bites of the molasses cookies one of the ladies of the town had brought. The smooth bite of the alcohol nicely matched the sweet crumbliness of the cookies. Meanwhile, the smell of roasting chicken from the kitchen filled the air delightfully.

For the first time in days, I didn't ache badly either. My cuts had closed and my knee felt fine. Only the wound in my arm pained me at times, but not all that often. Mostly, it reminded me how good it was to be alive.

That's when Jeremiah walked in the main door carrying Beth in his arms. She held crutches, and he set her down almost at once and waited until she had them under her.

"Jeremiah!" I called as I slammed the chair to its feet and stood. "Beth!"

I closed the distance between us and, the heck with propriety, I gave them both a big hug. Jeremiah laughed and Beth just looked amused.

"How're you feeling?" I asked Beth. "You, too," I added to Jeremiah.

Beth spoke first. "Wonderful! The doctor says I'll be off crutches in a few weeks."

"That *is* wonderful," I said. "And how's your Ma?"

"Good," she said. "She's resting, and she misses Pa terribly, but she'll be fine, thanks to you."

She was so earnest, I couldn't help chuckling. But then I turned to Jeremiah, who'd been standing patiently watching us, with an amused grin on his face.

"I'm good," he said. He touched his shoulder, just above a bulge in his shirt which had to conceal more bandages. "Maria says Beth here's hot water washes did the trick. The disease didn't take, and I'll be as good as ever."

"So you'll be able to write again," I said with a wry grin. God, it was good to see them.

"I'm already writing." His smirk was as wide as a canyon.

"Well, sit down, sit down," I said. "Here, at this close table. I'll fetch my glass."

While Jeremiah helped Beth into her seat, I quickly retrieved my drink and cookies and then swung by the kitchen to ask the cook for drinks and food for my guests. I found them comfortably waiting when I returned.

"So what are you doing here?" I asked him. "I thought you were headed to San Francisco."

"McNab went. Hickok caught up to us in Empire. We thought he'd do a better job with Congress than me."

It made sense. Hickok could charm the scales off a snake.

"Besides," he said, "I've been trying to find someone who could make sense of those words on the amulet, with no luck."

"But we wanted to see you!" Beth blurted. She immediately put her hand over her mouth, but I could tell she wasn't embarrassed. Not really.

"Well, I'm glad to see you, too," I said with a smile. "Tell me what happened after we parted."

Beth was all too happy to tell me about their ride over Berthoud Pass into Empire, and as we talked they asked for 'the real story' of what had happened with me. I was glad to tell the tales, since they understood. They knew all too much about harpies and cyclopses and witches and so I didn't have to cut down their disbelief or anything.

They also knew Cassidy, and when I choked up talking about his wounds, they understood. A tear even formed in Beth's eye when I described having to use the tourniquet. So when I got to the part about Cassidy climbing on the altar and got too choked up to continue … well, they understood.

Still, it was good to talk with them, and to be with them, such that I was a mite sorry when Beth's Ma appeared to collect her for dinner. I got a farewell hug and promised to visit her the next morning.

Jeremiah gazed at me intently once we were alone. "So, how are you *really* doing?"

I met his eyes and then closed mine. When I opened them, he was still sitting patiently, waiting.

"Not good," I admitted. "I have bad dreams a lot. Most of 'em are about Cassidy, but not all."

Jeremiah nodded knowingly.

"I also don't like the way people look at me, you know? Like I'm strange or something. It makes my skin crawl."

"You're a hero now."

I snorted. "I don't wanna be a hero. Not anymore."

Jeremiah leaned back in his chair. "You sound like Cassidy."

"Well, he more or less said so himself." I'd finished my whiskey over the long story telling but now I found myself with a powerful thirst. I went to the side bar and picked up another bottle. I had a feeling Mr. Lake wouldn't mind.

"If you don't want to be a hero," Jeremiah asked, "what do you want?"

"I dunno. What did Cassidy want?" I wandered back to the table. I wasn't drunk, and I wondered if perhaps for the first time in my life I wanted to be.

"What did Cassidy want?" Jeremiah asked. He then answered himself, "he wanted to help people. And kill giants. He had a powerful hatred of giants."

"Don't need to be a hero to kill giants." I poured a finger's width of whiskey into my glass. "An army sharpshooter gets to do that. Cassidy told me that's what I should do."

"True."

"So what do you think?"

"About what you should do? I don't know. But I do know that you saved Beth's life, and you saved a lot of other lives. You were brave and you were quick and you were clever. If people treating you differently is the price for that, I'd consider it a bargain."

"It wasn't the only price and you know it," I snapped back. "But … yeah …" Saving Beth was worth it, and in some ways worth it all.

"You did what had to be done."

"Yeah," I said with a roll of my eyes. "Now you sound like Cassidy."

"Who do you think taught it to him?" He looked so smug and happily self-righteous, that I couldn't help laughing a bit.

"He was a good man," I said at last.

"He was. Indeed he was."

We both sat for a moment, lost in our memories.

After a bit, Jeremiah cleared his throat and stood. "I'd like to write some of this down before it escapes me. Perhaps we can meet for dinner."

"I'd like that," I said. "And Maria, too."

"I'll ask her."

"Oh, and Jeremiah? I've thought of a title for your next book: Cassidy's Last Ride."

"That's a good one," he said with a smirk, "but I've already got one in mind."

"Oh?"

"Mmm hmm. The West needs its heroes, so I'll write about the new one. Sorry my friend. It'll be 'The Tale of Billy the Kid and the Giants of Colorado.'"

With that, he turned and walked out, leaving me staring at his back in surprise.

THE END

AUTHOR'S NOTES

Sidekick sprang from some musings about what it would be like to be the side character in the adventure. We frequently follow the hero. What would it be like to be just one of the people going with the hero? Of course, as the story evolved, Billy grew and moved into such a central role that I realized he had to become the star.

The *Mythic West* Universe was born from a handful of discussions with friends and a family trip to the YMCA Snow Mountain Ranch camp, which is not far from Grand Lake, Colorado. That region of the West is steeped in history of the late 1800's. I had an image of giants walking the land one day and the kernels of the story were sown.

Once I started, my goal was to make the Universe as realistic as possible. The history up through 1865 is identical to the actual history of the United States. All the history after the rift at Andersonville was opened is my best extrapolation of what was likely to have happened. The only major intentional alteration I've made is the mining camps north of Grand Lake did not start until 1879, a few years after when this story is set. I've pulled that forward for dramatic license and the hand-waving argument that silver certainly could've been discovered earlier with the population dislocation.

Otherwise, the city names and historical figures listed are as accurate as I could make them for 1875.

During my research, I discovered that Billy the Kid came through Colorado when he was ten years old, on his way to New Mexico where he would later gain infamy as a gunfighter. His presence at the time I was setting the Battle of Golden City was too good pass up and Billy became my main character. Cassidy and the rest of his band are purely fictional. The Cozens, Colonel Mosby, Tom, and Mr. Lake are not. In all cases, and particularly with Billy, I have taken the liberty of projecting their characteristics in ways that may not reflect the actual historical figures. There are elements of the historical Billy the Kid in my Billy McCarty, but since the timelines diverged at age ten, I felt free to mold his personality myself.

I also decided to make the monsters non-magical. I wanted creatures that could've lived in our universe, but don't. The Jotun and Cyclopses are the size of a Tyrannosaurus Rex with the thick hide of a rhinoceros. The harpies have California Condor bodies with rattlesnake venom and flesh-eating bacteria filth on their claws.

That left the nature of the rifts themselves. Since they were created by human sacrifice, souls had to be absolutely real. The rift at Andersonville was created by sacrificing all 45,000 Union prisoners at once, which was why the rift was large enough to allow an army of giants to spill through. All other rifts in history were never that big, which is why they played such a small part in the pre-1875 world. The rest of the nature of rifts was revealed in the story.

Finally, this novel pays homage to the dime novels of the late 1800's and early 1900's. The real Billy was a fan of them, and I easily imagined them being a part of regular life after the Battle of Golden City. There are times when people need a good story to take them away from the hardships and horrors of their every day lives. This novel was intended to be just such a tale.

ABOUT THE AUTHOR

Edward J. Knight writes fantasy and science fiction from his home in Colorado. He's put two satellites into orbit and is raising two children along with his partner, Sarah. He hates stories with idiot plots. More of his work and some occasional musings can be found at www.edwardjknight.com.

Want to keep on what Ed's writing, and when new releases will be out? Sign up for his monthly newsletter at:

https://mythic-western-press.kit.com/280d39ec48

Or via the links at: www.edwardjknight.com

ALSO BY EDWARD J. KNIGHT

Sharpshooter

Scout

Gunslinger

Ghosthunter

PREVIEW OF SHARPSHOOTER

The Second Novel in the Mythic West Billy the Kid Series

BY THE LAST day of saber training, I hated being in the army. I was sure that becoming an army sharpshooter was not the best way to kill giants. I hated army training with the same passion I'd felt when we'd confronted the witch back in Colorado. Of course, on a dusty, well-trodden field outside of Fort Chicago, there were no witches. Just a merciless sergeant, cussing us out every time we did something even the slightest bit wrong.

A sergeant I couldn't shoot.

Not like giants. Those I could shoot just fine.

It didn't help that Fort Chicago was humid and muggy in early September. My blue wool uniform clung to me from all the sweat and even that didn't stop it from scratching. The cap didn't keep the sun off my neck and left a vulnerable pink gap there when we did formation drills. At least I was comfortable during shooting practice, but that was because I was one of the best. I never missed at two hundred yards or less.

Saber practice was another thing entirely.

Besides the Winchester rifles, the army issued each of us one of the long curving swords. If we ever found ourselves in close combat with the giants, God forbid, we were to chop at their knees and ankles. Once they were down, we could stab them wherever we could reach, but our sergeants said that keeping them from walking around was what really mattered. Upright Jotun were hard to fight. Jotun on the ground were easy pickings.

So my squad of recruits stood in a skirmish line with our sabers extended. We were far enough apart not to smell each others' stink, which was appreciated, since we'd trod through the cavalry field muck to get to this training ground. We hadn't been allowed to get out of formation, to my disgust.

My right arm ached holding my sword, but the sergeant wouldn't let us lower it until he'd individually inspected each one of us to make sure we were holding it right. The same inspection he'd done every day for the past two weeks.

But the sabers were heavier and thicker than the ones used in the War Between the States and my wrist felt like it was going to break. I grimaced and held it as best I could as the sergeant worked his way down the line. I knew he was going to yell at me because I couldn't keep the tip up. Then we'd start slashing practice, and we'd keep at it until he was either happy or convinced we weren't going to get any better that day.

That could take a long time.

For better or worse, it didn't take more than a few minutes for him to get to me. He stood a foot from my side and looked out at my blade.

"Private McCarty!" he barked. "Point higher!"

I shifted the sword as directed.

"More left! Straighter. Get that point up, McCarty!"

I ignored the string of curse words that followed. Out of the corner of my eye I'd spotted one of the HQ messengers hastening over to us. The sergeant only had time to make me do two practice slashes, both horrible according to him, before the messenger pulled up huffing in front of us.

"Sir!" he said. "Private McCarty to report to headquarters

immediately, sir!"

The sergeant nodded in acknowledgement and then tilted his head while he looked at me. Out of the corner of my eye, I could see the envy in the other recruits.

"What'd you do?" the sergeant asked. "Kill someone important?"

"Yes, sir. Actually I did, but it was months ago." I saluted. "Excuse me, sir."

The sergeant stared at me in disbelief for a moment. "Fine. Dismissed."

With the glee of the paroled, I followed the messenger back to headquarters.

The sprawling Fort Chicago sat south of the actual city, with fortifications extending all the way to Lake Michigan. The army had expected the Jotun to push north once they'd crossed the Ohio, but instead the giants had targeted St. Louis, for reasons that were still hotly debated. As a result, the original complex had grown from hastily thrown up earthworks to an immense maze of interlocking walls and buildings.

Which meant it took us over a quarter hour, even at double time, to get from the training ground to General Sanborn's headquarters. Sweat beaded on my brow and I really wished I had an opportunity to at least wash my face, but the messenger wasn't slowing or stopping. We just jogged together in silence, pounding up the dust.

But that gave me time to think.

And I couldn't come up with a single reason the general would want me. He'd been briefed on what happened in Colorado long before I'd turned up to enlist. He hadn't expressed any interest in meeting me then. There were a few stares and rumors at first, but most everybody treated me as just another soldier.

Which is how I wanted it.

I could help protect the West against the Jotun, like Cassidy had wanted. Before Cassidy had... had died. He'd said I should try to be a sharpshooter instead of a hero like him.

I'd come to believe he was right.

And so did everyone else in Fort Chicago. Heroes got people killed. They drilled that into your head the first day. You followed orders, not your conscience. That's how you survived.

That was how we'd win the war.

Besides… after Colorado, all I wanted to do was kill giants. I wanted to aim my rifle, shoot them in the eye, and walk away knowing I'd done good.

The army thought that was just fine.

In the outer office, General Sanborn's aide sat behind a large rough-hewn oak desk. The skinny man, not much older than me, bobbled his head when he saw us enter. The rest of the room was sparse. Battalion flags covered one smooth plank wall, along with a portrait of President Stanford. The Stars and Bars stood on a pole discreetly in one corner. The room smelled of sawdust and coffee.

I pulled up in front of the desk into the stance I'd been taught and saluted.

"Private McCarty, reporting as ordered, sir."

He gave me a dour smile and a half-hearted salute in return. Clearly my fervor did not impress him.

"Go on in," he said. He gestured toward the door to his left instead of the one behind him.

I took a deep breath and marched on through.

The small conference room was nearly empty. It held a long table, and a handful of wooden chairs. Like the reception room, the walls were smooth oak planks with minimal decoration. A large map covered one side.

McNab, Cassidy's grizzled former quartermaster, stood in front of the map, casually studying it and rocking on his heels.

I took a moment to look him over. He'd trimmed the bushy salt-and-pepper hair that ringed his bald head and also shaved recently. He wore an army jacket and pants, though the high boots were decidedly his own and not government issue. Best of all, he actually looked relaxed.

He turned and gave me a broad grin.

"Billy! Good to see you!"

I snapped to position and saluted, and only then glanced at his stripes. Sergeant-Major? When did that happen?

"Sir!" I said. "Private McCarty reporting as ordered!"

"Oh, knock it off," he said with a wave. "They only gave me this," he touched his chevron, "because Mosby insisted. He said it'd make it easier for me to get him his whiskey."

I grinned. Colonel Mosby didn't drink whiskey at all, and McNab and I both knew it. But if McNab could joke about Mosby, that was a good sign.

He looked me up and down and a smirk creased his face.

"Looks like they made a regular soldier out of you," he said.

"They're trying. But I can't stand the army."

"That's too bad," he said with a grin. He nodded his head toward the table. "Your orders."

I spotted the small folded piece of paper I'd overlooked before. I picked it up and scanned it. My eyebrows went up as I did.

"Assigned to Mosby's Raiders." I set the orders down and turned to McNab. "What is this? Mosby's leaving Colorado?"

He chuckled and waved a hand dismissively. "He got his orders, too."

"And I suppose he requested me."

"You'd suppose right."

"I thought he didn't like me," I said, "after our 'talk' back at the beginning of summer."

"You weren't exactly forthcoming." McNab's grin reminded me all too well of Colonel Mosby's frown.

He was right, I hadn't been forthcoming, but not because I didn't want to tell Mosby, but because I didn't want to think about what had happened at *all*. Cassidy's face. The blood seeping from his arm. The knife.

Always the knife.

At least in my nightmares.

McNab picked up on my sudden sullen mood.

"It's okay," he said. "I don't think Colonel Mosby dislikes you for that. He wants you because he knows you're darned good in a fight."

I looked at him warily, but he just stood there, rocking a bit on his heels, clearly amused at my discomfort.

"At least according to his quartermaster." McNab couldn't hold back the teasing grin with that.

"You," I said.

He nodded.

"Fine," I said. "Who else is assigned to Mosby's Raiders?"

He held up his right hand. "Me," he said, ticking off a finger. "Jeremiah." He touched the next one. "And Luke."

I let out a deep sigh of relief. Then my mind raced.

"What about Maria?" I asked.

"Assigned to Sanborn's personal medical corps." His eyes twinkled. "But don't worry, you'll see her once we're out in the field."

I nodded. It wasn't that I was sweet on Maria, like McNab implied. I just knew how good her healing skills were and couldn't think of anyone I'd rather have around. Certainly not the sawbones I'd met here in Fort Chicago. They were way too quick to reach for the amputation saw for my comfort.

Apparently Sanborn thought so, too, if he was keeping her close. I wondered what McNab thought about that.

"Well," I said, "at least we'll be together."

"Maybe," he said. "We're all in the same regiment, but it's a big regiment. It's not gonna be like Colorado."

When it was just the six of us riding together. And Beth, the young girl we'd rescued. That I'd rescued. Of all the things that'd happened in Colorado, that was the one I was most proud of.

"Still," I said. "It'll be good to be out killing giants."

His eyes glinted knowingly, but he kept the grin off his face. I knew he felt the same.

"But first we've got a lot of work to do," he said. "Starting with recruiting."

I tilted my head and waited for him to go on.

"We got three companies at half strength," he said. "If that. We need to fill 'em with new recruits. Which is where you come in."

"Me?" I couldn't help but blink in surprise.

"Sure, kid. You've been training with 'em. Who's the best?"

"Me," I said. "Uh... at least in shooting. I'm not so good with the sword."

"You the worst?"

"Uh... no." I immediately thought of this kid from Minnesota. As skinny as he was, I was sure he'd lied about his age to join up. Not that the recruiter probably cared.

"Then you're the test. Any man who can beat you with a sword and come anywhere close to you with a rifle joins the Raiders. The rest can go to the regular infantry."

I shifted uneasily. There were easily three, maybe four, hundred new recruits in camp. And McNab wanted me to fight them all?

"C'mon." He strode toward the door. "Time's a-wasting. We've got two days to get our regiment into shape before we move out."

"Two days? That's not enough time!"

In the first two days, I'd barely learned how to march, much less how to fight. And I'd already known how to shoot.

"No, it's not," McNab said with an unsavory chuckle. "But if Sanborn doesn't attack the Jotun soon, General Lee and a bunch of his men are gonna die."

"And if he attacks with green recruits, a bunch of us are gonna die."

"You do see the problem."

He went out the door, so I hustled to catch up. As we left the building, he turned and gave me one of his most devilish smirks.

"I hope you're rested," he said. "With all the fighting you're gonna do, you're gonna need it."

I groaned. He just laughed and kept walking.

Available now!